ACCEPTABLE LOSSES

NIA FORRESTER

ISBN: 9798644635290

For my love.

PART I

1

———————

"You should meet my brother."

"Your brother?" Lena lowered her coffee cup and looked across the conference room table at Quentin. "I know I said the date was nightmarish, but ..."

"No, for real. Every Monday you come in here and tell me about these sorry-ass dudes, and now I'm starting to feel like you might need a little help, so ..."

"So you want to bring in your family as reinforcements? Great, thanks," Lena laughed. "Honestly, Q, it's not that deep. I mostly tell you those stories about my dates for our mutual amusement."

Quentin looked at her with narrowed eyes. "I don't know, Lene. You make it sound pretty dire. Some fool told you he *left his wallet* and made you pick up the tab?"

Lena shrugged. "That's what's out here right now, so you better count your lucky stars you're not in the dating game anymore."

Quentin let that comment pass. "You'd like my brother," he said instead.

"What's his name again? You don't talk about him that much."

"Darius. He's two years younger than me, so that makes him just about your age, and he's a very successful tattoo artist."

Lena laughed. "Wait, what? *You?* Have a brother who's a *tattoo* artist? Did you grow up in different homes?"

"Very funny."

"Q, you are *so* conservative. A brother who does tats for a living is not what comes to mind when I think of what your family might be like."

"He did *my* tats ..."

Lena almost spluttered her coffee onto the table. "*You* have tattoos?"

"Yeah. Why's that so surprising?"

"I just said why. You're conservative."

Quentin shook his head and gave a brief laugh himself. "You might not know what you think you know, girl."

Before Lena could get out her retort, three of their colleagues filed into the conference room at the same time, talking among themselves about their weekends, the weather, the kinds of things people talked about on a Monday morning. Quentin and Lena exchanged one last smile and then joined in the banter with everyone else.

For the next three or so hours, they would be sequestered in the conference room, going over their cases with the four partners who headed up the Antitrust Litigation and Civil Investigations practice in their firm, Fox, Cheatham & Lowe. As the only two Black associates in this division, Quentin and Lena bonded almost immediately when she joined the firm two years earlier. For Lena, Quentin thought it was probably reassuring to find someone who could be a mentor; and for him, it was simply a relief to see another brown face after several years of being the only one, apart from the partner who supervised them.

For the first few months as part of the team, Lena was the very picture of professionalism around him. She had more than kicked ass on the first case she was assigned to, working as second chair to Quentin as the lead. It was one of those distasteful cases where their client was undoubtedly on the wrong moral side of the conflict but on firm legal ground. Those were the ones Quentin hated—where someone had done wrong, but not broken the letter of the law and so it was his job to defend them.

Working with Lena had made the case not suck nearly as much as it would have under normal circumstances. She had a sharp legal mind, a killer sense of humor, and a knack for putting things in perspective. She didn't moralize or bemoan the ignoble nature of their task; she simply put her nose to the grindstone and got it done. And watching her do that helped Quentin remember to do the same, making it a lot easier for him to pore over documents that pretty much proved their client was a scumbag.

But by the time that case was over and settled, Lena had let the professionalism slip a little; only when they were alone, and only because she had come to trust him, and he to trust her. Now they were occasionally on the same cases, but were more often on the same schedule for coffee breaks in the Starbucks half a block away from their building. And in marathon meetings like the one they were about to have, Lena sitting across the table—exchanging looks with Quentin and having entire conversations without speaking a word—was a lifeline.

On Mondays, it had become their habit to get to the team meeting early, update each other on their weekends, and shoot the breeze before the business of the day got started. And occasionally, Lena's weekends were about some guy she'd gone out with. She got asked out a lot. Dudes at the gas station, in the waiting room at her dentist's office ... pretty much everywhere.

But that was no surprise to Quentin—she was gorgeous. With a head full of crazy, crinkly, massive natural hair that was always a show-stopper when she wore it out—which was far too seldom as far as he was concerned—she didn't seem to even fully grasp the scope of her gorgeousness. Whenever Lena walked into a room for the first time, it was like that old song: *The men all paused.* Even the ones who saw her on a daily basis couldn't help but look.

Her figure was on the leaner side of lush. Firm and well-toned legs that would do Quentin well not to check out too often, though he did anyway; a butt that swayed gently from side to side when she walked, and the posture of a prima ballerina. If it wasn't for the fact that in most other respects she was like one of the guys, Quentin would have made it his personal mission to avoid Lena at all costs.

Because, after all, he was a married man. At least technically speaking.

Quentin and Mara had been officially separated for nine months, but had been separat*ing* for at least two years; the love and closeness they once had dismantled brick by painful brick and replaced by anger and acrimony. But now the deal was all but done, and she was comfortably installed in her new place in downtown DC, and he was still in the house they'd bought together. That living situation was her choice.

Now, though neither of them had uttered the ultimate and final 'D-word', it seemed to be little more than an administrative detail at this point. It wasn't uncommon now for more than two weeks to pass without them speaking at all. And there was no longer much of a pretense that they were looking for ways to "work things out."

Quentin lived his life in limbo, waiting for one of them to finally admit that it was time to put their marriage out of its misery. But he was determined that it would not be him. The thing was, he meant it when he said 'till death do us part. He was riding it out, that nasty patch of arguments and coldness and sometimes outright cruelty on both sides. He had been just hanging in there, putting all his faith in the likelihood of better days. If marriage was a lifetime proposition, what were two years, three or even four, of bad times? There would be plenty of good around the corner—that was his philosophy.

Until Mara dropped her bomb—she wasn't sure she loved him anymore, and she needed to "get away" for a while to figure things out.

I just need you to let me go, Quentin, she'd said. *That would be the kindest thing for us both.*

In the end, he did what she asked; because it had been a long, long time since either of them had done anything for the other that could even remotely be considered 'kind.'

"So Quentin you want to update us on the Powell matter?"

Richard Lowe was one of the named partners and Quentin's mentor. He walked into the room and started talking before he even took his seat. Around the conference table, everyone sat up a little straighter, preparing to look attentive. Lowe cut an imposing figure, though he stood just barely over six feet tall. A former NFL player who had exercised his good sense to leave the league and return to school after just one bad hit, he was somewhat of a minor celebrity in the Washington DC area and rumored to be mulling over a run for mayor. Quentin respected him and considered him a friend, though they were separated by more than a dozen years in age.

"I think we have good news on Powell," Quentin said after clearing his throat. "We made the settlement offer last Thursday, and over the weekend, I got a couple questions for clarification from opposing counsel, which sounded to me like they're moving in the direction we want them to. Deadline for them to respond is today COB."

He answered a few more questions, and Lowe moved on to other cases and other members of the team. Quentin listened with only half an ear until it was Lena's turn. She was working on a complex case which, if she handled herself well, could help accelerate her rise, or even write her ticket at the firm. Occasionally, she'd called on Quentin as a sounding board, but the truth was, she didn't need one—her instincts were on point, and the only thing standing in the way of her going from being a good lawyer to a great one, was a few more years of practice under her belt.

While she was making her brief presentation and outlining her strategy, Quentin thought he could detect a very slight tremble in her voice. She was nervous.

When her eyes moved around the room as she spoke, he made sure he gave her the tiniest of winks, reassuring her that she was doing fine. In return, she gave him a barely detectable smile, and her voice steadied and grew just a smidge louder.

"You still at the office, Q?"

"Yup. Just squeezing a few more billable hours out of Powell. How 'bout you? You still around too?"

It was just past eight, and he was in his office still, having moved from behind his desk to the leather sofa in his sitting area, and loosened his tie about an hour ago. His cell phone rang just as he was beginning to consider calling it a night, and Lena's face flashed across the screen.

In the picture, she'd purposely crossed her eyes and stuck her tongue out at the camera in a selfie taken during one of the late nights on a shared case a few months ago. Though she'd begged Quentin to delete the shot, he'd instead assigned it to her contact information so it was the face he saw whenever she called; and it made him smile without fail, every time.

"Yeah, still here. About to kick my shoes off and order some Thai food. You in?"

"Thai Kitchen?" he asked.

"I guess. But there's this new place in Adams Morgan called Siam Orchid that ..."

"What'd I tell you about these new-fangled fly-by-night spots? I've been getting Thai food at Thai Kitchen since ..."

"Law school at Georgetown. Yeah, yeah ... you told me. Fine, Q," Lena sang. "Thai Kitchen it is. Same as always, right? Seeing as how you're averse to trying something new and all."

Quentin laughed. "Yeah. Same as always. Buzz me when they get here."

Less than an hour passed when Lena called him back to say their dinner had arrived—another reason he liked Thai Kitchen —and Quentin headed over to her office, which was on the other side of the floor, perpendicular to his. On the way there, it didn't surprise him to see that there were more than a half-dozen other associates working late.

After the 2008 financial crisis, a few medium-sized DC law firms had gone bust, and even some of the large ones found themselves staring down the barrel of bankruptcy. But Fox, Cheatham & Lowe hung in there, and even thrived because of a business model that didn't turn up its nose at smaller clients— family businesses, and not just multinational corporations; middle-class families, and not just trust fund babies. So while a lot of firms with larger footprints saw their too-big-to-fail clients do just that, the American middle-class—businesses as well as individuals—hobbled along, and still needed legal help to do so. There were a lot of loan modification cases in those years, but it paid the bills and paid for the considerable stable of attorneys who were still busy enough to have to work late on a Monday night.

"You weren't kidding about kicking off your shoes, huh?"

Quentin found Lena in her much smaller center office, her stockinged feet propped up on one of her extra chairs and eating directly from the carton.

"There's your boring-ass Shrimp Pad Thai," she said over a full mouth, indicating where she'd left it on a side table near the door.

"Thanks." Quentin willed himself not to look at her legs, stretched out in front of her.

"One of these days, I'm just going to fake you out and get you something revolutionary ... like the duck or something."

"See, this is where you got me all wrong," he said grabbing his food and taking the closest free chair—there were no couches like the one he had in junior associates' offices—to make himself comfortable. "I tried the duck. Hell, I even tried the octopus. But I happen to *like* the Pad Thai. And once I know what I like, I tend to stick to it."

"You play for keeps, huh?" Lena glanced up over the edge of her carton, chopsticks at her mouth.

"Generally, yeah."

"Hmm," she said.

"So you got your answer on Powell?"

"Yup. They took the deal. Didn't even counter."

"I thought they might." Lena got up and went behind her desk, reaching down and with a flourish, pulled out two bottles.

Seeing what they were, Quentin laughed out loud, throwing his head back.

"Moët, for you, my friend."

"Damn, you couldn't get the adult-size bottle?" he teased. "That was a five-million dollar settlement!"

"Yeah, but even these bad boys cost twenty bucks each, so ..."

Lena handed him one and he took it. It was ice-cold, so either she had bought them that way, or she had gotten them earlier in anticipation of his win and chilled them all day. Either way, Quentin was touched.

Together, they opened their respective bottles and whooped at the satisfying pop of the corks, then held them up to toast to his victory. Lena sobered up, moving closer, close enough that Quentin's nostrils filled with her perfume and he could see where her lipstick had gotten smudged from eating. The hint of color on her already pink lips was somehow more alluring than when they were fully-painted.

"To the best legal eagle I know," Lena said. "And the best friend I have at this godforsaken job. Here's to another notch on your belt."

They clinked bottles and took a swig, then sat down to resume their meals. The silence stretched on for a few minutes until Quentin cleared his throat.

"What if I didn't get the settlement done?" he asked. "You would've been out forty bucks for nothing."

Lena shrugged. "I knew you'd win this one sooner or later."

"Well, I guess you could always have saved it for your own win on the Braden Corp. matter," he said, referring to the case she'd presented on in the team meeting.

"I don't know. Braden isn't exactly a winnable case."

"Of course it is. What d'you mean? You know you're more than capable of ..."

"I'm not talking about that," she said, not looking up at him. "I'm talking about whether it's for a good cause. I mean, we're defending a company that had some poor guy hauling asbestos for years and acting like they didn't know it was toxic ... Sometimes it feels like to lose would be a win."

He remembered their first case together, back when she was new. Then, she had been the one to remind him not to take every case personally; and to turn his focus on one thing only—getting the win. Though he wouldn't say it aloud, he worried that it was a little soon for her to be getting disenchanted with the nature of the work. It didn't bode well for what she would feel about it in just another year or two from now.

Some lawyers, lured by the promise of a sizeable salary, jumped into this kind of practice before doing the all-important gut-check. And before they knew it, they had a big house, an even bigger mortgage, and astronomical payments on a luxury car tethering them to work that on a good day they didn't believe in, and on a bad day felt downright crappy about.

"C'mon, you can shake that off. There's always going to be one or two like that," Quentin said, trying to meet her gaze. "The ones that test your belief in our legal system and ..."

"I don't know that I want that kind of test, though, Q. I mean, I have a friend. Graduated with me, and works as a juvenile defender. She makes maybe a quarter of what I make. Less. And I never hear her sound anything but certain that her work is making a difference. I kind of envy her that, y'know? I wake up in cold sweats with pictures in my head of the poor guy who's suing Braden. You know what mouth cancer looks like, Q?"

He shook his head.

"Well, I could show you. But I like you way too much to do that. So just believe me when I tell you, gruesome doesn't even *begin* to describe it."

Lena took a deep breath and set aside the remainder of her food, reaching instead for her bottle of Moët.

Quentin watched her for a few moments. Her hair was coming loose from all the bobby pins or other accouterments she used to secure it. It was irrepressible, that hair of hers. He shoved aside an urge to reach forward and pull it free. If he had his way, she would wear it out, all the time. Without the control she tried to exert over it, it would spring high and away from her head like a halo.

"You ...." He started and then stopped, then started again. "Maybe you have too much heart for this job," he suggested.

Lena looked up at him, her eyes open and frank in their surprise. She leaned forward. "Q. You have a lot of heart too."

"Yeah? But I don't get tortured about these cases like you do, so ..."

Lena shook her head slowly. "I don't believe you," she said. "You do. I know you do."

And Quentin felt a chill, a literal chill run across the surface of his skin.

"So," he said to lighten the mood, "you want to meet my baby brother or what?"

2

———

AGAIN WITH THE BROTHER?

Lena tried to control her expression, and in the end wasn't sure she could, so instead took another sip of Moët. It shouldn't matter, but the idea that he would so easily hand her off to someone else caused a little ache in her chest. Not that she was surprised—Q was clueless that way. He would never dream how frequent a topic of conversation he was among the female associates at the firm. The consensus was that there was nothing quite as sexy as a man who was fine as hell and didn't know it, and who was humble on top of everything else. Quentin Thomas was that rarest of breeds—a bad-ass who either didn't know or didn't care how bad-ass he was.

"Why are you so sure I'd like your brother?" Lena asked once she'd swallowed her disappointment along with the gulp of champagne.

"I'm not sure you'll like him, but he's a good guy. Interesting. Decent. Funny. At a minimum, he'd keep you entertained."

You're interesting, decent, and funny! she wanted to scream. *You keep me entertained!*

More than entertained. Q kept her ... present. There wasn't a moment when she was in his company that she thought about what she had to do next, where she had to be, or anything other than just being there, with him. But apart from his *bad-assedness*, the women around the office also talked about his marriage. Lena had never seen the wife, but the word around the firm was that she was as striking as a young Grace Jones, and just as imperious.

Apparently, they'd been separated a while; but Q still wore his ring, and there was never any hint of him seeing anyone. Lena would have expected nothing less than that from him—loyalty, even in the face of what appeared to be a crumbling relationship. And though they'd been friends for a good amount of time now, he never talked about his wife at all. Never so much as breathed her name in casual conversation, which only made her gargantuan in Lena's imagination—more beautiful, more elusive, more impossible to compete with.

That is, if she were competing. And of course, she was not.

"So what're you thinking?" she asked. "You want to fix us up, or ... just meet? I would love to *meet* your brother, Quentin, but a fix-up, I don't know. And anyway, I'm thinking of taking a break from dating. It's too exhausting."

"Whatever you want to call it. You can meet him, and then the rest would be up to you two," he said. Then he put down his bottle and removed his cufflinks, unbuttoning the sleeves of his shirt and rolling them up to the elbows.

His forearms were large and sinewy and covered in a light layer of smooth hair that looked almost silky to the touch. And Lena *really* wanted to touch. Her eyes followed his every move as he reached for his Pad Thai once again and lifted the chopsticks to his lips, which were just ...

Married, Lena. He's married.

"Okay, sure. What could it hurt? I'd love to meet your brother."

"Cool," he said. "We get together every Friday at this dive bar he likes to go to. Maybe this week you can meet us there. No pressure. Just a couple drinks, and if you all hit it off, you can take it from there."

"Sounds like a plan," she said, trying to sound enthusiastic. "Cool."

"So let's talk some more about this case that's weighing on your soul ..."

<hr>

"YOU ARE *SO* STUPID. I CAN'T EVEN BELIEVE WE SHARE THE SAME parents let alone shared the same womb!"

Lena tossed a balled-up kitchen towel at her brother who was sitting at her kitchen table, watching rather than helping while she loaded the dishwasher. As usual, even though she'd gotten home well after ten p.m., it was to find that her twin brother, Marlon, had done virtually nothing but watch television all day and create little satellites of crap all around the apartment.

Marlon was in the middle of yet another interlude of under-employment, working as a waiter in an upscale restaurant downtown while trying to save enough money to go back to finish his Master's program.

"What was I supposed to do? Tell him I'd rather go out with *him*? What about '*he's married*' do you not understand?"

"He's separated. It's not the same thing. People don't separate to work on their marriage. They separate to work on their *divorce*."

"Maybe so. But he's *not* divorced. He even still wears his ring."

"Huh. He does?"

That factoid seemed to give Marlon pause. He scratched his

goatee thoughtfully for a moment and bit his lower lip. "Well," he said, "is the brother cute at least?"

Lena laughed. "See! So take back what you said about me being stupid. Stupid would be to sit around mooning over a man who is so clearly not available it's sickening. I don't even know why I keep hanging out with him."

"To torture yourself. You've always been silly like that. Remember Chuck Benson? How you could have even liked a white boy named *Chuck* of all things is beyond me. I almost disowned you."

"If you have to reach all the way back to high school, then that proves I'm smarter in love now," Lena pointed out.

"Smarter? Yeah right. In love with a married man who you practically begged to put you in the friend zone. Real smart."

"It's *because* he's married that I have to be in the friend zone, Marlon. Try to keep up."

"Whatever. That never stopped me."

"That's because you're messy like that. And because the married men *you* get involved with are married to women who probably don't even know they're gay."

"Technicalities." Marlon pushed himself up from his seat. "I'm going to take a shower and go to sleep. Don't be makin' too much noise out here."

"Yeah. Thanks for all your help cleaning up."

"You're welcome," Marlon sang, waving over his shoulder as he left the room.

Lena rolled her eyes and dipped her hands back into the sink to retrieve the remaining dirty dishes and cutlery that would need to be crammed into the already overcrowded dishwasher. She didn't really mind cleaning up on her own. Housework gave her brain the downtime it needed after working at an intellectually challenging job. And it gave her time to contemplate the dilemma she'd walked herself into.

She didn't want to date Quentin's brother. She wanted Quentin. It had been a hard road to even admit that to herself, let alone her brother. But after just three weeks of working with him when she was a first-year associate, it was a wrap—she was falling, and falling fast.

High-intensity cases like the one they were working on also came with high-intensity hours. For months, it was routine for Lena and Quentin to put in eighteen-hour days, eating, sleeping, and even showering at the office while they pored over reams of paper and complied with discovery orders.

It was complex litigation of a type Lena had dreamed she would be involved in when she went to law school—high-stakes and high-profile, with lots of players whose names were commonly seen in *The Washington Post*. Every day she went to work, she was on an adrenaline high.

And soon, Quentin became part of the reason for her high as well.

For starters, he was the most patient man she had ever met. With bloodshot eyes, clothes he hadn't changed out of in twenty hours, and fueled only by coffee and good intentions, he managed to answer every stupid little wet-behind-the-ears-First-Year-Associate question she asked him. And he did it with a calm, even tone, never betraying how tired he must have been, or how foolish she might have sounded. He treated their legal assistants with as much respect as he did the senior partners, and he even covered her with an afghan when she fell asleep on his office couch when she was supposed to be in the middle of supervising document review.

Lena recalled waking up in a panic, drool on her chin, looking around frantically for the two staff she was supposed to be working with. The only person there was Quentin, at his desk with a banker's lamp on but the rest of the room dim, reading documents under that poor lighting just so she could sleep.

Oh my god, Lena remembered saying as she sat up, hair and clothes askew. *I am* so *sorry. How much time did we lose while I was sleeping?*

Doesn't matter, he'd said smiling at her. *Go on get some more rest, Sleepfighter. Tomorrow we live to do battle another day.*

And it was then, in that moment, that Lena knew she was a goner.

After that, every second they spent together on the case was sweet torture. As time passed, the sweetness—and the torture—only deepened as she got to know Quentin better and learned to live with the knowledge that he was off-limits for her.

What only made matters worse was that the man was great-looking as well. Built like a titan, he had broad, square shoulders, and the lean, fit physique of a swimmer—well-muscled, but not too bulky. He had the cool, brown complexion of a pecan, wheat-colored eyes, and a strong, square jaw that was lightly bearded. But the facial hair didn't mask the dimples. Dimples, Lena always thought, made a man look almost pretty and tended to short-circuit their masculinity. But not in this case. Quentin's dimples were deep and long and only served to accentuate his jawline and punctuate his perfect, full lips.

Yeah, she had it bad.

The only thing that kept Lena firmly in her lane was that simple gold band on the index finger of his left hand, and the fact that she respected both him and herself, too much to do anything ridiculous. And hell, why ruin a beautiful friendship? Right now, there was no question in her mind that she was Quentin's closest friend at the firm. She loved that, and basked in it, even as she realized that there could never be more.

But now this thing with him wanting to fix her up with his brother was like salt in the open wound of her heart. Tonight was the first time she admitted to herself that she had been living on empty hope. If not hope for a relationship with him, it was the hope that he at least felt some semblance of a thing other than friendship for her. Maybe they would never act on it, but she would have liked knowing it was there. Quentin trying to get her to meet his brother pretty much ended that little fantasy.

Sighing, Lena leaned against the now running dishwasher and looked around. It was eleven-fifteen, and she could hear Marlon in the shower. She could use one of those herself. But why bother? She would be up for work in a mere six hours and have one then. So, shutting off all the lights in the apartment, she headed in to bed.

3

———

"When she gets here, don't be doin' no dumb shit, a'ight?"

"Like what?" Darius grinned, taking a gulp of his beer.

"Like, I don't know ... being ... yourself," Quentin said.

They both laughed, and Darius shook his head. "You know I would only do this for you, right? And you gon' owe me big-time."

"Whatever. This just evens us out because who was it that convinced Ma that you couldn't come to Thanksgiving because of *work* when your ass was in Vail with one of your playmates?"

Darius shrugged. "You know she never believes a word I say."

"Because you're a liar," Quentin said.

"Dang, why you gotta go there, bruh? Sometimes I conceal irrelevant details to spare her and Dad's feelings, that's all. You know how they worry about me."

"And it's not like you ever give them a reason to or anything," Quentin said sarcastically.

He shook his head and glanced toward the entrance to the bar and then at the clock. Fridays at seven-thirty were sacrosanct for him and his brother. Their lives had taken such divergent paths that Quentin knew he had to schedule time with Darius, otherwise, they might never see each other. This was their time —Friday, seven-thirty, Accra Café. It was a bar that catered mostly to DC's West African community, but also attracted the artsy crowd of which Darius was a member.

A very successful tattoo artist who had his studio in an enviable location right on Wisconsin Avenue in Georgetown, Darius made a living more than comparable to what Quentin was pulling in as an attorney. Though he would never admit as much out loud, Quentin admired his brother for how he had bucked the wishes of their parents and forged his own unique path.

In their teens, he and Darius could almost pass for twins, but in college was when their differences started to become apparent. By the time they were in their early twenties, Darius looked like a taller, buffer version of Lenny Kravitz and was immersed in a counter-cultural scene that made their parents lose many nights of sleep wondering and worrying about his future. And Quentin was in law school, falling in love and planning his future with a beautiful woman.

But through it all, one thing remained the same—they were each other's best friend and had a bond that was impenetrable, no matter what pressure was exerted on it.

"Here she comes right now."

Quentin had glanced up once more, just in time to see Lena enter. She had changed out of her work clothes and was wearing close-fitting, dark wash jeans and a snug, though not tight, black turtleneck sweater. On her legs were calf-high boots, which along with the jeans, made her legs look a hundred yards long. She had released her hair from the severe hair-tie it had been in at the office so that it was now an explosion of kinky, wavy awesomeness. Looking at her, watching her walk toward them, Quentin felt pride, the kind of pride that usually accompanied ownership.

But there was definitely no ownership between him and Lena. And even if there were, his mission tonight was basically to give her away.

"You must be Lena."

Darius hopped off his barstool and extended a hand as soon as it became clear she was coming toward them. And in doing so, he blocked Quentin's view of her entirely.

"I am," Quentin heard her reply. "And you're Darius."

"That I am. What're you drinking, Lena?"

"Can we get a table, maybe?" Quentin asked.

"Oh. Only if you guys want to," Lena said, leaning around Darius to offer Quentin a little smile. "I'm perfectly capable of balancing on a barstool if that's where you guys want to be."

"Nah, Q's right. Let's get a table. That way I can look right at you while we talk." Darius grinned at her, and Q recognized the way his brother's voice dropped, to the lower-than-usual baritone he reserved for women he was attracted to, or trying to charm out of something. It didn't always mean the woman was special.

Quentin had witnessed his brother use this same routine on meter maids, female cops who stopped him for speeding and even random women he wanted to give him a spot in front of them in the grocery checkout line. Darius couldn't know it yet, but Lena wasn't some basic chick—she was different, so this bullshit routine was not good enough for, nor was it likely to work on a woman of her caliber.

Sighing, Quentin waved over the bartender to settle their tab.

"They have pretty good music in here on Fridays," Darius said when they were getting situated at a table a few moments later. "You think you might want to hang around and check out this reggae band that's coming on?"

Lena shrugged. "Might as well. I love live music."

"You sticking around too, Q?" Darius asked.

"Yeah, of course. This is where I always spend Fridays, right?" he said.

Darius gave him a strange look, which he ignored, then returned his attention to Lena.

"They have food here, too. But nothing to write home about. You like African food?"

"Depends on what kind," she said.

Her lipstick was a deep, dark color which made the shape of her lips even more apparent. They were bow-lips, the upper an inverted W and the lower, a soft, symmetrical curve. Quentin didn't think she had ever worn lipstick this vivid to the office before. If she had, he definitely would have noticed.

Darius leaned in. "What kinds have you tried?"

One of Darius's ambitions was to travel to every country on the African continent. So far, he had been to ten countries in West and North Africa and amassed an enviable collection of art, and a vast palate from having tried dozens of new cuisines. Quentin, by comparison, had only been to Kenya, and only for a week on a very tightly-controlled resort-centered vacation with Mara for their honeymoon.

"I've had Ethiopian, of course. Lots of that in DC. Senegalese. Moroccan, Nigerian ..." Lena ticked them off on her fingers. "A few."

"The guys in here are Ghanaian."

When Darius leaned in and placed his forearms on the table, Quentin saw Lena's eyes flit along their length, taking in the complicated array of images. There was scarcely an inch of skin along Darius' arms that wasn't inked.

"You like these?" Darius extended his arm for her inspection, and Quentin tensed a little as she touched it.

"They're amazing," Lena said, nodding. "They look three-dimensional. Like they're leaping off your skin."

Darius grinned. "That's my art."

"Wait. You did your own tattoos?"

"Nah, girl. How I'ma do my own tattoo?"

Lena laughed. "I don't know how it works. You said it was your ..."

"You sketch out your designs before any inking happens. These are my designs."

"Well, they're really cool." Lena looked at Quentin, seemingly recalling for the first time that she and Darius weren't alone. "And you did your brother's too I heard?"

"Of course. I would never speak to him again if he let anyone but me do it."

Lena laughed again. She seemed to find Darius funny for some reason.

Lots of women found Darius funny. Until later, when the crying came because he broke their hearts.

What the hell was he thinking anyway, introducing Lena to Darius? His brother was a straight-up dog when it came to his personal life. Okay, maybe that was overstating things a little because Darius tended to let them know right away that he wasn't looking for more than a little fun. But that was the thing —no way was his brother ready for a serious relationship and Lena was not a woman to trifle with. And yet, the idea of Darius 'serious' with Lena ...

Now that they were in the thick of it, the whole evening was beginning to feel like a very, *very* bad idea.

"I'm serious. Tattoo art is a very personal thing," Darius was saying. "That shit ..." He paused and grinned. "Excuse me. I mean, that mess where you just stop in at some anonymous joint and tell some fat dude in a wife-beater to put a rose on your ankle ... that's not how my studio works."

Looking genuinely interested, Lena nodded and took a sip of her beer. "Okay. So how..."

"I do a consultation with every client ... not me personally all the time, but my artists, or me ... and we find out why they're getting it, what it means to them, and then we do a custom design. We never ink the same image on more than one person unless that's the point."

"What do you mean unless that's the point?"

"Like some couples get the same joint like a bond or whatever. Y'know, like a sign of commitment. Or we had a group of women come in one time who were cancer survivors who had been through chemo together, and we designed something for them that they all got."

"Wow, that's kind of cool."

"Yeah, it is. Sometimes you hear an entire life story while you're inking someone. They tell you about the journey that led them to you. It's almost spiritual. The permanence of the ink is like their ... battle scars."

A slow smile spread across Lena's lips, and she looked at Quentin as though he had been hiding something wondrous from her.

"I mean think about it—in some civilizations tattoos were the markers of warriors, of survivors. Why should *we* treat them with any less reverence than that, right?"

Lena nodded as though transfixed.

"And in some civilizations, they were just meant to make a human canvas—pretty pictures on skin," Darius said lightening the mood and winking at her. "So occasionally, we do that too."

Lena grinned.

She liked Darius. It was written all across her face, and it felt like someone had stabbed Quentin in the gut. Stabbed him in the gut with a rusty knife and then just twisted the *hell* out of that sucker.

She turned to look at Quentin again, smiling as if to say,

'how amazing *is* this guy?' He smiled back and took a long gulp of his beer.

"So, you two could not be more different. Or more similar. I can't wrap my mind around it," she said.

"Nah, Q's the uptight one," Darius said, grinning. "I think it was predestined. I mean, with a name like Quentin, it had to happen, right?"

Lena shook her head, smiling politely. "He's not that uptight."

"I'm sitting right here," Quentin reminded them.

"Oh, are you?" Darius said, his eyes never leaving Lena's. "I forgot."

———

Usually on Fridays, Quentin and Darius shut the joint down, and tonight was no different. Around one a.m. when the band was still going strong, Lena had begged off to go get some rest, but not before dancing to a few songs with Darius on the small, cramped, and very hot dance-floor.

While Quentin watched, they did a bump-and-grind to reggae and dancehall music, both of them sweaty and exuberant once they returned to the table. Lena's makeup had long perspired away by the time she left, and her big hair had become even bigger.

Quentin knew his mission was accomplished when Darius walked her out to get her a cab and took a suspiciously long time to come back in.

Now, it was three a.m., and they were finally leaving themselves. Quentin had a long drive back to Maryland, and would drop Darius off at his place on Capitol Hill on the way. But they were a little quieter than usual as they headed out to Quentin's car. It was only once they were inside, and Quentin started the engine that he could bring himself to ask the question that it had been killing him not to ask.

"So, you gon' call her or what?"

Next to him in the car, Darius leaned back into the seat and laughed. "*Hell* nah."

"Wait, *why*?"

"Q, I'm not stupid."

"The hell does that mean?"

"You know exactly what I mean. I don't even know why you would set me up like that, man," Darius said sucking his teeth.

"Set you ... what are you talkin' 'bout, D?"

"Quentin, remember the Hot Wheels set you got for your thirteenth birthday?"

"What?"

"Mom and Dad got you a Hot Wheels set for your birthday. And because you were turning thirteen, it was a year you got lots of cool stuff, remember?"

Quentin looked at his brother, wondering whether Darius had had more to drink than he thought.

"Remember?"

"Yeah, yeah, I remember. What's your point?"

"You got lots of stuff, but you never opened the Hot Wheels. I looked at that box every day for like a month after your birthday. And then because you never played with it, I asked Mom if you could give it to me. So she asked you ..."

"And I said yes."

"Yeah, you did. And do you remember what happened *after* that?"

"You played with it, got sick of it, and then gave it back to me."

"No, Q. I played with it, *loved* it, and then you asked for it back."

"That's not what ..."

"Yeah."

"Nah."

"Yeah, Q. You took the shit back!"

Quentin thought for a moment and then took his eyes off the road for a moment to look at his brother again.

"Wait a minute. Are you saying that Lena is ...?"

"Like that Hot Wheels set. Yeah. Exactly. So you ain't about to set me up like that."

"Wow. So you're comparing a woman to a toy. There're so many things wrong with your analogy I don't even know where to begin."

"Let's talk about how much of a sexist pig I am later. Right now, we're on why you even want to try to pretend that you're not into her like she's into you."

"I'm not into ... Wait, what did you say?"

"She's into you." Darius shrugged. "Amend that. You're into *each other*."

"That's not true." Quentin shook his head.

"Which isn't true?"

"Neither is true, Darius. I'm married, and she is definitely not into me."

Scoffing, Darius turned a little in his seat to look at him just as Quentin turned onto 14th Street to head toward the Northeast quadrant of the city.

"Let's start with you being married. I mean, why is that, bruh? One, you been separated for almost a year; two, Mara is a bitch, and ..."

"Whoa, man. Don't call her a bitch. She's still my wife."

"And not much of one. If I thought for a second you two would pull it out and reconcile, I wouldn't call her that. But I *know* her. She's been playin' you for years, Q. The only reason she hasn't filed is that she's out there ho'ing around looking for a better deal and hedging her bets with you in case she doesn't find it. *Divorce her ass!* Divorce her, and set yourself free."

"Free, huh?"

If only the word didn't sound so damned attractive.

"Yeah. Free to step to Lena, which you so *clearly* want to do. You were mean-muggin' all night. And she could barely concentrate on any conversation we were having because she was preoccupied with *your* ugly-ass."

"Didn't look like it to me when y'all was grindin' on the dance floor."

"See what I mean? Why would you give a shit what we were doin' on the dance floor? You wanted us to hit it off, right? Or maybe you didn't."

Quentin said nothing.

"I'm not calling her because you don't really want me to. That's the bottom line. And if I do, it'll just give you one more reason to hang on to your sham-marriage instead of getting out clean like you can right now."

They were closer to Darius' place now, and for a few minutes, drove in silence.

"Lena's not into me like that. Every Monday she comes in and tells me about her dates with all these losers, who ..."

"Because deep down inside, she's hoping you'll rescue her."

"I did. By introducing her to someone who's not a loser. You."

"I appreciate the vote of confidence, but you're my brother, and I know you. It would mess your head up if I dated this woman. I mean, she's cool as hell, and I could easily see myself getting ..."

"Then call her," Quentin said, raising his voice a little more than he intended. "Truth is, I don't know what'll happen with me and Mara. And even if Lena was into me like that—which I don't believe she is—I'm not available."

"A'ight," Darius said, sounding tired. "Y'know what? I don't want to talk about this no more. I can't stand when you martyr yourself for people. One day Q, you better learn to do you. I'm serious. First Mom and Dad, then Mara ... When you gon' stop being such a 'good boy'? I just ..." Darius broke off and sighed. "Anyway. Let's just drop it."

He leaned back in his seat and closed his eyes.

"Fine by me," Quentin said. "Fine by me."

4

IT WAS TIME TO TALK TO HIS WIFE.

All weekend, Quentin had been brooding over it and considering what Darius said, about him 'martyring' himself. It was true that he had no idea what she was up to while he had been practically living like a monk for the past nine months.

It wasn't like he didn't have opportunities, but call him an idiot; he was still a little squeamish about the idea of having actual intercourse with another woman while still legally married. There could be no coming back from that. It would be like waving the white flag and calling it quits on even trying to make his marriage work.

But Darius was right. By not even communicating, wasn't that pretty much what they had done already? Maybe the answer was 'yes', but it wasn't an answer he could reach on his own—he needed to talk to his wife. So he emailed her at her work and set up a call for 2:30, which was kind of a lame move, but he felt like he needed to prepare for the conversation. It had been almost a month since they'd even heard each other's voices, after all.

Quentin timed the call precisely before his coffee date with

Lena because he had a feeling that after talking to Mara, he was going to need some relief, the kind of relief only offered by Lena's smiles and laughter and hell, just her *presence*.

You're into her. And she's into you too.

Darius' words kept swimming around in his head, but Quentin wasn't going to allow himself to dwell on them. First things first: *deal with Mara*. She had emailed back right away and said she had time around two-ish for a call, so just before that time rolled around he sat at his desk, hand poised on the receiver, ready to dial her number.

"Quentin."

She answered almost immediately, her voice sounding as warm as it had been during the earliest days of their relationship.

For a second, he was disarmed and washed in a flood of feeling for the woman he honestly believed he would have spent the rest of his life with.

"Mara," he said in return.

"So, you said you wanted to talk? What about?"

"What about?" he asked. "How about our marriage?"

"Oh yeah, that," Mara said in a failed attempt at humor.

"Yeah. That. How've you been?"

"You know. So-so. You?"

"Okay."

The silence lengthened.

Finally, Mara broke it. "Are you planning to file?"

"I don't know," he admitted. "I guess I just wanted to see where your head is at."

Mara gave a long, deep sigh on the other end of the line. "Oh, so we're still doing that, huh?"

"Doing what, Mara?" A surge of the same impatience and exasperation that had marked his last year of living in the same house with her rose in the back of Quentin's throat.

"Playing this game of chicken about who'll throw in the towel first. Do you seriously want to stay married to me, Quentin? Or is it just that you don't want to be the one to cry 'uncle'?"

"I could say the same for you."

"I moved out!" Mara raised her voice for the first time. "I cried 'uncle' a long time ago."

"Then why haven't you filed?"

"On what grounds? You know the law in Maryland. It has to be separation for a year, conviction of a felony, emotional or physical abuse or extreme cruelty, or ..."

"Adultery."

"Are you accusing me of something, Quentin?"

"Not at all. Are you about to *admit* to something?"

Another sigh. "Quentin, I'm going to go. I'd hoped we could have a different kind of conversation than the one we've had for the last three years, but I see now that was expecting too much. So... you take care, and be well."

"No," Quentin said, his voice firm. "We're not doing this again. Don't hang up."

He waited, listening to make sure she was still on the line. She was. He could hear her breathing softly.

"Look," he said, making an effort to sound more conciliatory. "Whatever we ultimately decide, we don't have to go out like this, Mara. Like those couples who turn their divorce into World War III and forget everything that was good about their marriage. I don't want us to go out like that. No matter what."

Mara was silent for a long while, then sighed. "Me neither, Quentin. I've never wanted that. There was a lot that was good about us ..."

"So how about we meet? Face to face and just ... talk? Maybe we can ... agree on what we want to do next, where we want to go."

"If you're thinking that we might ..."

"I'm not thinking anything. Except that we'll have a conversation, maybe over dinner. And just break through all the ugliness. And then if we can do all that, it might be clearer, to both of us, where we should go next, what our next move should be."

"Okay," Mara said after a moment. "Where? When were you thinking?"

"No time like the present. How about Filomena, tonight?"

"You know I could never say no to that Linguini Cardinale."

In spite of himself, Quentin smiled. "And I'll have the ..."

"Misto de Mare Alla Filomena," Mara finished for him. Her voice was soft and warm again.

Through the telephone connection, Quentin could almost feel another connection—the kind that came from spending many years with someone and learning habits, likes and dislikes that no one else in the world was privy to. Apart from the bond between siblings, there was nothing that matched the institution of marriage for creating that kind of intimacy. It would be a lie to pretend he didn't miss that. The question, though, was whether he missed Mara.

Perhaps tonight he would find out.

"You ready?"

Lena looked up from her desk, surprised to see Quentin standing in her office doorway. Right on time at three p.m. like always, so it shouldn't have been unexpected. But after this morning when he'd been decidedly more distant before the team meeting, she honestly thought he might beg off their regular three o'clock coffee date, or worse yet, just not show.

"Yup." She shoved the papers she was reading aside and reached for her suit jacket.

"You won't need it," Quentin said. "It's real nice out."

"Oh. Cool." Instead, she grabbed her cellphone and followed him toward the elevator bank, feeling inexplicably self-conscious about her bare arms. Neither of them spoke, which was unusual.

Either Lena was crazy, or he'd been treating her differently since Friday when she met his brother. Like this weekend for instance. There were no text messages. Not a single one, when normally he might have shot off at the very least a few words, just as a *'hey what's up?'*

Lena spent much of Saturday arguing herself out of being the one to break the silence, telling herself it was her imagination. They didn't *always* text on weekends, and Quentin had a life after all, and was probably doing what everyone else did on weekends—running errands, going to the gym, hanging with friends ... The kinds of things she should have been doing, instead of obsessing about him.

Still, it was a little weird that even when they were alone before the team meeting that morning, Quentin hadn't even alluded to all that time she spent Friday evening with him and his brother. And that was actually kind of disappointing because, while she'd dreaded the conversation on some level, she was also a little eager to download with him a little and share her opinion of Darius. Her edited opinion anyway.

Truth was, Darius Thomas was pretty darn close to irresistible. Like Quentin, he was smart, funny, and comfortable to be around—and easy on the eyes for sure. But while Quentin was the kind of guy who looked amazing in a suit and maybe on weekends, in a little urban, edgy, preppy-wear, Darius was the one who should never wear anything but a t-shirt and jeans, with the occasional button-down, and only so he wouldn't taunt women with those guns of his.

When his hand was on the small of her back, leading her to

the dance floor, Lena felt a tiny tingle. And when they danced and he slid his thigh between her legs, she almost lost all common sense.

At the end of the evening, he led her outside, and they talked for a few minutes on the sidewalk before he hailed her a cab. All Lena could think about was not only how charming he was, but how *freakin'* sexy. And when he finally got a cab to stop and opened the door for her, leaning in the window once he shut it, she smelled his very subtle, clean verbena scent. Lena thought he might kiss her, but he didn't. Instead, he smiled and said, '*thanks for hanging out*' in that deep, gravelly, *hella*-sexy voice of his.

And Lena settled back in the seat as the cab pulled away, wishing that she *hadn't* been wishing the entire time that Darius was Quentin.

Why wish something so pointless?

So she decided right then that if Darius called, she would at least consider going out with him. *Why not?* Quentin was nothing more than a pipe dream, and his brother was available, possibly willing, and the kind of man that no sane woman would consider a consolation prize.

When she'd described to her brother how the night had gone, Marlon had made a sound of disgust.

And you call me messy? he said. *When you're considering dating the brother of the man you really want?*

But who cared what she really wanted? Life didn't always grant you that.

"How's the Braden case coming?"

The unexpected sound of his voice in the close confines of the elevator, and interrupting her thoughts, almost caused Lena to jump.

"Good," she said, clearing her throat. "Fine."

The air was quiet between them again, almost strained. Lena

was relieved that the elevator just then came to a stop at the lobby. When the doors slid open, she hesitated and Quentin extended an arm, indicating that she should exit ahead of him.

He wore an earthy, masculine fragrance that she could almost believe was his natural smell and not cologne. When she walked by him, she thought she heard him expel a soft breath, something that almost sounded like a sigh of frustration.

Outside, as they turned in the direction of Starbucks, they kept pace with each other as they walked, and Quentin's arm brushed Lena's occasionally, something she was painfully aware of but was sure he didn't even notice.

Ten paces. Twenty. Thirty.

Lena wasn't actually counting, but they had been walking for a while and neither of them spoke again. What the hell? This never happened, that she and Q had nothing to say to each, that they were ... uncomfortable. And there was no mistaking this feeling—neither of them were relaxed right now.

At Starbucks, a woman holding a coffee carrier nudged the door open with her hip and Quentin had to pull Lena out of the way, his fingers closing on her arm for a moment.

Lena swallowed. "Thanks," she mumbled.

They made their way to join the line and Quentin shook his head. "Just tell me what you want," he said. "You go grab a seat."

"No," Lena demurred. "Thanks, but I have a ... complicated order."

"A triple-shot, three-pump vanilla latte extra-hot?" he said, deadpan.

Lena looked up and him, her eyes slightly wider.

"C'mon. You must think I have a sieve for a brain," Quentin said, noting her surprise. "You only order it every single day. Talk about *me* not wanting to try something new."

"I'll have you know it's only the most delicious coffee-drink

like, *ever*. It shouldn't even be considered coffee. It's more like …
ambrosia."

Q rolled his eyes. "Okay, well find us a couple seats and I'll order the ambrosia. And I'll have you know there's no such thing as a 'coffee-drink', just real coffee and then that bullshit you get."

Lena laughed, relieved that whatever heaviness had been there between them seemed to have dissipated. "Whatever, Quentin. I'll find us a place to sit."

All of the outdoor seating was occupied because the weather was so pleasant, so they wound up sitting at the bar style seating that lined the plate glass window looking out onto the sidewalk. Sitting next to each other, they nursed their coffees in silence for a while, but this time it was companionable.

"So about Braden …"

"Why you clockin' my case so hard?" Lena said nudging him with her knee. "You're starting to make me think you doubt I can handle it or something."

"Nah, that's definitely not it," he said slowly. "But I don't know … I was wondering if you might want to someone to second-chair."

"What d'you mean?" she asked slowly. "Like you?"

"Yeah. After Powell, I want to take a slightly lighter load. But not too light. Braden's complex, but if I'm not the lead, you know …"

"No, I get it, Q. I would love that. But you'd want to second for *me*?"

"Lena, for the hundredth time, you're a damn good lawyer. You probably don't even need the help. You'd be the one helping me out."

She rolled her eyes. "Yeah. Sure I would."

"No, for real. Basically I'm not looking for anything too high-pressure right now, but I can't exactly sit on my ass either, so this would give me a break, without it looking like it's a break if you know what I mean."

"You think Rich would okay it?"

"He already did. I told him I'd see if you were cool with it first."

"I'm cool with it," she said taking a sip of her coffee.

"Don't try to act like you won't be excited to be working sixteen-hour days with me again," Quentin said. "Sitting in the office in our own stink, dying to go home ... eating three meals out of Styrofoam containers, never seeing the sun ..."

He was teasing, but she actually *was* excited. Still, even after all this time, Lena had never enjoyed her job so much as she had when she was working closely with Quentin.

"It'll be a'ight," she said, not looking at him.

Then he reached out and touched her arm, which had been resting on the bar in front of them, running two fingers over the area between her wrist and elbow. Lena held very still.

"Goosebumps," he said, quietly, his fingers still moving back and forth across the surface of her skin. "They really crank up the AC, don't they? I never should've told you to leave your jacket. Sorry. I thought we'd sit outside."

"It's okay," Lena said, her voice hoarse.

Clearing her throat she glanced up and Quentin's eyes met hers and held. Then one corner of his mouth turned upward in a smile.

"So me and you again, huh?"

Lena's heartbeat sped up just enough that she had to take a deep breath to quiet and slow it once again. "Yup. The dynamic duo."

Q finally pulled his hand away, and she felt the loss immediately and acutely.

"Cool beans," he said. "So once I get Powell signed, sealed

and delivered, we can strategize and you can get me up to speed."

"We could do that tonight," she offered, trying not to sound eager but probably failing. "If you're working late. And I definitely am, so ..."

"Tonight?" Quentin grimaced and put a hand up to the back of his neck. "Not tonight. I have a ... thing, but maybe tomorrow?"

"A *thing*?" she said, hoping to appear unbothered. "Sounds like a hot date."

"Yeah, I don't know about the 'hot' part, but ..." He let his voice trail off and then took another sip of his coffee.

Not hot, but ... *what?* A date, nevertheless?

Lena took a quick sip of her own drink to mask her disappointment.

And there it was—the line. They were friends, but not the kind that would make it okay for her to probe further. But it didn't take a genius to figure it out. Quentin was either going out someplace with his estranged wife, or with some other woman.

Lena didn't know which option hurt more. But she did know one thing—she had no right to be hurt by *either*. Quentin was not hers and he never would be.

And she was a complete idiot for sitting around pretending and hoping otherwise.

5

———————

Lena was emptying her glass of pinot noir and had just glanced up at the kitchen clock when her brother walked in. She had twenty minutes to decide. That was definitely not enough time. Reaching for the bottle, she poured a little more wine while Marlon unloaded his messenger bag and shrugged off his spring jacket.

Though they were twins, he and Lena barely resembled each other. He was darker in complexion by several shades and had jet-black curly hair to her kinky dark-brown. People frequently mistook him for Ethiopian or Southeast Asian and occasionally spoke Arabic to him on the streets of DC before realizing he was just plain ol' homegrown Black American. But he was cute, that much was unquestioned. Problem was, he knew it too, and was even a little vain about it.

"What the hell? Alcoholic much?" Marlon strode over to her and picked up the bottle. "This was almost full yesterday!"

Lena looked at the bottle. Damn. If anyone had asked her, she would have said she had only the one glass. Or maybe two.

"What's going on? Somebody die or something? Did our *father* die?" Marlon added hopefully.

"Marlon. Stop it. That's a terrible thing to say. Not to mention if anything happened to him, you'd be a blubbering mess."

"I never said I didn't love the bastard, I just don't like him very much."

Though Marlon and their father spoke, it was just barely. Winston Chambers hadn't quite come to terms with the 'Gay Son' thing just yet.

"And I was just kidding, of course," he added. "So if not a death in the family, what's the matter with you?"

"Darius called me."

"The sexy younger brother?" Marlon sat next to her, his eyes excited. "And? Is that a bad thing? I thought you said he was cool."

"He *is* cool. And he asked me if I wanted to hang out."

"And so the problem is what, exactly?"

"I don't know," Lena said truthfully.

"Do you like him?"

"Yeah, he's fun. And funny, and interesting. All the things Quentin said he was."

"But he's not Quentin."

Lena looked at her brother, her cheeks growing warm. "I need to give it up, don't I?"

"'Fraid so, sis," Marlon said. "I mean, I think it's probably a fair assumption that there's no way Darius called you without telling his brother. Am I right?"

Lena shrugged. "They do seem to be pretty close."

"So if Quentin isn't trippin' off you going out with his brother, neither should you. Let it go, Lene. As you keep pointing out, he's married, and honestly? The more you talk about him, the more it sounds like he wants to stay that way."

"You're right," Lena said quietly.

Problem was, it was one thing to give up all her secret hopes about Quentin, but it was quite another to blow-torch them.

And that's what going out with his brother would do. If she went out with Darius, that was it; she was putting to death every possibility, in some remote and implausible future, that she could ever, ever, *ever* be more than a friend to Quentin.

But maybe that was precisely what she needed. Even if nothing else came of her date with Darius, it would definitely help extinguish her pointless hope. And just how pointless had been made clear to her very recently when Quentin let her know he had a date.

Whether that date was a reconciliation with his wife, or with some other mystery woman didn't much matter. Either way, it wasn't with her. Reaching for the phone, Lena dialed Darius' number.

MARA LOOKED AMAZING.

She had colored her hair a reddish-copper shade that complemented her dark skin and gave it a subtle, bronze glow. When Quentin first saw her a couple nights earlier, it was a surprise. It was still short, the look she favored to accentuate her high cheekbones and full lips, but in a different, more modern style. And as always, Mara was flawlessly chic.

Sitting across the table from her in Kapnos, their second dinner date in three days, Quentin recalled what he used to feel like being the man with her on his arm. Ten feet tall, that's how.

Now, he observed her as though she was a beautiful stranger.

"What're you thinking of having?" She was looking down at the menu, chewing on the corner of her lip in the way she always did when she was concentrating on something.

"Those phyllo pies sound amazing," Quentin said. "You?"

"Something with lamb," Mara said, still not looking up. "Can't do Greek food and not have lamb."

Finally, she put her menu down and gave him her full attention.

Quentin instinctively smiled, but part of him wasn't even there.

After their first successful dinner at Filomena, they were both relieved and maybe even a little over-exuberant because the evening had been a good one. By avoiding talk of their marriage and separation, they actually managed to have some semblance of a good time. And when they parted in front of the restaurant, Quentin kissed her on the cheek and felt Mara lean into it.

For a few moments, he considered making the kiss something more, maybe even inviting Mara back to the house. She was his wife, after all, and he hadn't had any in *months*. But the thought that the same might not be true of her held him back.

The next day they talked again—still pleasant. So they planned, tonight, to go to the restaurant owned and operated by a celebrity chef they had watched together years earlier on a television cooking reality show. Taking baby steps, they might somehow, soon, get to a place where they could talk about the big pink elephant in the room. Without trying to use it to trample each other to death.

"So how's work been?" he asked. "We didn't talk about that Monday."

"The same. Lots of travel. But this year, thankfully, I might get to go someplace more exciting than Chicago or L.A."

Mara was a corporate event planner. When they first met, when Quentin was in law school, she was already well established in her career, putting together high-end events for Washington DC's movers and shakers. She had even done a few events for the firm after they were married, but now, for obvious reasons, someone else in her company handled the Fox Cheatham account.

Quentin couldn't say that the frequent trips she had to take were responsible for the cracks in their marriage, but they sure hadn't helped. After having a knock-down, drag-out fight with your spouse, it was generally better if they were around so the apologies could be made, and the make-up sex could be had. Instead, many of their fights ended with Mara having to get on a plane the next day, widening the distance between them, both literally and figuratively.

"So where to this year?"

"I might get to go to the UAE."

"Wow."

"Yeah. *Really* excited about that one."

"Going alone?" Quentin asked.

Mara's face fell. "It's for work, Quentin. So, yes, I'm going alone."

"And if it weren't for work?"

Mara leaned back, folding her arms. "There's a question buried in there."

"Does it sound buried? I thought I was being very direct."

"So you want to know if I'm seeing anyone."

"I do want to know that, yes."

"Quentin ..."

"We're not in court, Mara. You don't have to worry about saying anything self-incriminating. This is just me, just you. Talking."

"And we were doing so well," she said, almost to herself.

She picked up her glass of water and took a slow sip.

Then their waiter arrived and for a few minutes, they both busied themselves with asking questions about the menu, placing their orders and getting a wine recommendation. When they were alone again, the mood was different— taut and more than a little tense.

"You can ask me the same if you like," Quentin offered.

"I already know the answer," Mara said, squeezing her lips together in a tight purse.

"You do? How?"

"Because I know you. You wouldn't bring up seeing other people unless you were *certain* you had the moral high-ground. You haven't been seeing anyone, so you can't waste the opportunity to show how comparatively ... dirty my hands are."

Mara looked up at him, and her eyes had hardened into the look that he became familiar with as their marriage began to fall apart.

"That's your thing—being the good guy compared to everyone else. Your whole life is defined by that. Even with your family." She shook her head. "You're the 'good son', and Darius is the fuck-up, isn't that how it works? You're so used to being in relationships where the other party is cooperative about playing that role that you can't stand it that I won't fall in line."

"That's interesting psychoanalysis, Mara. But you haven't answered the question."

"Off the record, counselor?" she asked sarcastically.

"Yeah. Off the record."

"I *am* seeing someone. Yes. There. Are you happy now? Did that adequately *feed* your righteous indignation?"

Quentin leaned in closer. "Did you honestly expect me to not want to know if my wife has been fucking someone else?" he asked.

Mara looked down at her lap. "Why are you doing this?"

"Doing what?"

"Starting this fight with me. Quentin, by the time I left, you wanted out of our marriage so badly, I could practically hear you hyperventilating every minute we were together. But you had to cast me as the villain to make yourself feel good about it."

"That's bullshit."

"Is it? You need to feel like you're justified to want out, but you also want me to be the one to pull the trigger. So after we got along so well a couple nights ago, I guess I should have seen this coming—you orchestrating this argument to ...”

And for a moment, she stared at him and Quentin was shocked to see that there were tears in her eyes.

“You fell out of love with me, Quentin. I could almost *feel* when it happened. And then after that, you set about making sure I fell out of love with you ... you just ...” She stopped and took another sip of water. “Look, we’ve already been separated for nine months. In three more, we can get divorced without there being any admission of fault on either side. I suggest we agree to make that the plan.”

“You want a divorce.”

“Yes,” Mara said.

But what was curious about it was that she didn’t look relieved; she almost looked ... defeated. Tired, even.

For a fleeting moment, Quentin wondered whether any of what she said was true, that maybe he wanted out before she did, that he might have fallen out of love with her first.

“But what you said on the phone? That meant something to me. I want that,” Mara continued. “For us to not hate each other when all is said and done. So, yes, Quentin. You can have your divorce.”

“I don’t recall asking for ...”

His wife looked him directly in the eyes and offered a small, sad laugh. “Oh yes you did,” she said. “Maybe not in words, but yes. You did.”

In litigation, there were *wins* and then there were wins.

For Fox Cheatham’s bottom-line, there was no distinction between them. But in Quentin’s mind, there was a firm line of division. There were cases that he won on the law, and on his clever presentation of arguments, and on his ability to simply out-lawyer the other side. And then there were cases where some small technicality granted him the advantage—a witness for his opponent messed up on the stand or failed to recall key details while being deposed, or a judge made rulings in his favor that were just short of reversible error. In those cases, when Quentin won, the win didn't feel clean. In cases like that, a loss wouldn't have been welcome, but it would have been acceptable because the 'win' wasn't fully deserved.

Driving away from his dinner with Mara, he had the answer he had been seeking for months—she said wanted to divorce, and that she would file. *He* hadn't walked out on his marriage, and *he* wouldn't be the one to put the final nail in the coffin to end it.

He had won. But it didn't feel clean.

***

"This was *so* not what I was expecting," Lena said, laughing as she and Darius exited the fitness studio. "When a guy asks me out, I'm thinking wine ... fancy hors d'oeuvres, a complete meal maybe ..."

"We can do something like that next time," Darius said.

"So now that you sweated my tail off, am I free to go?"

"Nah. We're going to Jamba Juice," he said, inclining his head to the left.

Lena sighed. "Okay, you're in charge, so let's do it."

"You did well in there," he said as they started walking.

"Thank you. Was it a test or something? Something you put women through to see whether you want to take them on a real date?"

"Nah. Why would I need to test you? My brother says you're cool people, so you're cool people."

Lena shook her head. "That's all it takes, huh? Q's endorsement?"

"He's never steered me wrong." Darius shrugged.

"And is he in the habit of ... steering women your way?"

Darius laughed. "I do a'ight on my own."

Lena didn't doubt it. While they were working out, more than a few gym-bunnies shot envious looks her way, their eyes skimming Darius' frame, struggling not to stare. It was a special kind of high, she couldn't lie—being with That Dude at the gym, being the object of all that envy.

When Lena called him back to let him know she was free, Darius told her to "dress very casually, and for an active evening." So Lena had worn loose black yoga pants, her tennis shoes, and a long-sleeved, white Under Armour shirt, pulling her hair back into a high Afro-puff. She imagined he was probably taking her to play laser-tag or something, but when she met Darius at the address he gave her, she got out of the Uber and realized it was a Washington Sports Club.

We're gonna work out, he announced, looking pleased with himself.

And they had. After a half hour warm-up on the treadmill, Darius took her through his routine of dead-lifts, bench presses, squats, and flies. Somewhere about forty minutes in, Lena felt those endorphins kick in, and actually started to enjoy herself.

And it didn't hurt that she got to watch Darius's muscles ripple and tremble as he put them to work. Even the grunting and groaning as he handled the heavy weights was kind of sexy.

Now, as they walked down the cobblestone sidewalks of Wisconsin Avenue, Lena was glad she'd come. Working out was something of an afterthought for her most days since she worked long hours, so it was good to see how well her body held up under pressure.

"After we get our smoothies, want to see my studio?"

Darius was walking closely at her side, but not touching her. Lena pretended not to notice the looks he got from other women. His tattoos didn't just cover his forearms, she'd learned; they were all the way up to his shoulders and neck as well. And when he lifted his shirt in the gym to wipe his brow, there were even more on his chest.

"I would love to see your studio," she said. "But you're not going to talk me into getting a tattoo."

He grinned. "No authentic tattoo artist would do such a thing."

In Jamba Juice, they both got energy bowls and sat at one of the tables to eat, Darius's long legs stretched out beneath it, on either side of Lena's.

"So is this your standard Wednesday night?" she asked.

"This is my standard, any-day-of-the-week night. Except for Fridays. On Fridays, I hang with Q."

"Every Friday?"

"Without fail."

"That must get irritating for women you're involved with. Friday is supposed to be date night, couples' night. Do you ever bring your dates with you?"

"Nah. Friday is about me and Q. If she's not with that, she can't be with me."

"That's a pretty hard line to draw. I guess I should be flattered I was invited to hang out with you two last Friday."

"You should," Darius said, looking at her seriously for a moment. "He's never done that before. Neither of us has. That's how I knew you were important to him."

Lena looked down into her bowl and scooped up a spoonful

of strawberries and yogurt. "I don't know about all that. We're friends, and he wanted me to meet you, that's all."

"Hmm." Darius looked at her searchingly. "Y'know, I'm going to share something with you about my brother ..."

Lena looked up, waiting.

"He doesn't ... always know his own heart. So when he wanted me to meet you, like maybe so I could ask you out, I wondered, y'know. Especially when I saw you two together."

"What did you wonder?"

"Whether friendship was all either of you wanted. From each other, I mean."

"Did you ask him?"

"I did."

"And what did he say?" Lena asked, trying not to sound too eager to know.

Darius shook his head. "I'd rather hear what *you* say."

Lena forced herself to meet and hold Darius' gaze. "Your brother's married," she said. "And even if he weren't, we are most definitely just friends. I wouldn't have accepted your invitation tonight otherwise."

Every word of what she said was true, but then why did it *feel* like a lie?

Darius's eyes held hers for a few moments more. "Okay," he said finally.

Then he looked down into his bowl again and dug in, coming up with a heaping spoon of fruit and oat grain which he promptly ate, chewing like it was the most delicious thing he'd ever eaten.

When he swallowed, he leaned back and watched her eat a few bites. Lena pretended not to feel self-conscious at being so openly regarded, and kept eating, albeit more slowly and daintily than she might otherwise have done.

"So," Darius said, "you want to hang out again sometime?"

Moment of truth, Lena.

Darius was waiting, his light-brown eyes trained on her face. All the confusion about Quentin aside, he was the most attractive man who had asked her out in eons. And the most fascinating.

If she had met him any other way, and at any other time—like before she met Quentin—she would be jumping out of her skin to say 'yes'. But she *had* met Quentin first and had only met Darius because he was Quentin's brother.

Then she recalled what Marlon said earlier that evening: *He's married, Lena, and it looks like he's trying to stay that way.*

"Yeah," she said to Darius. "I think I would."

He grinned. "Hurry up and finish that," he said, "So I can walk you over to my studio. *And* talk you into that tattoo."

6

———————

"*You're* in a good mood."

Her brother was standing at the open refrigerator when Lena walked in humming. He was surveying the contents of the fridge with a grimace on his face, clearly dissatisfied with what it had to offer.

"As a matter of fact, I am," Lena said, tossing her sports bag on the sofa and collapsing next to it. "In a good mood and in even better physical shape."

"I thought y'all would have graduated to real date territory by now," Marlon said, shutting the door and turning to look at her. "Don't mess around thinking you have a new boyfriend, when maybe all you have is a new personal trainer." He laughed at his own joke.

Nodding, Lena accepted her brother's ridicule. "I know it's a little ... unconventional. But I kind of like this slow, meandering pace. Darius is ... a character. At this point, I don't know if I'd even like it if he invited me to a fancy restaurant and bought me a lobster dinner."

"Is he gay?"

"Marlon. No, he's *not* gay. Seriously?"

"Lemme meet him. I'll tell you if he is."

"He's not."

"Four dates now, and all of 'em at the gym? Does that even qualify as dating?"

"And then Jamba Juice. Don't forget Jamba Juice."

Marlon rolled his eyes. "Has he kissed you?"

"No, but ..."

"*Tried* to kiss you?"

"Well ..."

"Gay. He probably goes to the gym to check out other men," Marlon said with certainty. "I mean ... let's assess for a minute. When he asks you to meet him, does he actually *call* them dates?"

Lena thought for a few moments. "He says, '*want to hang out?*' or something like that."

"Lena. Something else is up. If he was dating you, he would've made his move already. Either in words or in deed."

"I think he's being respectful because he knows I work with his brother," Lena said.

But now she wasn't so sure. If she was inclined to be overly analytical—and she wasn't because that was what she did for work, and was trying *not* to do in her personal life—she would have to admit that Darius tended to treat her more like a home-girl than anything else.

They laughed, they joked, and they mostly steered clear of personal subjects except for that first time when he asked her about her and Q's relationship. And when he touched her, it was incidental, like when he ushered her through a door.

And why hadn't he tried to kiss her? Granted, the circumstances—working out together—weren't ideal for that, but then why wouldn't he change the circumstances?

"And what does Quentin say?"

"I don't know. He's been in New York for a week for a case. Since the day after the first time I ... hung out with Darius."

"Have you talked to him?"

"No. I'm not on that case, so no need."

"Mm." Marlon leaned against the kitchen counter and looked at her appraisingly.

"What?" Lena demanded.

"Maybe Darius is just your Quentin-substitute."

"My *what*?"

"You heard what I said. He's out of town and you miss him, so you're using his brother in the meantime."

"Using?"

"Let's put it this way," Marlon said. "You've rubbed a couple out with a picture of Quentin in your head, haven't you?"

"*Eww!* Shut up! I'm not talking to my brother about masturbating!" Lena tossed a sofa cushion in his direction, which fell far short of its intended target.

"And I don't want to hear any details, believe me. But I'm just sayin' ... if you're having such a great time with Darius, I wonder whether he's replaced Quentin in your nocturnal fantasies. And if he hasn't, then all this ..." Marlon gestured with his hand, "... is a mirage. A distraction. And you're just using him."

Lena shoved herself up from the sofa, suddenly feeling a lot less buoyant than she had when she walked into the apartment minutes ago.

"I hate you," she said to her brother as she headed for the shower.

"I know. But I *love* you. Hurry up and get clean so we can go get *tapas* somewhere. I'm starving!"

"I can't have *tapas* with you. I have to go back to the office to get some work done."

"It's Friday!"

"Well, no rest for the wicked. This case is kicking my ass so I need to finish up a few things. If I'm done by ten I'll give you a call and you can come get me."

In the shower, Lena lathered herself quickly. She was starving too, and it *was* Friday, so a few drinks with her brother and *tapas* in a trendy downtown restaurant sounded like as good a plan as any. Hopefully, she would be done early and they could hang out.

And then she thought about Marlon said.

He was right. Why *wasn't* she doing something with Darius? If they were 'dating' why was it that they had parted ways with a fist-bump when she climbed into the Uber, instead of with a kiss? Not even one on the cheek.

And most tellingly, why the hell was it that when she—how did Marlon put it—*rubbed one out*, she still thought only of Q?

She didn't need to ask those questions. She knew why. Marlon was right. Darius was a distraction. A pleasant one, but a distraction nonetheless. He looked like Q a little, sounded like him sometimes, and even shared some of the same cute mannerisms—like the way they both squinted when they were concentrating on something: Q when he was reading legal briefs, Darius when he was contemplating lifting a heavy weight. The way they both smiled with practically all of their teeth bared, you could almost hear the voice of a parent when they were kids, about to take a picture of them saying, '*Smile wide now!*'

They were both great guys. Either of them would be a great catch for any woman who was lucky enough. But neither of them could be the man for her— Quentin because he was married to someone else, and Darius because she was hopelessly in love with his brother.

"So how was NYC?"

"Same ol, same ol'," Quentin said, clinking his beer bottle against his brother's. "Got some settlement papers signed, took a victory lap around Manhattan, you know ..."

"*Damn.* Another one bites the dust, huh?" Darius said looking impressed. "You should be ready to run that joint soon, bruh. That partnership should be in the bag."

"You never know with stuff like that, but yeah, I think Rich was pleased." Quentin nodded. "So what's been up with you lately?"

Darius grinned at him. "Funny you should ask that ..."

"Oh! I forgot to tell you," Quentin interrupted. "I saw Mara. Just before I left town."

"Word?" Darius put his beer bottle on the bar in front of him and folded his arms, his expression sobering up suddenly. "And?"

Quentin laughed. "Don't look like that. It's not what you think."

"What do you *think* I think?"

"That we're getting back together or some shit."

"You're not?"

"No. She asked for a divorce. We had dinner a couple times before I left, and she agreed we should put ourselves, and each other, out of our misery."

Darius shook his head and looked down at his lap. "Damn." He looked up again. "And you're cool with it?"

Quentin shrugged.

The truth was, he hadn't given it much thought while he was in New York. He was working long hours combing through the final settlement agreement with a fine-tooth comb, then having heavy steak dinners with Richard Lowe, and finally collapsing into his hotel bed and waking up the next morning, bright and early, to do it all over again.

Mara hadn't even crossed his mind.

Instead, he wondered how Lena was faring on the Braden matter, and whether he should have stopped by her office on his way out the night before when he knew he was leaving. As it was, all he managed was one hasty text message letting her know he was gone, and that was after he already landed at LaGuardia.

She responded with one line: *Knock it outta the park, Q!*

That was all, and he hadn't seen or spoken to her since because he came back just in time to make it to his and Darius' weekly meet-up at Accra Café.

"You have to be sure," Darius said with uncharacteristic seriousness. "Because divorce is final."

"And so was my marriage. Or so I thought."

Now it was Darius's turn to shrug. "So it goes. But you're sure there's no part of you, no tiny part that wants to give it another shot?"

"What's up with you? You were the one who told me I should ..."

"Yeah, but what the hell do I know, Q?" Darius said impatiently. "This is *your* life."

"Okay, you want to know the truth?"

"Yeah. Please."

Darius turned his barstool around to face him, but Quentin kept his eyes trained on the television set, playing a soccer match with the sound turned down, above the bar.

"When we had dinner, Mara said some things. She said I fell out of love with her, and then did everything possible to make sure she fell out of love with me, too. I don't know," Quentin said. He took a long sip of his beer, a bitter, smoky ale that made his head spin a little when he drank it too fast. "But I remember ... I remember a time when I would stay in the office for just that one extra hour when I could go home, but I *chose* not to. And instead, I finished up that brief or wrote that last client memo ... even though I knew that it would mean Mara would be asleep when I got home."

He remembered way more than that. He remembered that Lena had been there at work on some of those nights, a salve to the unpleasantness that sometimes awaited him at home. A cute and funny counterpoint to his wife's increasing coldness and distance. Quentin wasn't even sure now when that had begun, Mara's coldness, or when he started thinking it was less trouble to avoid it than to deal with whatever might have caused it.

Darius nodded. "So you did fall out of love."

"That's the thing. Maybe it was that, or my drive to win cases outpaced my drive to make my marriage work. And that's the thing about marriage, man," Quentin said. "You always think there'll be more time to make it up, time to apologize, time to put her first again. If she'll only wait ... just that one more hour, or day, or week ... or after that one big case." He shrugged. "I guess she got tired of waiting. And truth be told, she wasn't exactly waiting. She was gone a lot too."

"You still haven't answered the question. When you guys split, were you still in love with her?"

Quentin looked at his brother and took a deep breath. Finally, he shook his head.

"I don't know. I just know that at some point, I guess I decided that even being away from her as much as I was, working as much as I was and not dealing with what was going on at home? The rewards would be ... worth the risk."

It was hard to admit it, but there it was. At some point in the pursuit of his career, the risk of losing his wife became an acceptable one.

But, no matter what his feelings, he never would have left Mara. Not because of a seasonal change in his emotions. Couples fell in and out of love all the time, but marriage meant you planned to stick with it until the love returned. He would have worked on their marriage until his last breath if his wife had been willing. Mara was the one who made it clear she had no plans to put that work in. *Not him.*

Darius sighed and nodded. "Okay. Then you're doing the right thing ending it. And now you're free to pursue ... other things."

Quentin laughed. "You still on that mess about Lena?"

"Well, if you wanted to, you could go for it, right? Now that you know what you don't want with Mara? So here's the thing, man. About Lena ..."

"I don't need you to tell me anything about Lena. Whatever you got to say doesn't change the fact that she and I are just friends," Quentin said.

"Hmm." Darius nodded and picked up his beer bottle again.

"What's that mean?"

"Nothing. Just ... *hmm.*"

***

"You sure you straight, man?"

Darius was frowning when he leaned in the passenger-side window. Quentin had just moments before pulled up at the curb outside his brother's apartment building, and was having a little trouble keeping his eyes open.

"Yeah, I'm good. I only had two beers."

"You could crash here, Q. I don't want to explain to our mother why you ran off the road after hanging out with me all night."

Quentin glanced at the dashboard clock. "It's just after midnight," he said. "You and me, we push on through till dawn sometimes, bruh. I'm good. And besides, ain't nobody want to sleep in your dirty-ass crib."

"A'ight ..." Darius still looked a little uncertain. "Call me when you get home before you shut it down."

"Yup."

But as soon as he pulled away from the curb, Quentin felt his eyelids growing heavy again. Without the accompaniment of Darius's idle chatter, he was feeling the long day, the trip from New York and the alcohol begin to catch up with him.

"Shit," he muttered, considering whether he should turn around and take his brother up on his offer.

But what he wanted most right now was his own bed; definitely not Darius's sofa with its stains of dubious origin. All he needed was something to help keep him awake for the thirty-five-minute drive back to Maryland.

Without stopping to second-guess himself, he reached for his phone, and at a stoplight, dialed Lena's number. If she didn't answer, he would resort to WHUR, Howard University's radio station, listen to some deejay prattling on, sing along to some R&B and before he knew it, he would be home.

"Hey! How's New York?"

The sound of her voice, piping directly into his head through his earbuds, made him smile.

"It was in pretty good shape when I left it," he answered.

"You're back?"

"Yup."

For a moment neither of them said anything. The sound of Lena's soft, barely audible breaths on the other end was actually having the opposite effect he'd hoped for, and Quentin felt sleep whispering his name.

"What're you up to?" he finally asked. "Out on the town, hittin' up some clubs ... sippin' on gin-and-juice?"

"I wish. Working on Braden."

"You're working?" he asked. "Where?"

Lena groaned. "The office."

"What the ... it's *Friday*, Lene."

"I know. I was supposed to go hang out with my brother. But then I got here and you know how it is—one thing led to another led to another, and now I may as well finish up."

"Want some company?"

Quentin thought he could hear her smile. But when she spoke, for *sure* he heard it.

"I would love some," she said. "But y'know what I would like even more than that?"

"What?"

"7-Eleven nachos, a Spicy Big Bite and a large Coke."

"I might be able to hook you up," he said.

Quentin made a U-turn at the next light, and headed back into the heart of downtown Washington DC, his exhaustion momentarily forgotten.

7

———

"WHAT TOOK YOU SO LONG?"

"First, I had to find a pig, kill it, skin that sucker, grind up the meat …stuff it into some sausage casing …"

"Smart-ass."

Lena grabbed the 7-Eleven bag from Quentin's unresisting fingers and opened it, closing her eyes in appreciation at the aroma of greasy, fatty, decidedly heart-*un*healthy, late-night comfort food.

"Damn. You really are going to eat that crap, huh?"

"Hell yeah." She looked in the bag and stuck out her lower lip, mimicking someone close to tears. "You got me *two* Big Bites," she said. "And *two* nachos."

"And a *two*-liter of Coke."

"Thank you."

Lena took the bag over to her desk and pulled everything out, shoving aside the papers she had been trying to read while managing her impatience for Quentin to arrive. She had been telling herself that it was hunger alone that made her eager for him to get there. But seeing him now, dressed in jeans and a dress shirt with the tail out, a five o'clock shadow dusting his jaw she had to admit, that the food was the least of what she had been yearning for.

"You look like half-baked cow-crap," she lied easily as she broke the seal on the Coke.

"Thanks," he said, impassively. He took one of her guest chairs, stretching his legs in front of him. "You do, too."

Lena grinned and looked down at her black leggings, over-sized sweatshirt and well-worn All-Stars, and suddenly it was all weird and quiet and they were staring at each other in a way they never had before.

Lena was first to break the stare, focusing once again on her meal. Such as it was.

"I wasn't planning on having company," she said, hiding her smile.

Somehow, she knew he hadn't been any more honest about how she looked him to him than she had been about how he looked to her.

Searching her office for a few moments she found a coffee mug that didn't look too dusty and poured some Coke. She extended the mug to Quentin who shook his head.

"So what's going on with Braden?" he asked. "Anything I can help with?"

There was the Quentin she knew—always reminding her in the nick of time that they were 'work-friends'.

"Your eyes are about to close, Q. You should probably just head home. I appreciate you doing the food run, but ..."

"Nah," he said. "It's almost one-thirty. I can't leave you here alone,"

"I'm fine," Lena said, hoping he wouldn't take her word for it. "I've been here all along, and it's a secure building. I'll just call the car service when I'm done."

"Can't do it," Quentin said, shaking his head.

His eyelids looked like they weighed a hundred pounds, and each time he blinked, Lena wasn't sure they would lift again.

"Actually, you probably *shouldn't* do it," she amended. "You look like you're ready to pass out."

"Because I am." He nodded slowly and then gave her a grin that had her stomach doing flips.

Between that smile and the sleepy eyes, Lena's imagination was running wild. She pictured Quentin in bed, waking up next to her, giving her that identical smile, his eyes sleepy like they were now.

"Go get some rest in your office, then," she said, pointedly turning her focus to her still-warm hot dogs. "After I eat, I'll knock out a couple more things and then I'll come wake you."

"Deal." Quentin was already shoving himself to his feet.

Lena made it a point not to follow him with her eyes as he sauntered out of her office, stretching as he went.

IF SHE HAD BEEN HOPING TO GET HER SECOND WIND AFTER EATING, that wasn't what happened. Instead, Lena was full, sluggish and beginning to feel tired herself. Even the caffeine in the soda hadn't helped, and by two-fifteen a.m., she was thinking about Quentin, peacefully asleep in his office and wishing she had a sofa of her own to collapse onto.

After a few pointless attempts to get back to work, she decided to throw in the towel. Anything she read this late at night was sure to fly out of her head immediately, and anything she wrote was certain to be gibberish.

Gathering the refuse from her late-night meal, she stuffed it in the trash can near her desk and grabbed her phone and pocketbook, heading down to Quentin's office. When she got there, she found him eyes closed, chest rising and falling in a slow, even pace, apparently sound asleep. His shoes were off, and he was stretched out on his sofa, as expected.

Lena stood at the door and studied him for a few minutes, relieved that there was no one else around to watch her at it. Quentin had longish lashes, and of course *that face*.

But it was the mouth that got her every time. Those full lips ...

"You here to tell me a bedtime story?"

Lena jumped, her face growing hot. How long had he been aware of her standing there?

"As a matter of fact, I am," she said, recovering quickly.

At that, Q opened his eyes. Barely. They were a little pink, and still *a lot* tired.

"Oh yeah?" he said as she came around to face him. "What's it called?"

He let his feet fall to the floor so he was only partly reclining now, and she sat at the other end of the sofa, so they were about three feet apart.

"It's called Quentin Kicks Ass. About an attorney who closes deal after deal, after deal ..."

"Sounds boring," he said, one corner of his mouth lifting in a half-smile.

"Maybe to him. But it's a story I never get tired of hearing," Lena said truthfully.

"Yeah?" Q's eyes opened just the teensiest bit wider.

"Yeah." She nodded, speaking quietly. "I'm proud of him. And proud to be ..." Lena shrugged, "his friend."

The smile on Quentin's face slipped and his eyes fixed on hers for a few moments, then his focus shifted to her lips. So Lena did what anyone does when someone stares at their lips— she licked them.

Quentin's eyes darkened, and he extended his hand, palm up. Lena reached out resting her open hand atop it. She held her breath. Curling his fingers, Q caressed her palm, then awkwardly interlaced their fingers. Switching tacks, he released her hand altogether and held her wrist, pulling her toward him.

Lena didn't think she had taken a complete breath the entire time, and that was confirmed when it all came out at once in a long, deep, audible exhale.

Q was still staring at her, his face unreadable. Or at least ... what she read, she was unwilling to believe.

"C'mere," he said, his voice throaty and hoarse.

Lena slid over, closing the distance between them and Quentin put an arm around her shoulder, pulling her against him so her head was practically resting on his shoulder.

"Thank you," he said.

He kissed her on the forehead, and the contact was white-hot while his lips remained there until—with her breath still hard to control and unsteady—Lena turned her head slightly and looked up at him.

"You ... you're wel..." The rest of her sentence seemed stuck in her throat because Q was leaning in, his face coming closer to hers.

"You smell *so* good," he said, his voice as quiet as hers had been. "Do you just wake up smelling this good?"

"Yes," she said, straight-faced. "Every day." And then, "what do I smell like?"

"Coconut. And cotton candy," he said without hesitation. "You smell ... sweet."

"Liar," Lena whispered. "I smell like 7-Eleven junk food and you know it."

Quentin smiled.

And that smile was the last thing Lena saw before his lips touched hers and her eyes fluttered shut.

Coconut oil. Every morning she mixed it with her unscented lotion to use after she showered. But today she had to mix it with something of Marlon's from The Body Shop because she was out of her unscented kind. Marlon's moisturizer bore the scent of some unidentifiable tropical fruit. Lena was glad Quentin liked it. Maybe she would steal Marlon's moisturizer when she got home.

Quentin didn't dive in deep right away. Instead, he brushed his lips back and forth against hers, the pressure light, and so damned sexy like he was deciding whether to kiss her and how far to take it. It was Lena who pushed in closer, and she was first to introduce tongues into the equation, pushing just the tip of hers between her lips until Quentin did the same. And once their tongues touched, something ignited in them both and they basically went wild.

Lena felt Q's hands in her hair, grabbing and holding; and hers were on his shoulders, then his back, then cupping his face. She had been dying to touch him for so long that she couldn't seem to decide where and for how long. And wherever he touched her it felt better than good, it was *amazing*. Now it was her jaw, her neck, her shoulders. Lena shifted, pushing her chest forward, feeling her nipples harden just at the idea that Quentin might make contact with them.

But whatever he might do, Lena knew what she wanted, and she wasn't about to wait. She slid her hands down over his chest, to his stomach, under the hem of his shirt and upward again. He tensed slightly at the contact with his bare skin and made a sound like a groan, his kisses becoming deeper and more insistent.

Under her hands, Lena felt a faint trail of hair, surprisingly soft at his abdomen that ran up his chest, becoming coarser and denser the farther north she went. She pulled back a little, intending to unfasten a button or two when Quentin grabbed her wrists.

"Lene," he said. His chest was heaving, his nostrils flared. "What're we doing?"

"I don't know," she admitted.

Their faces were close together, almost touching and Lena felt his warm breath on her cheeks. How long had it been since she had been fantasizing about being this close to Q, touching him this way and having him touch her?

No, she didn't know what they were doing, but she didn't care.

Tentatively, hoping he wouldn't push her away, Lena touched her lips to his again and Quentin heaved a quiet sigh and they were off once again—dueling tongues, wandering hands, panting and uneven breaths. He gently pushed her back so she was lying on the sofa and he was on top of her, part of his weight on one elbow.

Lena felt him, like a rod between her thighs and shifted so he was pressed directly where she wanted him. Quentin sucked on her tongue and her back arched off the sofa, her fingernails raking his scalp. His hair was low-cut and smooth and felt almost silky to the touch. She wanted to pause, to experience each sensation separately and to revel in them, but they just couldn't seem to stop kissing each other.

"Damn," Q breathed against her neck.

His hands were under her shirt now, and he was palming both her breasts, his thumbs skimming across her nipples through the fabric of her bra.

"You still tired?" Lena teased.

"Hell nah," he said, moving his lips to that sensitive spot just behind her ear. "And to think I almost wound up crashing at D's …"

At that, Lena froze. *Darius.* She had forgotten about Darius.

"Quentin," she said, swallowing hard. She put her hands up, palms pressed against his chest to get him to lift off her.

"What?" He dipped his head again, this time taking her earlobe between his lips.

"*Quentin*," she said again, this time, more forcefully.

This time, he pulled back, his eyes searching hers. "You okay? Did I ..?"

He sat up and Lena bit down on her lower lip, not quite knowing *how* to say what she knew she had to say.

"No," she said at allay his fear. "It's nothing you did. It's something I ..." She tugged at her sweatshirt, trying to get it righted again. "It's Friday. Did you see your brother?"

"Yeah. Before I came over here. Why?"

"Because ... did he say anything? About me?"

"About you? No, wh ..." Quentin sat up straighter as the realization of something dawned in his eyes. "What should he have said?"

Lena sighed, running a hand over her face. "He should have said ... that we've been hanging out. Darius and I have been ..."

Quentin stood so abruptly, Lena jumped. Then he was pacing the floor directly in front of her, a hand atop his head.

"You're ... kickin' it with my brother?"

"I don't ..."

She didn't know what to call it. Marlon was right. It was weird that Darius hadn't actually taken her on a *date*-date. But on the other hand, just because they hadn't been to dinner, or held hands, or kissed didn't mean that Darius wasn't trying to start something with her. And she was saying 'yes' to these offers to hang out, so from all appearances, she was interested in starting something with him as well.

At least that was how it would look to Quentin. And how it might ... not might, probably ...That was how it probably looked to Darius as well.

What the hell had she been thinking? If she had even an ounce of interest in Darius, she never would have wound up groping and grinding and sticking her tongue down Quentin's throat.

"Lena!"

Her head jerked up, and she looked at Quentin again. He looked pissed. Of course, he was pissed. *What kind of person did this?*

"Are you *dating* my brother?"

"We've worked out together a few times, and then he ..."

"Y'know what?" Quentin said, holding up a hand. "This isn't for you and me to talk about. This is something me and him need to discuss. Get your stuff, let me take you home."

He wasn't even looking at her now. And his voice was different. Lena tried to make eye contact but he evaded it.

"Q, I didn't mean to ..."

"Look, it's late. You ready? I need to ... let's just get out of here, a'ight? I know you must be tired too."

Lena nodded. "This is all I have," she said, indicating her long-discarded pocketbook on the floor next to the sofa.

I know you must be tired too.

He had to be angry and yet he managed to sound caring at the same time.

"I'm ... I'll meet you at the elevators," he said, his words tumbling one over the other.

And then he left her there, sitting on his sofa, lips still tingling from his kisses, the memory of his fingers still imprinted on her skin.

LENA PACED HER LIVING ROOM, PLAYING WITH THE TASSELS ON THE sleeves of her top. It was a white linen blouse she had bought during a vacation in Cancún, which doubled as a cover-up.

Underneath, she wore a white bikini under her denim shorts, and on her feet, a pair of brown sandals.

"You are a hot-ass mess, you know that?" Marlon said. "Going on a date in order to break up with the guy you're not even sure you're *actually* dating."

"Shut up, Marlon. I'm trying to think."

"What are you thinking about? When he called, you just should've said no! Or told him on the phone that you're not into this little *quasi*-dating situation."

"I feel like I owe him more than that. And besides, he's Q's brother, so I can't burn any bridges."

"Why not?" Marlon grabbed a couple grapes from the bunch on the plate in front of him. "Quentin is just your ... co-worker, sis. Lest you forget."

"He's way more than that."

She had been trying all morning to put out of her mind what happened on Friday evening, second-guessing her every move, wondering what Darius would think of her if he knew, wondering what Quentin thought of her. He had driven her home, with no more than a dozen words passing between them. When he got to her building he waited until she was inside and even texted her a few minutes later to make sure she wasn't just in the building, but in her apartment as well, with the door secure behind her.

"Oh yeah, he's your fantasy boo-thang. Emphasis on the *fantasy*."

"Didn't I tell you to shut up?"

Marlon didn't know, nor did she have any intention of telling him that at least for a little while, the fantasy had been made real. And that Quentin had more than lived up to all those moments in her imagination. Just kissing him, feeling his hands on her waist, on her breasts had been ... sublime.

But of course, that was all messed up now. Now she was the

chick who would be scandalous enough to be crawling all over him even though she was seeing his brother. She was *that* chick.

"Okay, shutting up right now." Marlon pantomimed zipping his lips shut, and Lena took a deep breath, resuming her pacing.

Just as she decided that she needed to stop pretending she could develop any feelings for Darius and make a gracious exit from their non-dating situation, he had called her and asked her to a cookout. Just talking to him made her feel guilty, knowing she had been lip-locked with his brother, tussling around on an office sofa. But that part of her messy situation would have to wait to be sorted out when she saw Q on Monday.

Today, her only mission was to look Darius in the eye and level with him. Whatever it was they had been doing, she couldn't do it anymore. She wasn't sure she was ready to tell him why, but either way, she had to end it. Marlon was right—she had basically been using him as a Quentin substitute.

And if there was any doubt about that, it had been thoroughly dispelled when Q called her during prime booty-call hours, and she hadn't even been able to make herself *not* respond. Hell, if he had been making a booty-call, her dumb-ass would probably have been more than happy to oblige.

So that was that—Darius was history, as was whatever they were doing. He was way too cool a guy for her to lead him on. She relented when he asked her to the cookout because he probably deserved to be told in person that she wasn't going to be 'hanging out' with him anymore; and because he was Quentin's brother, she definitely didn't want any hard feelings between them when the dust settled.

So now, here she was, pacing her living room and waiting for him to arrive, mentally rehearsing how to end a relationship she wasn't even sure had begun.

"YOU LOOK TIRED."

Quentin's mother ran a hand over his head, letting it come to rest at his cheek. She patted it, and Q smiled up at her reassuringly.

"No, I'm good, Ma."

Sitting at her kitchen table, he watched as his mother prepared the meats for their Sunday meal. His parents always liked to do a Sunday spread, no matter how many or how few people they had over for dinner. It was a ritual of Quentin's and Darius's childhood to sit in her kitchen and watch her work. Intermittently, their father would stop in, look over her shoulder, kiss her on the neck, wrap his arms around her waist, and their mother would shoo him away, blushing like a schoolgirl.

Quentin had always wanted that for himself. When the time was right, he planned to have the same kind of relationship with a woman who, decades into their marriage, would still blush when he touched her just so.

If that was what he'd wanted, he'd definitely chosen wrong with Mara. By the time they separated, she was flinching when he touched her or moving out of his reach while trying to make it seem like that wasn't what she was doing.

"How was New York? Your brother told me you closed another deal when you were there."

"That's basically all there is to tell. Closed a deal, hit up some New York restaurants and came home."

"I love that city. Your father and I used to go there for long weekends, to watch whatever show was the big deal on Broadway, and sometimes just for the excitement of *being* there, y'know?"

"Yeah, I know. It's a cool place."

"If we were younger and could afford it, I think we might even have chosen it as a place to live."

"Why didn't you?" Quentin asked, looking up at his mother now. "When you were younger?"

Turning to face him, her back to the stove, his mother's expression transformed, a soft smile curving her lips. Evelyn Thomas was a beautiful woman; there was no question about that. Only just having turned sixty, she looked like a woman ten years younger. She was trim, and still very active, joining whatever trendy fitness craze happened to be in vogue at the moment.

Right now she was into hot yoga and swore it had made her a new woman. She certainly looked amazing, with her new gray highlights, which she had jokingly said she added so that younger men would stop trying to hit on her.

Quentin and Darius had both inherited her pecan complexion and hazel eyes. Their height, imposing physicality, and square-jaws had all come from Darrell Thomas, their formidable and much darker-complected father.

"We wanted to be sure we would have lots of space to raise children—and safe neighborhoods both for you boys, and for your father to work in."

Darrell Thomas was a police officer, and when Quentin and Darius were growing up, had still been a patrolman. Now, he was just a few years shy of retirement and was the Deputy Chief in their parents' small, suburban village, just outside Washington DC.

"And remember when you all were growing up, that was the height of the crack epidemic," his mother explained. "New York was terrible. DC was terrible ... I couldn't sleep at night if I thought your father might not come back after his shift. That was a very real possibility back then. Police officers' lives weren't sacrosanct."

"Neither were young Black men's lives, Ma."

"No, that's true," she said nodding. "But the young Black

men I was most concerned about were my own. So ... living in New York, that just didn't seem like the most practical thing for us, for a young family. Why? Were *you* thinking about it?"

"It crossed my mind."

While he was in New York, one of the partners from their opponent law firm had given him a soft approach, mentioning that they were *'always looking for new members to join their team'* and that the perks in NYC, as compared to DC, were *'exceptional'*. It was the kind of approach that would be deniable later if Quentin was to mention it to his bosses, but that could become outright recruitment if he responded with anything like interest.

At the time, he'd actually been insulted, because of the obvious conflict it presented, and the implication that he could be simply 'bought' away from the firm where he'd cut his teeth and learned to be the attorney he was today. But later, he saw it for the compliment it was and pondered it a little. He'd been planning to tell Lena about it since he could hardly confide in Rich.

But then what happened between them on Friday night blew that plan out of the water. That, and the bombshell that came later, when she told him Darius and she had been 'hanging out'.

Quentin wasn't able to make himself call Darius just yet to talk about it. He had even avoided a couple of his brother's calls on Saturday, at first, afraid of what he might say and then later questioning whether he had the right to say anything at all.

And what if Darius was really into her? What if she—despite the make-out session—was into Darius?

"It could be a good, fresh start for you, Q. You know, after ... everything."

'Everything' was his mother's code for 'Mara.' His wife and mother had always gotten along fine, but that was just it—they 'got along.' Quentin knew his mother had been disappointed that the whole 'gaining a daughter, not losing a son' thing hadn't come to pass with her daughter-in-law.

Mara was always respectful and pleasant, but never really warm toward her. There were no girls' lunches or late-night telephone conversations; instead, there were carefully-chosen bouquets brought to Sunday dinner or expensive bottles of wine. Deep down inside, Q was pretty sure his mother had never believed Mara was the one for him, and that she was unsurprised by the end of the marriage.

"What could be a fresh start?"

The booming voice and formidable presence that was Darrell Thomas suddenly occupied the kitchen door, and both Q and his mother turned toward him.

Quentin stood to greet his father with an embrace. And his father, as he always did, kissed him on the cheek. He couldn't recall a time when his father hadn't kissed him and Darius, a habit that always surprised their friends—to see that huge, burly man with the James Earl Jones baritone lean in to kiss his teenage sons before heading out for a shift in uniform.

"Quentin was in New York last week. And was thinking about making a move there."

His father looked at him, brows furrowed. "Something wrong over at the firm?"

"Nah, nothing like that. Just a notion I had, that's all."

"It's a terrible notion," his father said, shaking his head. He ambled over to the stove and peered into one of the pots. "Your mother wouldn't like you being so far away. C'mon outside and help me get set up when you're done here."

He walked past them both and headed out to the deck.

Looking over her shoulder to make sure he was out of sight and earshot, Quentin's mother lowered her voice and shook her head.

"Don't listen to him," she said in a stage-whisper. "I know

New York's not too far up the road. He's the one who wants to keep you boys close. Turning into a big ol' sap in his old age."

Quentin laughed. "Duly noted."

Just then there was the cacophonous chime of the doorbell as someone repeatedly pushed the button, and then the sound of the front door opening. Only one person made that noisy entrance to their parents' home.

"Ma! It's your favorite son!"

Quentin watched as his mother left the stove and headed out to the foyer to greet Darius.

Good. Just the man he wanted to see.

"Darius, you're going to break that bell! I told you a thousand times not to ... oh!"

Quentin listened as his brother's voice mixed with another one, both of them greeting his mother. Because of Darius's loud mouth, he almost couldn't be sure at first, but then all three were heading down the hallway, the voices coming closer. And when they rounded the corner, Quentin's incredulity was validated.

Darius had brought along no other than *Lena* to the family Sunday dinner.

8

———

"I'M ABOUT TO HIT THE POOL," DARIUS ANNOUNCED, AS SOON AS the introductions to his parents were done. "You want to come with me?"

Lena shook her head, not sure whether she felt up to stripping down to her bikini with both Quentin and his father out on the deck that overlooked the pool area. If she could, what she really wanted to do was duck into a bathroom, call an Uber, and take her butt back home.

They were literally *standing at the front door* when Darius had broken the news that they were at his parents' house, and by the time Lena processed that little nugget and realized that it was likely Quentin was planning to be there, or already was; Darius was charging into the foyer and hollering for his mother.

Now, he was acting like everything was everything and she just wanted to choke him the hell out.

The minute she and Quentin lay eyes on each other, it was just ... awful. Q gave her a weird smile and said something like, 'small world' or 'funny running into you here'—Lena didn't even know precisely what he said because she was preoccupied with the sheer horror of it all—and then he came over and awkwardly hugged her.

Then Darius was decoding for his mother the tangled web of relationships, and there were pleasant exclamations of 'how nice!' and what-not, and then Q disappeared.

He finally re-emerged just after Lena met their father—as handsome a middle-aged man as Lena had ever seen, unsurprisingly, given his sons' hotness—and helped set up the barbecue grill and get the coals started.

Lena escaped back into the kitchen where she sat with their mother, trying to collect herself. Now Darius was asking her to go for a swim like it was the most normal thing in the world for him to have sprung her on his brother, and their parents on *her*.

"Not right now, thanks," Lena responded to his offer for a swim. "Maybe in a bit?"

"Okay. But it's hot as balls so ..."

"*Darius!*" his mother chided.

"Sorry, Ma. C'mon out whenever you're ready, Lena."

Lena gave him a flat, fixed stare, one that made her displeasure impossible to miss. But Darius only grinned at her and gave her a quick wink before ducking out of the kitchen once again.

"Your gardens are very beautiful, Mrs. Thomas," Lena said, for want of something better to say.

"Thank you. I wish I could take credit. That's Darrell's handiwork. I have a brown thumb, so I just concern myself with what's inside the house."

Lena laughed. "Okay, well that's beautiful too, and I'll be sure to compliment Mr. Thomas on his work."

"Please do. He's very into his ... tea roses and impatiens lately." Mrs. Thomas shook her head. "Like a little old English lady."

She turned away from the stove and pulled out metal platters upon which she began to arrange shish kebabs for grilling.

Lena stood to help and was waved away.

"No, no. Sit and relax. If you work at that firm with Quentin, I'm sure you can use the downtime."

"It is a challenging job ..." Lena said letting her voice trail off. "And ..."

"And?" Lena said, confused.

"And you love it? Isn't that what people say: '*it's a challenging job, but I love it*'?"

Lena smiled politely. "I could say that, I guess. But it wouldn't be exactly true. I can't say I love my work there. It's teaching me a lot, but ... love? No, not really."

"I was just having something like this conversation with Quentin before you got here."

"About him not loving his job?" Lena asked.

Quentin had never admitted as much to her, though she'd certainly suspected as much.

"Not so much that. But I think that's what might be under his curiosity about New York."

"New York?" Lena sat forward.

"Oh." His mother paused what she was doing and looked little flustered. "It was just an idle conversation, I'm sure. But he said he'd had thoughts about maybe moving there. Again, I'm sure it was just idle talk."

"*Moving* to New York?" Lena put a hand to her chest, and then realizing how that might look, let it drop to her lap again.

But not before Mrs. Thomas noted the gesture. And then something in her expression changed, and she smiled, letting her eyes shift once again to the task of arranging skewers on the platter.

"Idle talk," she said yet again. "But I wouldn't want that rumor to make its way back to his workplace. So, please ..."

"No. I wouldn't think of mentioning it," Lena said right away.

At least not to anyone at work. But to Quentin? That was another matter. *How the hell could he be thinking of* moving *to New*

York and not have said anything? Maybe all along she had been overestimating this 'friendship' of theirs. Maybe that was a fantasy as well.

After all, if you went by his actions alone, she was probably nothing to him—first, he fixes her up with his brother, and now he plans to move to another state without even mentioning it?

What were all those nights in his office talking, then? All those text messages throughout the day, kvetching about their cases? Their coffee dates? Nothing, obviously. She was probably just his little workplace pet. But on Friday when he held her, and when he kissed her, it felt like something real was happening between them.

Even with the misunderstanding about her and Darius being together she was hoping ... Hell, it didn't matter what she was hoping. If he was thinking of moving to New York, it may even have something to do with the wife. Maybe they were reconciling, and New York was to be a new start for them.

Suddenly, a swim in the cool, cool water seemed like precisely what Lena needed. Because she wasn't sure she could stand even another few minutes sitting there and pretending she wasn't hurt.

Standing she stretched her arms above her head. "I can hear Darius out there in the water," she said, trying to sound casual. "I think I'm going to join him after all. Do you need me to ...?"

"No, go enjoy yourself. He's right. It *is* hot as balls." Then Mrs. Thomas chuckled to herself, shaking her head in amusement. "*My* sons ..."

Lena had a fleeting thought that she wasn't just referring to Darius's colorful language, but rather than ponder it further, headed out back to hopefully swim her worries away.

EIGHTEEN.

That was how many laps Lena took without stopping. Quentin knew because he counted, his eyes on her as her strokes cut cleanly through the water. It was easy to watch her without giving himself away because the pool was just below the deck. Her swimsuit wasn't exactly made for this kind of swimming. It was made for lounging by the water and looking cute. All it was, really, was four triangles stitched together, and some strings. Two triangles for the bottoms—front and back—and two for the top, one for each ...

Swallowing hard, Quentin forced himself to look away as Lena turned easily and began doing the backstroke. Just as the freestyle had offered a view of her firm, smooth ass, the backstroke had its own benefits.

But he was better off not looking unless he wanted to embarrass himself in front of his father. He remembered what it was like to have his hands ...

Shaking his head, he forced his mind in another direction.

Poolside, Darius was on his phone, openly watching Lena as she swam. He didn't seem to have any of Quentin's reluctance to stare. But then Darius had always been the one to go all in for whatever he wanted, while he, on the other hand, stood back and waited. This time, though, the waiting had cost him. The idea that Darius and Lena might actually be together caused his chest to tighten.

Quentin sighed and circled his neck.

Funny thing, though, Lena didn't seem to talk to Darius too much since she'd been there. In fact, knowing her as he did, Quentin could almost believe she was a little pissed about something. He recognized the stillness of expression on her face, the unmoving rigidity of her posture. Quentin had only ever seen her pissed once before when a legal assistant had messed up something on a case, and this was how she'd reacted—with steely silence rather than an explosion of any kind.

But why would she be pissed at Darius? Seemed a little early for a lovers' tiff. Lovers. *Shit.* Was it possible that in the week since he'd been gone, Lena and Darius had done the deed? Unlikely. Because she had been all over him on Friday. And Lena was definitely not that chick.

But something was up because Darius didn't bring women to their parents' house. Never. In fact, unless he was planning to propose, Q would wager that Darius wouldn't even consider it.

"What're you grunting over there about?"

Quentin lifted his head and looked at his father. "Huh?"

"Huh." His Dad mimicked the sound he'd made and grinned at him. "What's going on with you and your brother with this girl, Lena?"

Q looked back down at the grill, needlessly turning a chicken shish kebab. "Nothing."

"This is the same Lena from your job you keep mentioning to me, right?"

"I never mentioned Lena to you." Quentin looked up in surprise. "*Did* I?"

His father nodded, slowly. "Yeah. You did."

"In what context?" Quentin was honestly curious now.

His father shrugged. "Let's see ... *every* context? She comes up a lot."

"Well, we worked on a few cases together, so ..."

"I know." His father nodded. "You said."

"What're you trying to say, Dad?" Quentin put down his tongs and folded his arms.

"Nothing. Why're you so defensive?" He looked amused.

"I'm not being defensive. You asked me what's up with me and Darius *and* Lena. So I just wondered what that meant, that's all."

"All it means is, I never heard *Darius* come in here talking about this girl. I never saw *Darius* grinning into his phone sending text messages to her every other Sunday he's over here. And yet, here she is ... with Darius."

"How would you know I was texting with ...?"

"Because if I asked, you told me."

"It was probably about work," Quentin mumbled, picking up his tongs again.

Damn. *Had* he talked about Lena a lot to his Dad? It was hard to say. Because he talked to his parents about pretty much everything, his father most especially. That was his boy, for real.

When they were together, the details of Quentin's life flowed out of him in almost stream-of-consciousness fashion. No editing, nothing left out. So if he talked to anyone about Lena, after Darius, it wasn't surprising that it would be his father.

But what about the texting? He didn't think he texted her *that* much. They played around a lot. Sometimes she sent him funny pictures or one-liners about her brother's antics, or she asked him to call her to interrupt a bad date. Or maybe he was just standing in line at the grocery store and she would idly drift across his thoughts, so he might reach out. But ...

"I had a work-wife once," his father broke into his thoughts. "Her name was Carrie Anastos. Cute little Greek girl."

"Hold up." Quentin held up a hand. "Are you about to tell me something I wouldn't want to know?"

"Shut up, boy. We talkin' man-to-man now."

Bracing himself, Quentin listened, hoping he wasn't about to have his illusions about his parents' marriage shattered. Having his image of his own marriage smashed to pieces was plenty enough.

"So Carrie Anastos," his father continued. "Her family owned ... probably still owns one of the most popular Greek restaurants in Bethesda and everybody works there—Mom,

Dad, brothers, sisters, cousins ... everybody. But she wanted to strike out on her own, so she got a job as a secretary at the department. And she loved it. You could tell ... always laughing, always smiling ... flirting with the guys as they came on and off their shifts.

"She had a smart mouth, too. And she got the gallows humor that cops have ... jokes about car accidents and shootings, things that regular folks can't laugh at and don't understand, but that we *have to* laugh at ... just to keep sane on the job, y'know what I mean?"

Quentin nodded.

"Anyway, Carrie had this lunch box she brought in every day, with Greek food that her mother made her at their restaurant. I mean, the *good* stuff, right? And I came in with stuff I picked up to eat before my shift—burgers, fries, sometimes Jamaican food, Chinese ... whatever. And we ate at the same table in the break-room occasionally. And she always wanted to taste what I had. I asked whether I should bring her stuff, and she always said no, that she didn't make enough to eat out for lunch.

"But after a while, it was obvious she was more interested in my food, and I was more interested in hers. So we got into this habit of trading lunches like kids do, y'know. Just sliding what-ever we had across the table and swapping. And that's how it started."

"How what started?" Q asked, not sure he wanted to know.

"Our connection. Our conversations. And I mean, *deep* conversations. Intimate conversations, even. About our lives, our families ... You were just a baby then; I was a new father, and I was scared out of my damn mind. You were so ... little and help-less, and your mother wasn't working, and you both depended on me. I was crazy about your mother ..." His father paused to collect himself for a moment. "And crazy about my new baby son, but it was terrifying, too. I was the only thing you both had to count on. That kind of thing you can't always share with your wife, Q. You want her to feel secure, so you can't always go confessing all your fears. So I told Carrie."

"And then …?"

"Then I started watching for her," his father said with a laugh. "Looking forward to going to work so we could have these long, deep talks we shared. She was like a sweet relief for me, an outlet where I didn't always have one with your mother. And I could tell from the way she looked at me that she had some of the same feelings. According to what she told me, Greek culture can be very insular, very … clannish. And she was looking to break free a little. I think I represented some of that for her."

"Did you guys ever …?"

"No." His father shook his head emphatically. "At the end of the day, I saw that Carrie could be as big a threat to my family as a bullet from some perp's gun. So, I asked my sergeant to change my shift, and then later, I transferred to a new precinct altogether.

"After that, no more lunches, no more deep, intimate talks. But my family was intact. And that was the most important thing. I *had* a wife. I couldn't afford to risk that for a work-wife."

Down at the pool, Lena had stopped swimming and now was sitting at the edge of the pool, legs in the water. Darius was sitting next to her, and they seemed deep in serious conversation.

"I guess I could've shared this story about a year and a half ago when this name, 'Lena', started creeping into your conversation. But I figured if you and Mara were having problems, it probably had nothing to do with …"

"Wait. *What?* You think Mara and I broke up because Lena became my *work-wife*?"

"I don't know, son. I don't know what was going on with you and Mara. And I didn't see all the texting and stuff happen until after she left, but I don't know ... I guess I wondered once she was gone whether that might have ..."

"No," Quentin said, his voice firm. "What happened with me and Mara had nothing to do with Lena. She was my subordinate and a member of my team at the time. Nothing more than that."

"Okay." His father shrugged. "But are you sure that's how you still feel?"

***

"Mr. and Mrs. Thomas, this was *so* good. Thank you for having me."

Lena leaned back in her chair and shook her head in appreciation, smiling at both his parents, and Q thought for the hundredth time how damn pretty she was. Before she jumped in the pool earlier, she had fashioned her hair into one thick braid that rested on her shoulder. It was loosening at the end and looked a little puffy, but now her face was sun-kissed, and she glowed.

"You're very welcome, Lena," his father said. "I hope we'll see you again."

"Don't make it sound like you're kickin' us out, old man," Darius said. "I know Ma has some dessert in there somewhere."

"I do. A couple choices as a matter of fact: some red velvet cake and a rum-n-raisin pudding, heavy on the rum, so none for you boys since you're driving."

"I'll put some ice cream on top of it and it'll be fine," Darius said, sliding his chair back from the table.

"No," Lena said. "Let me. Dinner was delicious. The least I can do is help bring out dessert for everyone."

They had all eaten at the table on the deck, everyone making pleasant conversation about the election cycle, and work, and Darius's planned trip to Thailand in the fall. His wanderlust prevented him from staying any place for too long, even though in deference to their parents, he had planted his roots in the Washington DC area.

Quentin sometimes envied him that—his firmly established reputation for unpredictability. Darius could do anything, go anywhere, and no one would be surprised. He was completely free and unfettered. Even his business could pretty much run itself.

"No need, dear. Let the boys handle it."

Quentin watched the way his mother smiled at Lena, with real warmth. She liked her. And all through dinner had asked a lot of questions, genuinely curious about Lena's work and life. She asked questions Quentin had never asked, and quite a few he wished that he had.

"I insist," Lena said smiling.

"I'll help you find everything," Quentin said before he had a chance to think too long and hard about the wisdom of it.

Lena's eyes dropped and she nodded. "Thank you."

She looked a little unsure of herself and he realized for the first time that she probably thought he was angry. After all they had barely exchanged ten words the entire afternoon, and none at all in private conversation.

He wasn't angry at her. He was angry at *Darius*. She at least had mentioned that things with Darius had accelerated. His brother, on the other hand, had kept mum on the whole darn thing, including the fact that he intended to bring Lena to their Sunday family dinner. *That* at least warranted a phone call, a little talk. But he would deal with Darius later.

Once in the kitchen, Lena turned to face him, awaiting instructions about where to find everything. Instead, Quentin leaned back against the kitchen cabinets, his arms braced behind him.

"So ..." he began, "this is ..."

"Awkward," Lena finished for him. "I know. I'm sorry. I had no idea that ..." She stopped and sighed. "Just ... I'm sorry."

"It's okay," Quentin said, wondering why it was that he *wasn't* angry at her.

She at least knew on Friday when he leaned in and kissed her that there was one very good reason that they shouldn't. *His* hands were clean in all this if anyone's were. And yet, he wasn't mad.

Lena gave a small, derisive laugh. "No. It is definitely not okay, Quentin. I mean, I'm here with your brother. And on Friday night ..."

"Let's not talk about Friday night," he interrupted her.

A look crossed her face then that was unmistakable. It was hurt.

"Of course," she said. "We should just forget it ever happened. It was wrong, and it shouldn't have ..."

"No, Lena, I didn't mean ... What I mean is ..."

He took two steps toward her, and then stopped. He didn't know what he meant. But he did know that what happened on Friday, he didn't like hearing described as 'wrong.' Shit, it was complicated, no doubt about that. But it didn't feel wrong. Kissing her, being that close to her actually felt very, very right.

Even now, as colossally fucked-up as this whole situation was, all he could think about was how pretty she looked right now, her crazy hair all messed up, her skin dark and sun-kissed, and her legs in those shorts ... He wanted to tell her that she was beautiful, that he didn't regret a moment of Friday night though he knew he should.

But how the hell was he supposed to say something like that when she was only here because she was his brother's woman? Or maybe, please God, it hadn't gone *that* far. And there was some way to ...

Taking a deep, ragged breath, Quentin ran a hand over his head.

"Look," he began. "You and me, we need to …"

"You know I don't do sugar like that, right? But Ma with these damn *puddings*, man."

Darius walked in just as Quentin was about to stumble through the rest of his sentence which he hadn't even thought through. Something about them needing to talk. But maybe it was just as well. This wasn't the time, and it sure as hell wasn't the place.

Lena took a breath as well. But hers sounded like relief.

"I'll let you guys take it from here," she said, turning and heading back out to the deck.

"What the hell, D?"

"What?"

"You know what I'm talkin' 'bout."

"Spell it out for me. You know I can be … slow sometimes." Darius's head was in the fridge, looking for something.

"I thought you said you weren't going to call her. Let alone bring her over here for Sunday dinner …"

"And I thought you said you didn't care." Darius emerged from the fridge with a cake box in hand. "You making the coffee or am I?"

"I didn't say I didn't care. I said …"

"See what I mean? It's the Hot Wheels set all over again."

"*Man* …"

"Either I can check for her or not. It's not complicated, Q. Or did you expect me to get your *permission* before I actually dialed her number?"

Quentin opened his mouth but nothing came out.

Darius shrugged. "*You* lit the match. Don't be mad now that there's a fire, man."

Narrowing his eyes, Quentin took a couple steps closer. "What the fuck does that mean? Are you two ...?"

"I'ma make the coffee real strong. I need to hit the gym later, and I think all this food might make me pass out."

"Darius. I asked you something."

"And it would be tacky of me to answer it."

Quentin leaned back against the kitchen counter and exhaled. That could only mean ...

Darius clapped him on the shoulder. "Look at it this way, bruh. At least she's still close. In the family, practically."

"I didn't think she ..."

"Huh?" Darius was pulling down coffee mugs now and setting up the Keurig. "You didn't think she *what* now?"

"I don't know. I thought ..."

"Thought what?" Darius turned to face him full-on, folding his arms. "*Say* it."

Quentin looked up at his brother and realized for the first time that while he may have sounded glib, Darius was, in fact, a little pissed himself. His nostrils flared and he'd pulled his lips into a tight line, the way he did when he was about to say or do something ill-considered and was trying to hold it back.

Quentin wondered whether, during that conversation by the pool, Lena had spilled everything about what happened Friday night. As it was, he wasn't sure how or whether he could sit on that information himself for much longer. He had never lied to his brother before and didn't intend to start now. Suddenly, his plan to confront Darius didn't seem like such a great idea after all; and his 'clean hands' felt more than a little dirty.

"I thought she might be ... a little ... into ... me," Quentin admitted.

Darius nodded. "Yeah. Exactly. And yet, you brought her around, introduced her to me, and damn near begged me to take her out. How *fucked up* is that?"

"Look, man. I was in a … things with Mara were just …."

"So if you couldn't have her *at the moment*, you thought I would be what? A *placeholder*?" Darius demanded. "And what if I really liked her, Q? What if she really liked me? What was your plan then, huh?"

"I didn't know that's what I was doing, D. I'm just … Wait. So she doesn't like you? So …"

"She basically blew me off today. Down at the pool. Let me know she likes me '*as a friend*', but that her feelings are otherwise occupied."

"Occupied … where?"

"She didn't say. But what do *you* think? Stupid-ass." Darius turned back to the coffeemaker.

Quentin reached out and put a hand on his brother's shoulder which he shrugged off. "I'm sorry, man. I didn't mean to put you in a position where …"

"And you didn't," Darius spoke without turning around. "I knew the whole time what was going on. She was using me as a placeholder too."

"Man, that's … I'm …"

"Shut up, Q." Darius turned to face him again. "My feelin's ain't *hurt*. I was just kickin' it with her till you came to your damn senses. Why you think I brought her over here?"

Quentin exhaled an exasperated breath and ran a hand over his face. "If that's the case, why you so mad?"

"Because the only person in this equation who won't admit what they want is you, Quentin. As usual. Mopin' around thinking about what you *should* do instead of doing what you *want* to do."

"A'ight, that's enough of that shit. You made your point."

"Did I? Because it was getting real hard to keep my hands to myself, Q. *Real* hard."

"But you did," Quentin confirmed.

Darius sighed long-sufferingly and looked up at the ceiling. "I'm your brother ain't I?"

Quentin held out a hand to give Darius some dap but instead pulled him into an embrace, one hand on top of his baby brother's Mohawk'ed head.

"I have something to tell you," he said before pulling away.

Just then, their father walked in. "Are y'all in here *baking* the damn cake?" he demanded, not commenting on the moment he'd interrupted.

Darius and their father took the pudding and cake back out to the deck while Quentin hung back to finish up making coffees for everyone. Everything was different now. He and Mara had an understanding about the ending of their marriage, his brother wasn't interested in Lena after all, and he ... was.

The admission excited him, motivated him, and yeah, something about it troubled him a little as well. Something about that story his father told him, about his "work-wife" felt unsettlingly familiar.

9

———————

CLOSING HER APARTMENT DOOR AND SLIDING OFF HER SANDALS, Lena was relieved that only silence greeted her. She didn't feel like being subjected to Marlon's interrogation just yet. First, she needed a little space to think about what she felt before having someone tell her what she should feel.

The afternoon had been a confusing mix of emotions—excitement at meeting Quentin's parents; fear and apprehension at how he would react to her unexpected appearance at a family gathering; and trepidation at the conversation she needed to have with Darius, mixed in with a fair amount of annoyance at him for using her to bushwhack his brother.

For ages now, Lena had been curious about the kind of family Quentin came from. In all the time they'd known each other, he talked about his parents and his brother only in the most general terms, casual references sprinkled here and there, which she had been left to patch together to create a picture.

She had gleaned from what he said that his brother and he were close, but it was only in the last few weeks that she realized just how close, and learned more about what Darius did, and the kind of person he was. And she knew he considered his parents the bedrock of everything that was good in his life, but until today she hadn't known their names, where they lived, or even what their professions were.

How was that possible?

They talked all the time, every day at three for sure during the work week, and on some weekends, on and off. But Lena now saw that Quentin had concealed all the important things from her, maybe even deliberately. What *was* she to him anyway? He was married, and she knew next to nothing about that as well.

Was his separation from his wife his idea? The wife's? Was he happy about it, or heartbroken? She had no earthly clue. And all this time, she had been comforting herself with the fact that if she had nothing else from Quentin, at least she had his friendship. Now it felt like she didn't even have that.

Shedding her blouse and loosening the button of her jeans, Lena headed for the bathroom. She would take a long shower, wash the chlorine out of her hair, and go to bed. Tomorrow was work, after all, and she would have to find a way to shed this funk.

Seeing Quentin in the morning was going to be difficult. She wasn't sure she could head to the conference room like she always did, cheerful and ready to shoot the breeze. *That* Quentin, her work-friend, seemed a fiction. The real Quentin was the guy she saw today with his family—the Straight-Man to Darius's Cut-Up, their father's compatriot, and his brother's best friend.

What the hell had they talked about, if all this time, Lena had missed all of that?

The hot shower felt good, as did using her nails to scratch and stimulate her scalp with the minty, lemony shampoo she favored. By the time she got out and dried off, Lena was feeling a little better and thought that after twisting her hair, she could collapse into sleep, even though it was only 7:50 p.m. Things always looked different—and better—after a good night's rest.

But she knew one thing for sure: she was going to wake up with a different attitude about Quentin Thomas. All of that crazy fantasizing and mooning over him were done with. Now, he would be a close colleague and that was all. And she would start by putting an end to those stupid three o'clock coffee dates.

THE SOFT VIBRATION OF HER CELL PHONE WOKE LENA FROM THE light sleep she had fallen into after twisting her hair. It was on the pillow next to her head and sounded for a moment like a housefly buzzing in her ear.

Turning, she looked at it, and when it wouldn't stop, picked up.

"Hello?" Her speech was garbled, clogged with sleep.

"Did I wake you?"

Her eyes opened fully at the sound of his voice.

"Yes," she said. "You did." And waited for him to go on.

"Well, I'm outside, I'm at your door, so..."

Lena jerked upright, her head swimming for a few seconds at the sudden motion. "Outside *here*?"

"Yeah. You going to let me in?"

The room was pitch-black almost. And she was certain the apartment was too. Reaching over, she flipped on her bedside light. It was a little after nine-fifteen. She would have slept on if Quentin hadn't called. And that would have been fine by her. And why had he called anyway? What did he *want*?

"What d'you want?" she asked.

"Open the door and we'll talk about it," he said, sounding unperturbed by her snippy tone.

"Can't we talk about it tomorrow? At the office?" she asked, looking down at her ratty t-shirt and faded black Capri leggings.

"No," he said simply.

Sighing, Lena hung up without bothering to say goodbye and headed out to the living room, turning on lights as she went. Marlon still hadn't come home, so he was probably working this evening. She had long stopped trying to keep track of his spotty work schedule.

Standing at the front door, she looked through the keyhole and took a deep breath. Quentin was standing there alright, looking all kinds of good.

He had changed since the afternoon and now was just in washed-out jeans and a plain, white t-shirt. Lena was unaccustomed to seeing him so casually dressed. Only once before today, in fact, had she seen him in a t-shirt.

It was at the firm picnic when he had played basketball with Rich, a couple of the other partners, and some of the other senior associates. Lena recalled that he'd done a lot of yelling and shit-talking, complaining about calls the ref made and shouting at his teammates when they didn't hustle. She remembered she had been one of maybe three female associates who were watching the game, just to watch Quentin.

But while she kept her attraction under wraps, the others had been shameless about making comments and giggling with each other and flirting with him when he wasn't in active play. Lena had been so jealous that day she'd accepted an invitation to dinner with Pete Lucas from Accounting. He'd taken her to a movie and tried to stick his tongue down her throat even before the closing credits were done.

Opening the door, she stood with her weight on one leg and looked up to meet Quentin's gaze. She noticed that his eyes ran over her length, taking every detail in. She couldn't recall him ever looking at her like that before, so openly ... appreciative.

Except for Friday night at the office, which she was determined to put out of her mind if it killed her.

"Quentin," she began. "What ...?"

And then he kissed her.

Crowding her back into the apartment, he kept his lips locked with hers, and Lena vaguely heard her apartment door slam behind them.

Her thinking self was frozen in place, and the rest of her responded on instinct, her arms going up and around his neck, her body pressing closer so she could feel him, and her lips frantically, greedily tasting his, opening when he sought entrance. His tongue tasted like toothpaste and felt divine. And as the bristles of his facial hair scored across her skin, Lena reached up to instead cup his jaw and feel their coarseness on her palms as well.

When he pulled away, it was slowly, momentarily capturing her lower lip between his. Lena's heart was beating fast and her chest was heaving. *And* she felt like slapping the *shit* out of him.

Instead, she stepped back and put a hand to her lips, as though they had betrayed her by being such obvious willing and wanton participants in what had gone on moments before.

"Quentin!"

He blinked slowly, and his tongue slid across his lower lip. "Sorry," he said. "I just thought it best we get that out of the way right off the bat."

Lena let her head fall back, her eyes trained on the ceiling, not knowing what to say.

"Actually, I'm not sorry. I've been wanting to do that all day. And not just today. For a long while."

Her head snapped back up.

"Yeah." He nodded and advanced toward her, as she took corresponding steps back. "For a *long* while."

"And so you decided to ... fix me up with your *brother*?" She felt angry tears rising to the back of her eyes.

"That was stupid of me. I don't know why I did it. I guess I was trying to ... kill this thing, whatever it is, that's going on between us. But I think Friday night proved that wasn't ever going to work."

"*Kill* it?" Lena gave a harsh laugh.

But hadn't she been trying to do the same by agreeing to meet his brother? It was crazy. Quentin was finally saying things she had wanted him to say for ages now, but now, she wasn't sure. After meeting his parents, suddenly their friendship seemed less true than it had mere weeks ago. Maybe this wasn't true either.

"Did I?"

He had backed her all the way against the pass-through between the kitchen and living room, and now was just a hair's breadth away.

Lena had to look up to see his face. Without the benefit of the heels she wore in the office, he seemed that much taller.

"Did you what?" she asked, stalling for time.

"Kill it. Or is there still ... something ... there?"

"You can't just pass me between you and your brother like a baseball card, Quentin."

"I know. That was messed up. But I was ... I wasn't thinking straight. And there was all this other stuff going on with ..." He stopped abruptly.

"Finish what you were about to say. With you wife, right? Because that's another thing; you're married. I know you're separated or whatever—not that *you* told me that—but you still wear your ..."

He held up his left hand, displaying the finger, naked where his wedding band had once been.

"That doesn't mean anything." Lena shook her head.

"It means a lot. To me. It means that I'm finally in a place where I know it's over. And where I can move on, and give someone else, someone I care for, what they deserve."

Lena looked down, not wanting him to see the hope in her eyes. Not wanting him to see the tears.

"What do they deserve?"

Quentin leaned in and spoke against her neck. She literally tingled when he did that.

"Everything," he said. "They ... you deserve everything. All I have to give."

Lena blinked away the tears that were now threatening to fall.

"Darius said you told him your feelings were otherwise occupied," Quentin continued. He tipped her chin upward. "Are they occupied with me?"

He seemed to be holding his breath, and his eyes looked the way she'd been frightened hers would look if he saw them.

Lena nodded, just barely, and watched as Quentin's face broke out into a smile. Then he was kissing her again and she was kissing him too, no longer pretending that she was holding anything back.

"I'm sorry," he said against her lips. "I'm sorry I almost fucked this up ..."

Lena cupped his face, kissing him back.

It didn't matter any longer what he said. All that mattered was that he was here, and how he was making her feel. And how she seemed to be making *him* feel. She'd never seen Q like this before, stumbling over his words, not knowing what to say, or how to say it.

For so long, she'd wondered what it might feel like to have Quentin touch her, that it never occurred to her that he might want it as well. And what happened in the office she had almost dismissed as a fluke—maybe brought on by low inhibitions and exhaustion—but this was felt like it was for real.

They were still doing the tongue-tango when the front door opened, and Marlon came spilling in. Quentin had her pressed against the wall, his thigh between hers, their arms wrapped around each other, and there was no time to disentangle before her brother spotted them.

Marlon stared for a moment, frozen in place, and Lena rolled her eyes when she took in his state. He was drunk.

"Oh. My. *God!*" Marlon kicked the door shut behind him. "So ... which one is this, then?"

"Marlon ..." Lena began.

"I'm Quentin." Q stepped out from her embrace and extended a hand which Marlon took, shaking it slowly while he looked Quentin over.

"Oh, yes. Now I see," her brother said. "Because you look a little too square to be a tattoo artist."

And Quentin—God bless him—actually laughed. "And you must be ..."

"What she said," Marlon said, his words slurring a little. "Marlon. Her twin brother."

"Twin?" Quentin looked over his shoulder and narrowed his eyes at her. "You never told me you were a *twin*."

"We never told each other a lot of things."

At that, Quentin turned to face her again, his eyes meeting hers.

"So let's start now," he said, his brow furrowed. "Telling each other the things we never told before."

"I can't speak for why you didn't tell her *your* stuff," Marlon said from somewhere in the background and far away. "But when you're a young, Black, gay man, you get used to being omitted from conversations, if you know what I mean."

Quentin's eyebrows rose at the additional revelation, but he said nothing.

"He's going to be like this all night," Lena warned, rolling her eyes. "Chatty. He gets like that when he's had a few too many. And alcohol brings out his persecution complex. Like anyone *cares* who he sleeps with."

"Still here!" Marlon sang. "Still here and still *hearing*. So ..."

"Want to come to my place?" Quentin asked.

"We have work tomorrow," Lena pointed out.

"Then stay over," he suggested, his eyes never leaving hers.

"Okay. I'll go pack a bag."

Lena turned and headed for her bedroom with Marlon close on her tail. Once inside, her brother shut her bedroom door and sat on the bed, laughing with a hand over his mouth.

"Bitch, you didn't even take a *breath* when he asked you to stay over. This is the most ho-ish behavior I have ever seen from you. I am *so* proud. Did you not leave here with one brother? Now you come back with the other one, and then going to spend the night? I never knew you had it in you, Lena!"

"Shut up, Marlon. And sober up."

"Girl, the afternoon I had. But from the looks of it, it was nothing compared to yours! So what happened? You kicked Darius to the curb or what?"

"He was probably always on the curb, but I can't talk to you about all that now."

"No, you can't. You have to prepare for your ... rendezvous." Marlon stumbled over the word, then stood and went to rifle through her underwear drawer, finally looking over his shoulder at her in frustration. "Where's all your slutty stuff at?"

"Give me that!" Lena snatched a pair of white cotton underwear from her brother's fingers. "Get out of here!"

"Fine, I can go interrogate the lawyer instead ..."

Lena grabbed the tail of Marlon's shirt and yanked him back. "On second thought, you just sit right here."

Marlon cackled and then fell back onto her bed, his eyes closing as Lena moved about the room grabbing things and shoving them into an overnight bag. Her hands were trembling in her excitement so she kept dropping things, but finally, she was all done.

"Marlon," she whispered sharply. "I'm out."

"Okay," her brother moaned without opening his eyes. "Have fun. And remember the key to any successful relationship. Fellatio. Early, and *often*. Remember that line, from ... what *was* that movie?"

Lena rolled her eyes. "Goodnight, Marlon. And you'd better not throw up on my bed!"

Lena hadn't driven in Quentin's car with him before tonight. She didn't think she even knew what kind of car he owned before now. An Audi SUV, a very adult, very responsible car.

Darius drove a Saab that was so old and beat-up that he said the next time it conked out on him he planned on abandoning it on the side of the road, removing the license plates, and taking the bus home. And she believed him, too. He was the anti-Quentin in a lot of ways— a rocking, rollicking ball of unpredictability, in contrast to Quentin's steadiness.

Lena liked the steadiness. Even the way he held the steering wheel right now—ten-and-two, by the book. Steady. Then one hand moved, and he released the steering wheel altogether, putting his hand instead on her thigh.

Lena held her breath and then, eventually, had to release it in an audible, shaky sigh. At that, Q looked over at her and grinned.

"You nervous too?"

"Too?" she echoed. "*You're* nervous?"

"Of course, I am. For a lot of reasons."

Lena put a hand over the one on her thigh. "Tell me some of them. Maybe it'll make me feel better."

"Because it's been almost ten years since I've been with someone other than Mara ..." Lena took note of the name she had never heard him speak before. "Because we're friends, and I don't want to mess that up. Because we work together, and I don't want to mess *that* up. Because ..."

"That's plenty," Lena said stopping him. All his doubts were mirror-images of hers, and the last thing she wanted was for him to talk either of them out of what was likely to happen tonight.

"But I want this," Quentin said. "I want *you*. *That*, I'm sure about."

"Okay," Lena said quietly. She shoved to the back of her mind the worry that in saying he was sure, Quentin only sounded less so.

About five minutes from his house, he stopped at CVS and told her he'd only be a minute, looking a little embarrassed and apologetic. Lena was pretty sure she knew why.

Married men probably didn't have a cache of condoms on hand. And if things went where they both obviously wanted it to go tonight, they would need some. In the modern world of sex and dating, it was a necessity until a couple made explicit commitments, but still, Lena wished it didn't feel so tawdry.

His house was beautiful. Clearly a house for a family, though; or for a couple that intended to start one. When he let her in and locked up behind them, Quentin walked her through all the rooms—four bedrooms, one of which was a home office, formal living and dining rooms, finished basement, and a sunporch and deck off the kitchen to be exact. The tour was a transparent attempt to get them both to loosen up a little, but for Lena it did the opposite.

"It's beautifully decorated," she said when they were done.

It *was* beautiful, and had to have been decorated by someone other than Q. They wound up in the kitchen again, and she couldn't shake the feeling that she was poaching on the territory of some other woman while she wasn't home.

"Thank you. But I hardly use any of it other than the bedroom, the home office, and the kitchen. I'm thinking of selling it and moving into the city. Maybe a condo, or something like that."

Lena nodded, and looked down at the terrazzo tiles beneath her feet, wondering whether she should have come.

"What're you thinking?" Quentin asked quietly.

He walked into her so their chests were touching, and tipped her chin upward so she was looking at him.

Lena shook her head, not answering.

"This is like the battlefield of the end of my marriage," Q said, wryly. "To tell you the truth, I don't much like it here either. I wasn't thinking ... *again*. I just ... I wanted to be alone with you."

This was the Quentin she never saw at work. The one who was uncertain, just like everyone else, who didn't always know the right thing to do or say. This was the Quentin she saw hints of all along; the one she loved, and would be a fool for if it came to that. She was probably being a fool just being here. After all, the ring may have come off, but he was still very much a married man.

Rising onto her toes, Lena kissed him. She meant it to be a softly commiserative kiss, but it turned hot within seconds, and then Q was putting his hands in her hair, pulling her closer, pressing her against the kitchen cabinets.

Then she was pushing him away, but only so she could shove her tank top up and over her head.

Quentin watched her, his expression so intense, it made Lena blush.

Could she have missed it? Had always wanted her like this, and yet she missed it?

His head bowed and he kissed her breasts, taking in a nipple and sucking it through the fabric of her bra. Lena gasped and thrust her chest toward him. Quentin's hand fell to her ass, pulling her closer, then grappling with the waistband of her leggings and forcing them down and over her hips. Lena helped as much as she could without pulling her lips away from his, occasionally pausing to take a breath.

When his hand moved between her legs, she inhaled loudly and moaned, incredulous at just how good that alone felt. She was so wet, his fingers glided across her, almost frictionless. Soon she had to turn her face away from him, just so she could breathe, short, hard bursts of air while Quentin's mouth was on her neck.

"Upstairs," he managed. "Let's ... upstairs."

"Okay ... yeah," Lena said.

And he lifted her, kicked her leggings and underwear aside. Lena wrapped her legs around his hips. Quentin grinned as she did and paused to grab the brown paper bag from CVS before carrying her off.

Upstairs, he set her down in the center of his bed, and Lena watched as he undid his jeans and slid them down with his boxer briefs. His erection sprang free, and she sized it up while he watched her watching him, a grin on his face.

"Like what you see?"

"Don't know if I can handle what I see."

He laughed. "Pretty sure we'll make it work."

When he shrugged off his t-shirt, Lena saw that his chest was decorated on one side with Darius' handiwork, a fire-breathing dragon.

"What does that mean?" Lena asked. "The dragon."

"Does it have to mean something?" Quentin crawled up onto the bed, spreading her legs as he did.

"Yes. If your brother did it, I'm pretty sure it does."

"It's something he likes to say about me, that's all." Quentin lowered his head to her breasts again, finally getting around to reaching behind her to remove the bra altogether. His tongue, on her raw and now bare nipples almost made Lena lose her train of thought.

"What does he like to say about you?"

"That I have the heart of a dragon, even if I have the attitude of a lamb."

"You don't have the attitude of a *lamb*," Lena said, almost insulted on his behalf. "Does he know how amazing of a litigator you are?"

"I let him pick it. And that's what he came up with. So he gave me a dragon, right over my heart. But ..." Quentin raised his head. "I don't know how I feel about talking about Darius right now."

"How about we not talk *at all* right now," Lena suggested.

"Deal," Quentin said. Then he slid down her body, lifted her legs over his shoulders and dived right into her.

Lena was torn between wanting to watch and wanting to just close her eyes and ... feel, because it was amazing. Quentin was stroking, tasting, penetrating her and nothing had ever felt this good. But to look down and see his large hands gripping her thighs, his head between her legs ... how could she *not* watch?

The approach of her orgasm, building as a ball pressing at the base of her stomach was actually unwelcome, because if she came, he might stop, and she didn't want him to. It was too good for him to stop.

But he did. Lifting his head, Q licked his lower lip and smiled at her.

"You taste ..." he said. "Lena, you taste so ..."

But he didn't even finish his sentence, he just went at her again. Ten seconds. It took ten seconds and Lena was screaming, her back arching like a bow off the bed. Slowly, she relaxed, letting herself fall back into the sheets. Quentin kissed her inner thighs, each touch of his lips feeling like a tiny electric shock.

Lena smiled, letting her head fall to the side, hearing a sound like a purr escape her lips.

"Come here," she said, and Q slid along her length so they were face to face once again, the rough hairs on his chest tickling and stimulating her nipples.

He kissed her, both their mouths wide open and greedy. He sucked her tongue, her lower lip, and then moved to her neck. She felt him everywhere, and was only remotely aware when he fumbled with something nearby, and lifted his hips for a moment.

When he entered her, it was swiftly, and there was almost no resistance. Lena's hand fell to his ass, gripping and holding him in place.

"I told you we'd make it work," Quentin breathed against her temple.

Lena smiled against his neck. She felt stretched around him, and he was pulsating inside her, matching the rhythmic gallop of his heart, thrumming against her. He seemed to know that she needed to feel this, and experience it, so for a long time, he didn't move. He waited until she did. And when she did, it was because she couldn't help herself.

While they had been still, she was growing hotter and more liquid around him, and they had both begun to perspire. Lena clenched, felt his response, and couldn't wait any longer. Lifting her hips, she began slowly gyrating against him, and he raised himself a little, easing some of his weight off her and giving her room to move.

Soon, he was moving with her, and they were in perfect sync. Quentin's breaths against her ear became increasingly ragged, and he turned his head so their lips were joined, just as the rest of them was, until finally, eventually, and at long last, they both collapsed into completion.

10

"So ... coffee at three?"

Quentin stuck his head in the doorway of Lena's office and found her standing over a row of documents, lined out on the carpet in front of her desk.

"Huh?" She looked up and smiled when she saw it was him. "Sure. Of course."

He winked at her and then resumed his game-face—the one he had been careful to maintain at work over the past month and a half since they'd been together. He was a lot better at it than Lena was, though.

Whenever they were in a room together, she blushed a lot, couldn't make eye contact with him for very long, and sometimes even stuttered. If Quentin had to guess, he would say they weren't exactly keeping their new relationship status under wraps, particularly since he had stopped wearing his wedding ring.

But appearances had to be maintained. At least for now.

"Meet at the parking garage?"

"Quentin," Lena lowered her voice. "Sometimes I actually need *actual* coffee."

The first time it happened, it was kind of an accident. They'd walked out of the building together to head toward Starbucks, and on the way back, he remembered some papers in his car that he needed for later. Lena walked into the underground parking garage with him; they got in the car, and few kisses led to him hiking up her skirt, pulling aside her underwear and her mounting him, hand braced on the ceiling while they ground into each other.

Afterward, panting and fumbling to help get her clothes back in order, Quentin apologized.

I shouldn't have done that, he said. *Treated you like a cheap prom date or something.*

Are you kidding me? Lena had laughed, leaning in to give him a deep kiss. *That was the most erotic experience of my life.*

And so what was a man to do? He recreated it for her at every opportunity. Even though they saw each other outside work a few times a week, and Lena stayed over on weekends, their three o'clock coffee date had come to mean something else entirely.

"Okay, so today, actual coffee," he said grinning at her. "You coming over tonight?"

"No, not tonight. Since you're probably going to be yukking it up with Darius until late anyway, I may as well hang out with my brother for a change."

"You could come with us," Quentin suggested.

"No, that's your and Darius's thing. Tell him I said '*hi*' though."

"Yeah, I will. So see you at three?"

"Yup."

Quentin turned to leave and then noticed the documents on the floor again. "What's this?"

"A timeline. For Braden."

"Let me know if you change your mind and want some help. You know I got you, right?"

"Yeah, but I think I'll fly solo on this."

Once they'd gotten involved, they mutually agreed that working on the same cases together should probably be avoided, so Quentin let Richard know he thought Lena was good to go on her own for Braden, with occasional consults when she felt a need for them. And so far, it had worked out fine, drawing this line between the professional and personal. If Lena wanted him as a mentor, he would be there, but for now, he vastly preferred just being her man.

JUST AS HE WAS ABOUT TO ENTER ACCRA CAFÉ, QUENTIN FELT HIS phone vibrating in his pocket and paused at the door, reaching in to fish it out. If he went in before answering, he wouldn't have a chance in hell hearing the person on the other end with all the loud music. And since it might be Lena, he checked. But it wasn't Lena.

Mara.

Quentin let it ring until it went to voicemail and put it back in his pocket, curious about why he would be hearing from his wife at all, but not curious enough to interrupt and possibly ruin his time with his brother. They had two more weeks before they could file with the court, and the last time he'd heard from her, Mara emailed to let him know the papers were drawn up and ready to go, which was good news since he was more than ready to be divorced.

He and Lena hadn't said a word about any future beyond the next weekend, but there was something in him that didn't sit right, being with her while married to someone else. And while he had long lost any feeling of loyalty to Mara, he wasn't too cool with the idea that Lena might be compromised by people finding out she was with a still-married-no-matter-how-long-separated man.

As it was, she had been back to his parents' house twice, now with them as a couple, and Quentin felt the question hanging there in the air, though it had never been asked aloud: *when are you going to make this thing legit?* Not as in married-legit, but at least legit enough to walk into church together for Sunday services, hand-in-hand.

He wanted that for himself, but more than anything, he wanted that for Lena. She deserved that. He still couldn't believe that he had her. And that she had been waiting for him, hoping for him. That she had passed up his brother for him.

Not because he didn't think much of himself, but because he thought so much of her. She was beautiful, smart, funny, cool to hang out with, and to top all that off, a straight-up freak in bed when she wanted to be. And now that they had opened up to each other on a whole different level, Quentin found himself thinking crazy-ass thoughts sometimes—of cohabitation and permanence. But he knew they were crazy. They *had* to be since he was just getting out of a marriage.

Spotting Darius over at the bar tossing back a beer, he waved and then signaled for his brother to instead take one of the tables. He was hungry and preferred to have more room than the bar provided when he ate.

"What's up, man?" They greeted with their customary hug and kiss, and then both sat down.

"How's things with my girl?" Darius asked.

Quentin looked at him. "I hate it when you call her that."

Darius laughed. "You know I don't mean it like *my* girl. I just mean ... my girl. Although let's face it, if I had actually *applied* myself, she would be."

"Shut the hell up," Quentin said matter-of-factly.

Even though he now knew nothing of consequence had happened between his brother and Lena, just the *thought* of what might have happened was too close for comfort.

Darius laughed again and motioned for the waitress. "Glad to see you like this, though, bruh. All ... loved-up and whatnot. So tell me, what's good?"

"I can tell you what's not good. Mara just called me."

Darius shrugged. "Well, the deal's almost done, so it's whatever. Unless you're ..."

"Nah, nothing like that. There ain't nothin' in the *world* she could say right now that would make me consider going back to that. Especially not with what I got going on right now with Lena."

"So what'd she say? Mara, I mean."

"I don't know. Didn't pick up. It's Friday, I'm not trying to let anything disturb my groove."

"Wow. Lena must be really puttin' it on you. I ain't *never* seen you look so mellow."

"Will you stop talkin' 'bout my woman?"

Darius leaned back as the waitress approached. "I can't," he said. "I'm starting to feel some type of way about it, the more I see how she got you all giddy. Wondering if I gave up too soon."

Quentin smirked before looking down at the menu and pointing out his selections to the waitress. "Wouldn't have mattered, man," he said. "She was always mine. Just ask her."

Darius took a sip of his beer. "Cocky motherfucka."

"So, here's the thing. There's something I should've told you a while ago," Quentin began.

Darius barely glanced at him. "So tell me."

"Remember that night I came back from New York and I met you here?"

"The weekend I took her over to the house?"

"Yeah. Well, that Friday night on the way home I called Lena."

Darius turned now, looking marginally more interested.

"I called her and she was at the office, and I went to meet her there, just to ... you know, to keep her company." Quentin cleared his throat.

Given how things had turned out, and the fact that Lena was with him now, it shouldn't have bothered him but he still couldn't stomach keeping something like this from his brother. It had been eating at him for weeks.

"Yeah, and?"

"And that night Lena and I, we kind of ... you know."

Darius pulled back. "You mean you hit it that night? Before I took her to ... No wonder she dumped me."

"Nah, nobody hit anything. It didn't get that far. It might have. But then she told me that you and she were hanging out and that pretty much put a stop to that."

Darius contemplated for a moment then laughed out loud. "Q, you are such a boy scout, man. I always knew Lena wasn't into me. Now, don't get me wrong, it was foul for you and her to be off behind my back feelin' each other up or whatever, but ..."

"As soon as I brought you up, she stopped it," Quentin said again. "She felt bad, I felt bad ... And nothing happened again until after you and me talked that Sunday. I just want to make sure you knew that."

Nodding, Darius took a gulp of his drink. "Glad you told me, man. But ..."

Quentin waited.

"You need to start being honest about your feelings. At least to yourself. And I don't know ... maybe you start with doing some more thinking about what happened with your wife. So you don't make the same mistakes."

"Mistakes? Whatever happened to Mara being a bitch and ..."

"Don't get me wrong, she's got her dirt. I'm damn near sure of it. But that doesn't mean you're all squeaky clean either, Q."

***

"What d'you want, baby?"

"Just vanilla. Vanilla with strawberry topping."

Lena collapsed and took one of the seats outside the yogurt shop while Quentin prepared to go inside to order for them, leaving their bags on the table. They were at the Mazza Gallerie Mall in DC because somehow Lena had gotten it into her head that on the weekends, they spent too much time inside. And in bed.

Quentin was having a hard time believing they could spend *too much* time in bed, but whatever she wanted, he was happy to oblige. In fact, he was beginning to think he was a little bit of a sucker where Lena was concerned. While walking through a department store with her, bored out of his mind, he bought a couple shirts she said she would like on him, just because she said she would like them on him.

Truthfully, it didn't matter what they did. Being with her outside of work was just as easy as it had been when they were at work. The silences were as comfortable as the conversations, and when they did talk, there seemed no end to the ground they could cover. And the sex ... it only got better the more they did it.

While he placed their orders, Quentin watched her, sitting at the table with that day-dreamy look on her face that she some-times got. At work, she got the same look, sometimes drifting away to parts unknown, eyes glazed over and twisting a strand of hair around her fingers. When they were alone together and she drifted away like that, he asked her what she was thinking, and was surprised that he actually cared what the answer was. It was the first time since the earliest days with Mara that he could recall wanting to know a woman, truly and really *know* her.

Quentin turned away and focused on ordering and then paying for the frozen treats and bringing them back to the table. Sitting across from Lena, he slid her the cup with her 'just vanilla' yogurt.

"Y'know what I thought we might do?" she asked, digging in.

"What?"

"Go on a date."

"Oh-*kay*. You don't think we're way past that?"

"Yeah. And that's why I think we need to do it. We just jumped over that part. I was in your bed after two kisses and a little groping in the kitchen. Even my brother called me a 'ho."

Quentin laughed. "If you are, then so am I. I didn't even play hard-to-get for a while."

"Are you kidding me? You were *very* hard to get."

"I didn't know you wanted me ... gotten," he said leaning in.

"Seriously?" Lena looked skeptical. "Me and just about every other woman in the firm who isn't otherwise attached."

Quentin narrowed his eyes. "I find that hard to believe."

"You would. You don't always pick up on cues or signals."

"Were you putting out cues and signals?" he teased.

"I don't know," Lena said, her face growing serious for a moment. "I kind of hope I wasn't."

Quentin leaned back, surprised. "Why would you hope that?"

"Because you were ... you *are* ... married. I'd hate to think I'm the kind of woman who would try to unleash her ... feminine wiles on a man who has a wife."

He didn't know what to say to that.

Truth be told, he'd wondered the same thing. All this time, had he used Mara's minor misdeeds and her frequent absences as an excuse? Was he falling for Lena even then? Mara had said as much—that he fell out of love with her and tried his darndest to make sure she fell out of love with him. It still bothered him to think that Lena might be the reason.

"Lene, no amount of feminine wiles in the world could lure me away from you. So if things were the way they were supposed to be with Mara, then ..."

"I didn't bring that up to get you to talk about her," Lena said speaking over him. "I actually don't think it's a good idea that we do. Not until ..."

The divorce.

It hung over them sometimes—the *one* thing they didn't really talk about. Once in a while, at his house, Lena would run across something of Mara's. Something feminine that obviously didn't belong to him—a stray piece of clothing among his, an old forgotten bottle of half-finished perfume, and once, a pretty floral coffee mug that didn't belong to the set in the cupboards, probably something Mara picked up in Marshall's where she was always finding what she called "cute knick-knacks" and bringing them home.

And every time she ran across one of those relics of his marriage, there was the slightest change in Lena's demeanor. At times like that, Quentin wished he could explain to her—his marriage was decidedly over, and he was happily moving on. The divorce was imminent, and he wasn't looking back. But he was quite sure those were the kinds of empty promises that married-but-separated men made to women all the time, and didn't mean.

"Okay, so you want to go out on a date," Quentin said, bringing the conversation back around to a more pleasant topic. "Where d'you want me to take you?"

"Surprise me," Lena said. "And I want you to take me home

after this so I can get dressed up and you can pick me up later like, you know, normal couples do."

"What do you mean normal couples?" Quentin grinned. "So ... do 'normal' couples spend the night together after their date?"

Lena rolled her eyes. "Is that all you can think about?"

"Yeah," he said, lowering his voice. "With you ... that's pretty much all I can think about."

Lena smiled and leaned in. She kissed him. She tasted like strawberries.

QUENTIN SURVEYED HIS REFLECTION IN THE MIRROR AND TURNED away from it, shaking his head. Lena had him so spun out, he was wearing one of the shirts he bought this afternoon. It wasn't bad, just not necessarily his usual thing. Even for Casual Fridays at the firm, the most he could bring himself to do was not wear a tie.

But he could get used to this crewneck look. Not too dressed-down and not too dressed-up either. He was due to pick Lena up in about forty-five minutes, and then he would take her for a pricey dinner at The Oceanaire Seafood Room, not too far from their office.

It'll be like any other date, she'd teased him when he dropped her off. *If you spend a lot of money, I'll put out.*

Oh, you're puttin' out anyway, he said, leaning in to kiss her before she got out of the car. *And you're staying naked. All day Sunday.*

His doorbell, sounding just as he was about to pick up his wallet from the bedside table, startled him because he so rarely heard it.

Shoving the wallet into his back pocket, Quentin headed

downstairs to get the door, stopping only to make sure he armed his security system, as it was just beginning to get dark. Whoever it was would have to be quick, because he was almost certain to get caught up in weekend traffic headed into DC.

Opening the door, Quentin stood stock still as he looked over his visitor. In retrospect, he would think about that moment and recall that he wasn't even surprised to see her.

Standing there at the threshold of the home they once shared, wearing jeans and a long-sleeved pink shirt, her face streaked with tears, was Mara.

11

———

"Something had to have happened," Lena said. "He wouldn't just not call. And not answer his phone."

"Okay, but stop calling *him*. You're turning into like, a stalker or something."

"I'm not *stalking* him, Marlon! He was supposed to be here almost two hours ago, and this isn't like him. I'm worried!"

And angry. Let's not forget angry.

When Quentin dropped her off at home after their shopping trip, Lena had been positively giddy. She forced herself to nap, anticipating a late night doing ... whatever, then woke up to shower, spent an hour doing something different to her hair that she didn't think he had ever seen before, and another picking an outfit.

While the last month and a half had been amazing, sometimes it definitely felt like they'd skipped over the usual relationship rituals. She wanted to walk into a restaurant with Q next to her, to see other women's faces darken with envy.

She wanted to walk by the Canal in Georgetown, holding hands and enjoying the spring evening. And then afterward, Lena wanted to go back to his house and watch his face transform the way it did every time she undressed before him. Except this time, she would be wearing something feminine and delicate and sexy.

She had the pictures in her head and knew that whatever happened, it would exceed her expectations, just like everything else about being with Quentin. If what she felt for him before was mere infatuation, now she was downright besotted.

Seeing him with his parents and brother, sitting in their childhood living room and looking at family pictures, she imagined a future where the pictures might include her. Just thinking it felt silly and premature, and not just because their relationship was so new, but because he was still playing out some of an old relationship with someone else.

And now, sitting in her kitchen wearing a white lacy shift dress and pewter high-heeled sandals, she felt like a stone was lodged at the bottom of her stomach. Something told her Quentin had been waylaid, not by an accident on the Beltway, nor by something else out of his control, but rather, by *someone.*

It didn't matter how many times he tried to pretend otherwise, he wasn't the kind of man to walk away from a commitment easily. With the right words, he could be ... swayed. Not because his feelings changed, but because his sense of responsibility was triggered.

Quentin had an almost militaristic sense of duty—to be a good brother, son ... and most likely, husband as well. Lena's blood positively boiled with jealousy she knew she had no right to feel whenever she was reminded that Quentin, for all intents and purposes, belonged to someone else.

Marlon was watching her, eating slow bites of a piece of cheesecake Lena had brought back from the Mall but not eaten. He had to have sensed that she was really worried because he had momentarily gone completely silent.

"Maybe I could call Darius and ask *him* to check?" she suggested aloud. "Just to make sure. Just in case something ..."

"I think you should wait another couple of hours," Marlon said quietly.

She didn't know if she could survive another couple of hours. Her heart was clenched like a fist in her chest, and she was breathing a little faster than usual, almost hyperventilating. What if he *had* been in an accident? It wasn't as though she would be his ICE contact, and it might take his family ages before they even thought of letting her know.

"I can't just sit here," she said. "I need to do something."

"If you need to do something, go take that dress off and put on something more comfortable. You're looking like Miss Havisham waiting for the wedding that's never going to happen."

"Marlon, would you just *shut up?!*"

"God, I'm just *sayin'* ..." Her brother ambled off into the living room, turning on the television set and settling on the sofa in front of it. "You're not the first woman in the world to be stood up. I'm sure there's a good reason. Or *some* reason anyway."

Feeling tears begin to sting her eyes, Lena got up and went into her bedroom, slamming the door behind her. Standing there for a moment, she tried to control her breathing and then slowly, methodically, removed her dress and laid it over her armchair, careful not to crease it as she did.

Finally, she took off her sandals and lay across her bed, shutting her eyes and praying for sleep. It was only a little after nine, so that seemed a vain hope, especially since she'd slept earlier in the afternoon.

When she opened her eyes again, Lena felt that it was much later. The apartment was completely silent and her room was dark though she couldn't recall having turned off the lights. Maybe Marlon had.

She tried to avoid looking at the time but couldn't. The red numbers displayed on the digital clock mocked her: 10:46 p.m. Grappling for her cell phone, she finally found it, deep in her bed sheets. The face only confirmed what the clock had already told her: it was almost eleven o'clock.

And furthermore, there were no messages.

Sitting up, feeling a sudden surge of anger, Lena dialed a number. She didn't give a shit *what* was going on. This was *unacceptable.*

"Hey," Darius answered on the first ring.

"When you see him, you can tell your brother for me ..." Lena began.

"He's with me," Darius said, interrupting her planned diatribe. "He's right here."

"*He is?*" Lena felt her heartbeat increase in pace once again. "Is he okay?"

Darius hesitated for a moment then sighed. "Yeah. He's fine."

He sounded somber, and Lena wanted to ask him what was going on, but she was still floored by the revelation that Quentin was with him. *With him!* If he could be with Darius, he could be with her. He could have at least *called* her!

In the background, Lena heard a muffled voice. *Quentin's voice.*

"He said to let you know he's coming to you right now."

"Wh ... *no!* Tell him don't bother!" Lena ended the call and held the phone up, planning to throw it across the room until, at the last second, common sense prevailed.

If he was in an accident or hurt, she would understand. She wouldn't have *wanted* that, didn't want that. But she would have understood. Anything else, barring—God forbid—something happening to one of his parents or Darius, and this was unacceptable. *Who the hell did he think he was?*

Getting up, she went to the bathroom, washing her face and

brushing her teeth, and willing herself to calm down. She was going back to sleep, and when she woke up, she would think about all this. But not tonight. Because if she thought about it, she would only come to outlandish conclusions.

Like maybe the prospect of having an actual 'date' with her had highlighted for Quentin that he wasn't actually ready for a real relationship. Or maybe their conversation at the Mall had reminded him of Mara ... See, her imagination was already running amok. So it was better not to think. Instead, she would just go to sleep. If she could.

"Lena."

Somehow, she had managed to drift off again. And now, opening her eyes in the darkness of her room, Lena found herself staring at Quentin. She could barely make out his features, but in the instant before she came to full wakefulness, all she felt was relief.

He was fine. It was just like Darius said. He wasn't hurt.

Then it all came back. Sitting up, she shoved against his chest.

"Get out," she ordered. "I told your brother I didn't want you to come here. Get *out!*"

"Lene. Let me explain ..."

"I don't want you to explain. I want you *out!*"

"No."

"No?" she practically screeched. "*Marlon!*"

Quentin tried to put a hand on her shoulder, and she shoved him again, practically flapping her arms to avoid having him touch her.

"Will you just calm *down?*" Quentin hissed. "Marlon let me in, so he isn't coming to your rescue."

"Well, I don't want you h..."

Lena tried to get up from her bed, but Quentin pulled her back down, and suddenly the room was flooded light. He had reached over and flipped on her bedside lamp.

Squinting in surprise, Lena's eyes took a moment to adjust, and then she saw him. He looked terrible. His face was drawn, his eyes rimmed in red. He looked like someone who had just received life-altering news.

"Q, what ...?"

His shoulders relaxed when he saw she wasn't about to make a break for it, and then he leaned back against the headboard, exhaling deeply.

"I'm sorry," he said, sounding defeated. "I should've come sooner. Or called you. But ..."

Lena glanced at the time. It was after midnight, well after she'd called Darius, so he must have lingered there even longer, even after knowing she was worried and looking for him. Her anger flared once again for a moment, but then she looked at Quentin's face and saw there, and in his eyes, that he was lost.

"What happened?" she forced herself to keep her voice level as she asked the question.

"Mara stopped by."

Lena sprang back from him as though stung. "I knew it," she said. "I *knew* it! I just ..."

"Will you listen to me?" Quentin asked, reaching for her.

"No! What's there to listen to? You were never over her, were you? I should have kn ..."

"Lena, *stop!*" Quentin grabbed her, pulling her back down onto the bed and, grabbing her face between his hands. "*Look at me!* It is over. Are you listening to me? *It's over!*"

She stilled, but her chest was heaving. Lena braved a look at him and saw that along with the pain, there was certainty.

"Then what ..."

"That's what I've been trying to tell you. But you keep flipping out on me."

Lena bit her lower lip, feeling silly all a sudden. "Tell me," she said quietly.

"Will you listen?" he asked, carefully.

"I'm listening, Quentin. You don't have to hold me prisoner. I'm listening."

Slowly, he released her and Lena folded her arms, preparing for bad news. Quentin was watching her, his eyes cautious as though he thought he might be being tricked.

"Mara stopped by just as I was leaving to come get you," he began. "She said she wanted to talk, and that she thought she made a mistake ..."

Lena braced herself for what she was fairly certain she knew was coming.

"She wanted to call off the divorce."

Exhaling, Lena shut her eyes and leaned back against the headboard. Quentin moved closer to her.

"Then she told me that ... she told me that while we were together, about two years ago now, she met someone. And that it wasn't planned ... you know the rest, all the shit people say when they fuck around." Quentin's voice was bitter. "But she said it turned serious, and they were planning to be together, but it was *complicated*. And it was going to take some time, so they agreed she should hang in there."

"Did she say who it was? Whether it was someone you know?"

"Yeah. That's the kicker. She said who alright."

"Who?"

"Rich."

Lena leaned closer, not sure she heard right. "*Rich*? Like ..."

"Richard Lowe. Our boss. Partner at Fox, Cheatham & Lowe. One and the same."

"Quentin ..."

"Yeah," he said. "I know. It's been him. All this time."

"And now?"

"Now it's over. He ended it. They've been together for the last two years on and off, and last week he ended it for good. Seems that the minute he heard she was actually about to be free, he developed a little belated remorse."

Lena didn't know what to say.

She thought of Richard Lowe and the special interest he took in Quentin's career; the praise he lavished on him and the hints about the prospect of an even brighter future at the firm. *Was all of that out of guilt?* But no, it couldn't be because Quentin was good. He was the real deal. Everyone said so, and Lena knew so.

"But there was something else. When I was in New York with him, someone approached me. It was, I don't know, an overture like they were interested in making me an offer to leave Fox, Cheatham ..."

Lena remembered the conversation with Quentin's mother and the mention of him considering a move to New York. Funny, but she had all but forgotten about that. She was sure, now, that if Quentin was seriously considering a move to New York, he would tell her. And he hadn't, so she put it out of her mind.

"I didn't think Rich knew anything about that. But apparently he got wind of it somehow. He told Mara ... he told her that he realized he didn't want to take the risk of me leaving. That I was too *valuable* to the firm. And that if ..." Quentin broke off and gave a harsh laugh. "And that if I heard that he and Mara were together, even if I never knew it started before we split up, I would leave Fox Cheatham. He told her he couldn't take that chance, that having me walk away from the firm was an ... 'unacceptable loss'."

"God," Lena said. And just like that, every ounce of respect she ever had for Richard Lowe was gone in a puff of smoke.

"So Mara showed up tonight crying. And y'know what she thought? She said she thought I should know—*she actually said this*—that if I stayed at the firm, it would be working for the man who had screwed my wife and destroyed my marriage."

"*Quentin*." Lena put a hand over his. It felt cold.

"You should have heard her, Lene. She said I should reconsider the divorce because she'd made a mistake ... a *mistake*. She said she made a mistake because she thought Richard loved her, but in the end, he chose business over their relationship. So I should quit my job, and we should try again because she now realizes she was wrong." Quentin shook his head, the incredulity written all over his face. "Man ... I almost fucking hit her. My whole marriage was a lie. Everything I thought about why we split up was a lie ..."

"Why did you think you split up?"

"Honestly?" Quentin turned and looked at her.

"Yeah. Honestly."

"Deep down inside, I felt guilty as hell. I thought Mara and I split up because ... because maybe I fell in love with you."

Lena swallowed hard.

She knew she should be focused on what Mara told him, and on the ramifications for Quentin's career, but for the moment, only one thing penetrated.

"You are?"

"Are *what*?" he asked, sounding almost impatient.

"In love with me."

Quentin looked at her. "Of course I'm in love with you. What did you think was going on here?"

Lena shook her head. "I thought ..."

He looked at her expectantly. "You thought what? That we were just screwing around?"

"No. I mean, *I'm* not. But ..."

"But I *am*?"

"No, Quentin, I ..."

"Jesus." He let his head fall back against the headboard. "What a fucking day *this* turned out to be."

"I'm sorry." Lena squeezed his hand. "I'm making this about me, and there's so much more going on. Like what to do about your job, and about Mara ..."

"About Mara?" Q erupted. "Is there any question what to do about Mara? I'm going to divorce her ass. Just as quick as I can make it happen. And as for the job ..." He exhaled. "I don't even know if I can go in there Monday. I mean, how the hell am I supposed to ...?"

"Don't think about it now. We'll figure it out. We'll figure something out."

"There's nothing to figure out. Whether I'm with Mara or not, I can't stay there. How the hell could I?"

Lena didn't have an answer for that. Because she agreed with him.

"Take your clothes off," she said instead.

Quentin looked at her, lifting his eyebrows.

"*Off.*"

Shaking his head, Quentin sat forward and pulled his shirt over his head, toed off his shoes and socks, unbuttoned and pulled down his jeans and boxer-briefs while Lena watched. Just as he was about to lay his clothes across her armchair, he noticed the lacy dress she had shed earlier.

"Is that what you were going to wear to dinner?" he asked.

Lena nodded.

"I bet you looked beautiful in it."

She gave him a wan smile and reached over, turning out the light. The room was thrust into darkness.

"There'll be other dinners, Q. C'mere."

She felt as Quentin made his way closer to her on the bed, and Lena arranged her body in front of his so that he was spooning her. They lay there for a few moments, saying nothing, the only sound that of their soft breathing. Lena took a breath.

"You really love me?" she whispered.

"I *really* love you," Quentin confirmed. "It would scare you if I told you how much."

Lena smiled. "I doubt that. Tell me. How much?"

Quentin shifted so that she was on her back instead of leaning on him, and then Lena felt his weight on her, his knee parting her legs. He settled between them, his semi-turgidity pressing against her and awakening her libido.

"I love you white-picket-fence much. Babies-and-a-pet-dog much. I love you cazy-enough-to-be-thinking-about-weddings-in-the-middle-of-a-divorce much. How's that for scary?"

Lena swallowed the lump at the back of her throat.

"Pretty scary," she admitted. "But … pretty amazing too."

"*You're* pretty amazing." Quentin was kissing her neck, then her collarbone, then removing her top and kissing between her breasts. Lena put her hands atop his head. "And I'm sorry I missed our date."

"It's okay," she whispered.

"No, it's not. But we're going to have lots of dates," Quentin said. "Just as soon as I find a new job to pay for them." He laughed mirthlessly.

When he seemed intent on making his way further down, Lena stopped him, pulling him back up to her and finding his lips. Arching her back, she worked her underwear over her hips until they were low enough to shimmy off altogether. Spreading her legs wider, she reached for him. He was completely hard now. Guiding him toward her, she felt him hesitate. They had no protection.

"It's okay," she whispered. "I want to feel you."

"I haven't been with ..."

"I know. I haven't been with anyone either. Not for a long time. I'm good. We're good ..." Lena lifted her pelvis off the mattress and sighed as Quentin sunk deep inside her.

He exhaled a long warm breath that stirred her hair.

"God, baby ..."

"I know," she breathed. "I know ..."

It was exquisite. Lena moved her hips in time with his, meeting every thrust, her arms tight around him and low on his back, trying to get him deeper and closer still.

"God, Lena ..."

"I know," she said again. "I love you."

Quentin's mouth on hers swallowed whatever else she might have said, which was just as well since she was pretty close to speaking gibberish. As his pace increased, and he gripped her ass hard with both hands, fingers digging into her flesh, Lena knew he was about to come. She felt his hesitation, and knew he was remembering that there was no condom.

"It's okay, Q ..." She held him tighter, not wanting him to pull out, knowing the risk and accepting it. "Stay with me ... stay ...."

With a deep groan, Quentin went stiff as a board, and Lena felt him erupt. Turning her head, she kissed him, ushering him gently down from his orgasmic high.

Finally, he collapsed atop her, and moments later propped himself up on his elbows, kissing her brow, her cheek and finally her lips.

Rolling over onto his side, Quentin pulled her toward him, and Lena felt his lips pressed against the back of her neck.

They were silent for long minutes until finally he spoke.

"Lena."

"Yeah?"

She felt a little drowsy now, drowsy and complete. Now that Quentin was with her, she could sleep, *really* sleep. Now that she knew he loved her, everything else felt surmountable. Even the mess with Rich and Mara and his job. They would figure it all out together.

"I have to say something. It's true, y'know?"

"What's true, baby?" she asked sleepily.

"I can't blame this all on Mara."

Lena's eyes opened a little wider. She listened a little more closely.

"I was talking to D about it tonight. And ... I don't want to sugarcoat it. She was wrong. There was no question she was wrong, but ..."

"But what?"

"I left myself open to it. To falling in love with someone other than my wife. I let myself fall in love with you."

Turning in his arms so they were facing each other, Lena stared into his eyes, hoping that she wouldn't see what she feared she might—regret. What they had would be marred if he regretted it.

"But we never ..."

"I know. We had some conversations. A few afternoons of coffee. Some late nights working on the same cases. But I wasn't being honest about the feelings I was starting to have for you. By denying they were there, I made things worse."

"But you didn't *cheat* on her," Lena said.

"Didn't I?" His eyes met hers. "I wouldn't have left her. But now I'm not so sure I didn't ... orchestrate her leaving me."

"So what're you saying? You're ..." Lena swallowed hard, not knowing what she wanted to ask.

"I'm saying I love you. But the way we got here scares me a little bit. I let the distance between me and Mara grow, and she let Rich crawl right into that space. And then, somewhere along the way losing my marriage became ... acceptable to me."

A lump formed in the back of Lena's throat. "So are you ashamed of the way we …?"

"*No*, baby, no. That's not it." Q pressed his lips to her forehead. "Just … let's not let that happen to us, okay? Let's not let anything come between us."

"That's not going to happen to us," Lena said, trying to sound firm.

"Good. Because losing you … that's something I couldn't accept."

12

____

"THIS IS SOME *BULLSHIT*," DARIUS SAID. "SO YOU TOOK THE OFFER, man?"

"Couldn't pass it up. The perks were just ... sick. And the salary was definitely New York money."

"Ma's gon' freak. Her favorite son moving to New York."

"Ma'll be fine because *you're* her favorite son. But Pops might freak."

Quentin dodged his fellow pedestrians on the already crowded pavement, dancing out of the way of sidewalk vendors, tourists, and commuters as he held the phone to his ear.

"And this is the only way?" Darius asked.

For a fleeting moment, Quentin felt a sense of loss, and the full expanse of the distance between him and his brother, talking to him from his studio in Georgetown, two hundred miles away. He would miss their weekly meet-ups, the shit-talking and the times they didn't talk, but just listened to live music in a crowded bar, and took comfort in each other's presence.

"No, but it's the best way," Quentin said. "The DC law scene is too small to try to avoid someone you hold a grudge for."

"Yeah ..." Darius sounded unconvinced. "And Lena?"

"Haven't told her yet. I'm taking the three o'clock so I'll have time to see her before I meet you at Accra."

"Damn. How you think she'll take it?"

"She'll take it fine."

"I don't know, man. You two are joined at the hip lately. Even more ever since ..."

"We'll be a'ight. This is a good move for me. She'll be on board because of that. But look, let me hurry up and make sure I catch this train. I'm about to duck down in the subway anyway, so I'm about to lose you ..."

"Okay. Catch you later at Accra, man. Travel safe."

Quentin hung up and took the stairs down into the Chambers Street subway. He would have to get used to this—the smell, the grime, the sheer grittiness of New York's subway in comparison to the relative crisp cleanliness of DC's Metro system.

But he liked New York. It was alive, and raw, and real. And though it was expensive as hell, his new employer was paying a generous signing bonus, relocation expenses and a salary that would improve rather than diminish his current standard of living. Looking for a new place, learning a neighborhood—its haunts and hideaways—was going to be a cool adventure. And it would get him away from the ruins and reminders of his old life.

Lately, he'd been thinking about it less. In the final month before the divorce hearing, Mara had gone all out ballistic on him, threatening to stall the divorce in whatever way she could. In the end, she couldn't get past it, the humiliation of knowing that the man she had left Quentin for had in essence decided he would rather leave *her* than lose Quentin.

But eventually, her threats had amounted to nothing, because a year of separation had passed, and he could get a divorce under Maryland law whether she wanted one or not.

And if she made things too difficult on property settlement issues, he made it clear he would get the divorce on grounds of adultery, calling none other than Richard Lowe as a witness.

Despite his best efforts, Quentin's divorce *had* turned into World War III. But at the end of the day, it had been a gift—he need not feel an ounce of guilt about falling for Lena, because her threats in the last month made it clear his ex-wife had never been the woman he once thought she was.

And as for his career at Fox Cheatham, it ended after one very tense meeting with Richard in his office. Quentin had cleared his desk, called all his former clients, and made a clean break of it. Rich, in a belated show of decency, had sent word through Lena that he was prepared to give Q an unreserved recommendation to anyone who might ask.

In the weeks that followed, Lena toyed with the idea of quitting herself, pointing out that she had been considering it anyway; and that her coffee breaks just weren't the same without him. But Quentin talked her out of it, reminding her that no matter where she went, it would be unwise to burn any bridges before she left. So, she stuck it out and even got another junior associate to work with her on the Braden matter. Wherever she landed in the end, a win on that case was going to help establish her value.

Quentin made it onto the Amtrak train with minutes to spare and after grabbing a sandwich in the Café, made his way to the Quiet Car where he ate and took a nap. He slept the entire way, waking up only when the train pulled into Washington DC's Union Station. As planned, he made his way to the Starbucks on the ground floor.

From a distance, as he approached, he spotted her—Lena with her formidable hair. She was wearing yellow today, a dress that looked like it had little white blooms printed on it and pumps in a pale color. Her legs were tucked to one side, and as always, Q's eyes were drawn to them.

He smiled, feeling proud that the beautiful woman sitting there, with the amazing hair and golden-brown skin, was *his* woman. He walked up behind her, touching her lightly on the shoulder. Turning with a look of slight alarm in her eyes, Lena smiled when she saw it was him.

"Hey." He kissed her on the lips and then joined her at the table.

"So?" she said, without greeting. She chewed her lower lip, her eyes fixed on his.

"They made me an offer," Quentin said.

Lena sighed, and then smiled. "That's amazing, baby." She leaned forward, kissing him at the corner of his lips, resuming her seat and picking up her coffee cup to take a long sip.

"It's cool, right? One interview and ... slam-dunk."

"That wasn't an interview. That was a courting process," she said, attempting another smile. "I didn't really doubt they'd want you. It's ... exciting."

"What's wrong? You say you're excited. But you don't look excited."

Quentin tipped her chin upward, and Lena swallowed. There were tears in her eyes.

"You're moving to New York." She shrugged.

"That's where the job is, so ... yeah."

Lena nodded and looked around the station as though searching for someone. "So ... you and Darius tonight, right? It's Friday."

"Yeah." Quentin looked at his watch. "In about an hour. But afterward, I'll come by you. If you don't mind him dumping me drunk at your doorstep at three in the morning."

"I'll take you however I can get you," Lena said.

"Baby ..." Quentin put a hand on her cheek. "C'mon. Cheer up ..."

"*Cheer up?*" That seemed to be the last straw. Lena shoved his hand away. "You're moving to New York, Q. How can I be *cheerful* about that? I mean, I'm glad about the job, but you'll be ... you'll be so far away. We said we wouldn't let anything come between ..." She stopped herself and leaned back in her seat, biting her lower lip.

Quentin leaned back. "Well, *that's* disappointing," he said, looking at her.

"I know," Lena said. "And I'm sorry. I know it sounds selfish, but it's the truth. I wanted you to get the job. But part of me wanted you *not* to get it. Because now you're moving and who knows what'll happen then."

"No. I mean, it's disappointing because you're acting like you aren't coming with me."

Lena's head snapped up. "Coming with ..."

"Lena." Quentin shook his head. "You think I'd go *anywhere* without you? If you're not coming, I'm not going."

He shrugged, and the tears that had been threatening for the last few minutes spilled over and down her cheeks. Lena made no move to wipe them away.

"But ... are you sure? I mean ..."

"*Baby.* What did I tell you? How much did I say I love you?"

Lena smiled, and this time, the smile touched her eyes as well. "*White-picket-fence much. Babies-and-a-pet-dog much.*"

"Yeah. *That* much. So how the hell would we do all that if you're here and I'm in New York? Huh?"

Quentin moved his chair so that it was next to, instead of across from hers. Nuzzling her neck, he pressed his lips into her skin and inhaled her minty, lemon scent.

"I'm not going anywhere without you. *Believe* that," he said, speaking against her skin.

"But how do you know you want that so soon? That it's the right th…"

"Because my heart said so," he said, pulling back a little and brushing away her tears with a thumb.

"I love you, too. But … you're sure you want me to come with you?"

"Even if I was a million miles away, nothing could come between us. But I don't want us to be in some bullshit long-distance relationship. I know what's most important to me, and you're it. And once we get to New York, we'll get started on all that white-picket fence stuff. I promise."

Lena shook her head. "We don't have to rush any of that, Q. As long as I'm with you, we can …"

"It doesn't feel like a rush," he said as Lena cupped his face in her hands and kissed him. "It feels overdue."

DARIUS WAS SITTING AT HIS CUSTOMARY PLACE IN ACCRA CAFÉ, sipping a beer, watching a soccer game, soundless, on the television mounted above the bar. Quentin paused for a second to take in the moment.

He would miss coming here every Friday and knowing that his brother and best friend was there waiting. He was supposedly the steady one, and Darius the one that folks would do well not to count on. But Quentin knew that wasn't true. It never had been.

As if feeling that he was being watched, Darius turned and looked toward the door. Spotting his brother, he gave the broadest of grins, and stood, opening his arms. Quentin walked into them and they hugged. Darius kissed him on the cheek and spoke into his ear, one hand on top of his head.

"Congratulations, man," he said. "You did a'ight."

"Thank you, thank you," Quentin took a mock formal bow.

"So c'mon, let me buy you a drink. Sit your ass down! Tell me what's good."

Taking the seat next to his brother, Quentin nodded. "Everything, man. Everything's good."

PART II

13

Lena looked around the living room, spinning in a full circle, trying to manufacture some enthusiasm. After all, this was her new home. Quentin had warned her that in New York, the price of a decent amount of square-footage was much higher than either of them were used to spending in the Washington DC and Maryland real estate markets. But it wasn't just the size. The apartment was boxy, bland and unimaginative.

A brand-new two-bedroom unit in Brooklyn Heights, it had large windows in every room, bamboo floors, classic pewter fixtures in the bathroom, and new appliances in the kitchen. It was clean and bright, and looked like a pleasant enough place to lay one's head, but not at all like a warm home.

When she asked Q if he'd gotten any furniture, he told her he had, but Lena arrived to find that by furniture, he meant the king-size bed, sitting ungainly and unadorned in the center of the larger of the two bedrooms, and a very basic pub-style kitchen table with two high-backed stools, set out in what was supposed to be the dining room.

Sighing, Lena dropped her purse on the floor in the middle of the living room and in exhaustion, sat next to it. Tomorrow, her father and Marlon were driving her things up, but she hadn't packed that much. Marlon had taken over her lease and inherited all her furniture, so she had mostly clothes and personal effects. Now she wondered whether letting all her stuff go had been premature. Quentin clearly hadn't done much of anything since moving here. She should have asked him to take pictures so she would have known exactly what she was up against.

It had been only three months since he'd moved to New York to take the new job and they promised to give it at least six months before making any firm plans. But neither of them had been able to last that long.

After Quentin's initial, impulsive suggestion that she come with him, commonsense had prevailed—there were arrangements to be made, Lena had to give notice at Fox, Cheatham, and she needed to find a new job. But after lots of frustrating weekends of Quentin taking the train to DC to spend time with her and having to rush back late on Sunday, all while trying to adjust to a new job; or Lena taking the train to Manhattan and the two of them staying in hotels to try to make it romantic, the stress of a long-distance relationship had begun to wear on them.

It all came to a head Labor Day weekend, when Q made the trip to DC despite telling her that he had loads of work to do. Lena remembered being excited when she heard his key in her apartment door. But when he walked in, she could see from the slump of his shoulders, one weighed down by his weekend bag, the other by his laptop, that he was tired and probably in a bad mood.

You mind if we stay in? he'd asked, before he even unloaded his luggage.

No, of course not. Lena agreed, even though she had been looking forward to being out with him, and hanging out with some of her friends and their spouses.

It was still new, having someone who was her plus-one, who could round out all those couples-laden events her girlfriends planned, which she had often bowed out of. And it was Labor Day, the last hurrah of summer. For all the folks who hadn't gone out of town on holiday, or who had just returned, there were late-night cookouts, or outdoor cocktail parties—the kinds of events Lena would have attended alone and feeling awkward; or with a date she didn't always know well enough to feel comfortable with.

But what did a party matter, when Quentin was there?

So instead they ordered in and ate on the sofa, Lena resting her legs across his lap. The trouble started when after dinner she suggested a movie and he gave a long-suffering sigh.

A television movie, Quentin. I know you don't want to go out. I meant something on cable.

I'm wiped out, he said running a hand over his head. *You mind if we just ...?* He inclined his head in the direction of the bedroom.

Even though it was only around nine p.m., Lena gave in. After all, he was the one who had taken the almost four-hour train ride directly after a full day's work. But when they were in her bedroom, he'd pulled her down to the bed, kissing her, and reaching for the hem of her shirt.

Wait, she stopped him. *I thought you were tired. Too tired to go out. Too tired to even watch a movie on the sofa. But you're not too tired for ...*

That's different, Quentin said, his eyes at half-mast.

How is that different? she demanded, thinking of the evening plans she had just canceled. *You're perfectly willing to exert yourself for something* you *want to do, but if it's something I want, then ...*

I had no idea you didn't *want it,* he said. *If it knew it was going to be a chore ...*

Now you're just twisting my words!

And that was it. They were off, and within minutes were smack-dab in the middle of the worst fight they had ever had. Over practically nothing.

And when all was said and done, Quentin had slammed his way out of the apartment and Lena wound up clutching her pillow, fighting back the fear that their relationship was already cracking under the pressure of a mere few weeks' separation. She fell asleep alone and didn't even hear when Quentin returned, nor feel when he crawled back into bed with her.

In the morning, she awoke to the aroma of breakfast and coffee and joined him in the kitchen. Marlon was with him, sitting at the dining table, looking uncharacteristically somber. Quentin didn't kiss her good morning, the way he normally might have. Instead, he looked a little sheepish as he handed her a mug of coffee.

Can we talk? he asked. And Lena felt her heart rate immediately double.

Sure, she whispered hoarsely.

Quentin gave Marlon a look, and her brother quietly left the room.

Look, Q began. *This isn't working.*

And Lena felt the tears gathering.

We're all out of whack, he continued, as Lena's eyes filled, threatening at any moment to spill over and onto her cheeks.

She nodded, waiting.

I don't think we should be apart any longer. I don't like it. He shrugged. *I mean, I hate it. I want you to come to New York, like, now.*

What? Lena had asked, hardly daring to believe what she was hearing.

I know what you're thinking, Quentin said quickly. *That I'm just saying this out of convenience, or because I don't like the travel-*

*ing, but that's not it. I just ... not having you around, as part of my
daily life just ... it sucks.*

After that, things shifted into high-gear. Within a week, Lena gave her bosses one month's notice, and even without a job lined up, made plans to move in with Quentin in Brooklyn.

Now, here she was.

Her life in DC was over, and she was officially a New Yorker. With her new apartment key, and a few days' worth of clothes, she had taken Amtrak's early Acela Express to the city and then the subway to her new home.

It was rainy and cold as Lena trekked the five blocks over from the Clark Street Station, and she wasn't dressed properly for the weather. By the time she fidgeted with the lock to the outer door and trudged upstairs to the apartment, she was already a little irritable.

Quentin hadn't been here to greet her because he had to be at work, but now Lena thought that was probably for the best since he would have been disappointed by how underwhelmed she was. He had Fed Ex'ed her a set of keys a few days earlier, the way a real estate agent might have done, with little tags affixed to each to tell her which was for which door.

Shoving herself to her feet with a sigh, she looked around once again and tried to imagine the place furnished. She would paint the walls, which were now a bland eggshell, and find cool decorative objects at weekend flea markets. She and Q would go shopping for linens and crockery and cutlery. They would set up house together, like the newlyweds they would one day be.

And tonight, she would cook for him. There was a grocery store about five blocks away, and a florist about a block from that. She could make him his first full home-cooked meal in his new—*their* new—place. And she could breathe a little life into this bland and ascetic space with some flowers. And then, together they would make plans.

Lena took another breath, this time smiling as she did.

What was she so gloomy about? This was good. She was going to be living with Quentin. For the first time, they would wake up together every single day, go to sleep every single night ... as a couple. It was going to be way beyond cool. It was going to be amazing.

All she needed was a hot shower, and an attitude adjustment.

———

"SO D'YOU LIKE IT?" QUENTIN HAD ROLLED UP HIS SHIRTSLEEVES and was leaning on the table between them as he dug into his dinner of lamb chops, garlic smashed potatoes, and brussel sprouts.

Lena had gone on a cooking and homemaking tear for the rest of the afternoon so that by the time he got home, the apartment smelled like a home.

"What? The place?"

"Yeah. And Brooklyn. You think you'll like it here?" He looked up at Lena and paused, waiting for her response.

"Sure. Yeah. From what I've seen," she said vaguely with a shrug.

"You don't like it," Quentin said.

"No, I do. But we need furniture." Lena looked around the almost empty room. "Stuff. We need more stuff."

"You'll take care of all that, though," Quentin said, his mouth full. "You can be like a housewife."

Smiling, Lena shook her head. "No thank you. I need to find a job."

"Yeah, but while you're looking. You can shop for furniture, paint, decorate ..."

"I want to do all that with you, though."

"And we will, Lene. On weekends. But during the week, you can get some of it done, right?"

"Yeah, I guess."

Quentin put down his fork and gave her his full attention. "What's the matter?"

"I don't have a job yet, Quentin. It wouldn't feel right going off on my own and spending a bunch of money on furniture and decorations without you being around so we can agree on cost, and ..."

Quentin shook his head as though exasperated. "I trust your judgment. And besides, I got a good amount from my share of the sale of the house, the signing bonus and moving expenses. So it's not like we're hurting for cash."

"It's not like *you're* hurting for cash. My savings are ..."

"Wait. Let's get something straight. Are we getting married, or not?"

"You haven't asked."

"I'm asking," he said, his eyes penetrating hers.

"That's not the most romantic proposal I've ever heard," Lena teased.

"How many have you heard?"

She rolled her eyes. "You know what I mean."

"I'm serious. Have you ever been eng ... has anyone ever ...?"

Five months. They had only been together for five months, and yet it seemed so much longer. Here they were, living together, talking about furniture-buying, and having conversations like this one. Theirs was the very definition of a whirlwind relationship, and yet it didn't feel fast. It felt like it had been a long time coming. But occasionally, they stumbled upon an issue like this one, which reminded them of all the things they had yet to learn about each other.

"When I was in college, I had a serious boyfriend sophomore through senior year. We talked about getting married after grad school." Lena shrugged. "But then we were living in different cities and gradually, we just ..." She shrugged again.

Wade. Lena hadn't thought about him in ages. They were inseparable, the kind of couple that seemed so stable and well-suited that there was no question they would be together over the long-term. In the end, it had only taken them a year to unravel. Wade had grown distant and uncommunicative and then there was that one, last awkward dinner when he let her know exactly why.

I love you, he'd insisted. *I always* will *love you, but ...*

You're not in *love with me*, Lena had finished for him.

And he nodded, his face drawn, sad and a little ashamed. It was that last emotion—shame—that let Lena know that there was probably someone else. But she didn't ask, and Wade didn't tell.

That was it. Her four-year relationship ended with lines that could have been written for the screenplay of an unimaginative, low-budget chick flick. It had to have been among the most civilized and anticlimactic breakup as ever occurred in the history of human relationships.

"So how did he propose?" Quentin asked.

Lena noted the overly casual way he asked, and almost smiled. Q was jealous! Of some old, college boyfriend who hadn't even amounted to anything more than a growing pain of young adulthood.

"He didn't. Not really. I guess it was just understood or something," she admitted. Then she shook her head, shaking off the memories and refocusing the conversation. "But anyway, back to us ..."

"I'll give you my card. Buy the furniture. When we get married it won't matter who paid for what."

Lena forced herself not to ask whether that was true given his recent, messy divorce. But they tended to steer clear of that topic. Mara, his ex-wife, was the one subject guaranteed to change his mood. As much as he liked to pretend he didn't care, Quentin hated the bad blood that had developed between them during the dissolution of his marriage.

"But you can't pay for everything, Q. I want to do my fair share."

"So get the other stuff."

"The 'other stuff'?" she mimicked. "You have no idea what that entails do you?"

Quentin smiled that smile of his. The one that made her feel like she was thirteen again and in the throes of her first crush. His hazel eyes crinkled at the corners and Lena's stomach did a little flip. For a few moments, they sat there, staring at each other across the table. There were still times—like this one— where Lena looked at him and almost couldn't believe he was looking back at her with exactly the same hunger in his eyes that she felt for him.

"You ready for me?" he asked, his voice barely above a whisper.

She smiled. It was what he asked when they were about to get frisky. He asked that a lot.

"Yeah," she said. "I'm ready."

14

———————

"Come on through, man. Lena would love to see you."

"It's just for one night. But you sure you got room for me?"

"We haven't furnished the second bedroom yet, but she bought a sofa last week, so yeah ... as long as you don't mind sleeping on that," Quentin told his brother. "How long you plan to be gone again?"

"Six weeks. Can't do Thailand right in less time than that."

Quentin leaned back in his chair and bit his lower lip, suppressing the urge to tell Darius to be careful. Didn't matter how old they both got—he still felt like he had to look out for his baby brother. But given Darius' twice-a-year trips to some of the most obscure parts of the globe, telling him to take care of himself was about as much 'looking after' as Quentin could manage. That, and doing Google searches to check for recent bombings, political unrest and the like, just to set his own mind at ease.

"Flying through Hong Kong," Darius added. "I might take an extra week on the way back."

"Sounds cool, man."

"Yup."

There was silence for a few beats.

"So how's she adjusting anyway? Buying sofas, huh? Sounds like you done turned her into a housewife."

"Nah, man. Being home all the time is driving her crazy. So of course she's driving me crazy. Calling me six times a day to ask me shit like whether I want white or fried rice for dinner."

Darius' rich, deep laughter traveled through the phone lines. "No. But I can imagine. She hasn't found anything yet?"

"That's the thing. Far as I can tell, she ain't even lookin'."

"What's that about?"

"She's not admitting it to herself yet. But I don't think she wants to go back into private practice."

"What's that leave? Staying home? Taking care of the babies y'all ain't even had yet?"

"No. I don't think so. She just needs to figure some things out, that's all. And hopefully she won't drive me out of my mind while she does it."

"But otherwise how's things with you two? Cool?"

Quentin smiled.

Yeah. Things were cool.

It was cool coming home to the smell of curried chicken, and walking into the kitchen to be greeted by the sight of Lena's firm derriere wearing only those little cut-off denim shorts and a tank top while she stood at the stove, barefoot, hair wild.

It was cool opening the bathroom door and having the scent of coconuts and passionfruit assail him, and seeing lacy underwear and bras peeking out from under the lid of the hamper.

Or climbing between the sheets each evening after working late in the living room, and having Lena turn instinctively toward him, slinging a leg over his, and wrapping an arm round his waist.

It was *all* cool.

"We're good," Quentin said.

"So you met her pops? How'd that go?"

"It was a'ight," Quentin said.

Actually, it went about as well as one could expect it to go when you were inveigling a woman to leave her home, her stable, secure, and prestigious job to live in sin while unemployed. For all those reasons, Winston Chambers hadn't taken to Quentin too much. It didn't matter how many times he tried to allude to the certainty of marriage and permanence with Lena, Mr. Chambers spent most of the afternoon that he was helping move his daughter's things glowering at Quentin and responding to direct conversation with grunts.

Finally, as Marlon and Lena were saying their goodbyes, Quentin took the older man aside to assure him that he loved Lena very much and would look after her.

I know you must be worried, he said, trying to maintain steady eye-contact. *But I promise you, I'll look after her. I'm as committed to Lena as though she was my wife. And as soon as she's ready, she will be.*

Winston Chambers had openly scoffed at that. *But you're just barely divorced from your last wife, are you not? And I didn't raise my daughter to be … 'looked after' by a man, thank you very much.*

So much for reassurance.

Later, when Quentin ran the conversation past his own father, he hadn't gotten much solace there, either.

I know you love Lena. And I know the kind of man you are, because I know the kind of man I raised you to be, his father said. *But if she were* my *daughter? None of this nonsense y'all doin' right now would be going on. You should've taken some time. Used the distance to heal from what happened with Mara, and then married Lena if that's what your heart still said you should do.*

Quentin knew what his heart said. It said that Lena was supposed to be his wife. He didn't need time to date other women, or to 'heal.' He knew what he wanted. But he supposed he understood how it must look. Like he was rushing things, like he and Lena weren't being deliberate or thoughtful enough.

"So tell Lena I'll be coming back with y'all after Thanksgiving, and ..."

"She's going to Florida for Thanksgiving. To spend it with her parents and her brother," Quentin interrupted.

"She's not coming to our house?"

"Nah."

Joint holidays would have been Quentin's preference, but in this case, he didn't want to further incite Mr. Chambers' wrath. So Lena was going to see her family while he spent the holiday with his.

Quentin thought he could hear impressions being formed in Darius' silence. Grown couples, mature relationships tended to include shared celebrations. What they were doing, was the kind of thing couples did in college—*'You go see your family while I go see mine. And afterward, we'll play house again.'*

"Anyway, I gotta get back to work, man. Hit me up later."

They talked a few times a week, but generally only for a few minutes at a time. Neither of them were phone people so after every conversation, it felt like there was a lot that they needed to tell each other but hadn't managed to share.

Quentin hung up and swung his chair around to look out the window. The firm was in a large high-rise, overlooking Old Wall Street. There were still cobblestone side-streets where, against all odds, small Mom-and-Pop stores still survived, selling cigars, soda, newspapers, candy and various other odds and ends. He liked that at lunch time he could wander through those streets and discover small hidden gems, thriving among the massive buildings that symbolized the power of American capitalism.

A few afternoons, Lena had come to meet him so they could have dim sum together, or grab a couple hot dogs before he had to run back to the office. But she didn't like Manhattan nearly as much as he did, and had, after only three weeks, sworn her allegiance to Brooklyn. Now that she wasn't working, Quentin watched her metamorphosis with wonder and some pleasure—she didn't restrain her hair as much as she used to, she wore sandals, and jeans, soft cotton t-shorts in earth tones and earrings made of raw materials like wood, unfinished copper and burlap string. Her makeup was bolder, and darker, her smiles more frequent, her spirit lighter.

Whether she knew it or not, Lena was coming into her own.

But she still worried, and sometimes voiced those worries, about work and her career path. They both knew what neither of them said—that if she wanted to work in a firm, all she had to do was say the word and Richard Lowe would help her get a position within weeks.

Within a month, she would be back in suits and four-inch heels, and smoothing her hair away from her face into a severe, but professionally-appropriate bun. She would command a hefty salary and could probably carve out a solid place for herself at a firm that would value her Washington DC insider knowledge and contacts.

But she didn't want that. Quentin was just going to have to be patient until she was ready to speak that new truth.

"Quentin?"

He spun to face the owner of the voice, and smiled at the young woman standing in his doorway.

Wearing an inexpensive dark-blue suit and black pumps, she seemed ill at ease. April Garner was one of the first-years he was supervising. Petite and cute as a button, he had to restrain the urge to pat her on the head every time he saw her.

"Hey, April, what's up?"

"I was about to head downstairs to get a coffee and wondered whether you wanted something."

"That'd be cool. Thanks. A grande dark roast would be great," he said, reaching for his wallet.

"No, no," April waved the gesture away. "It's on me."

"No," Quentin insisted, his voice firm. "It's on me. You're the one going to get it, so it's the least I can do." He found his wallet and pulled out a bill, extending it toward her.

April hesitated for a second then stepped forward to take it. Their fingers brushed.

"So how're things going back there?"

April was working on a large document production along with a few other first-years. It was the kind of grunt-work that was a rite of passage for new attorneys, and helped weed out those who were team players, and those who might be prima donnas later. So far, April looked to Quentin to be in the first camp.

"Pretty good," she said.

She even managed to sound cheerful about it, he noted. Document production was among the most mind-numbing of tasks a lawyer could perform. It was the kind of work that made you wonder whether your law school tuition had been wasted.

"Great. Well ... hang in there. Only a few hundred thousand more pages to go."

April smiled. She had a little gap between her front teeth. It made her stand out among the multitudes of orthodontically-perfect smiles.

"I'll be right back with your coffee," she said as she ducked out.

When she was gone, Quentin reached for the phone and dialed Lena. It was almost three p.m. This was around the time she and he used to go for their coffee dates and his internal clock always seemed to reach for her at this hour, like a conditioned yearning.

She picked up on the second ring, her voice sounded slightly breathless and hurried.

"What're you doing?" he laughed. "Sounds like you're running from a pack of wild dogs."

"No. In the hardware store. Looking at paint colors," she explained. "And guess what."

"What?"

"We have plans for tonight. We're going out to a neighborhood open house."

"Cool." Q smiled at the excitement in her voice. "An open house for what?"

"A transitional home for girls."

"What're they transitioning from?"

"Different things. Bad homes, foster care ..." She paused at the last one. "Jail. Prison. Stuff like that."

Quentin's eyebrows raised and his interest piqued. "How'd you come to hear about it?"

"Talking to a woman in the park near our house. I go there to walk every morning, and we've run into each other a few times. Turns out she lives a few blocks from us, in the house."

"In what house?"

"The transitional house, Quentin. Are you listening? She owns it. Her grandmother left it to her with a request that she turn it into a program for girls. And she moved all the way from Baton Rouge to carry out her grandmother's wishes and set everything up."

"Cool."

Already, he had an inkling that Lena's interest in this place was more than casual. And if he was correct, he should definitely go with her to check it out.

"So what time is the open house?" he asked.

"Seven to ten. You think you can make it home before then?"

"Yeah. Definitely. I'll get in around six-thirty and we can go check it out."

"Okay. So I'd better go …" Lena said, still sounding a little rushed. "I still need to pick out some colors to show you when you get home."

***

THE BROWNSTONE WAS AN IMPRESSIVE, 19TH CENTURY, RED BRICK edifice on Remsen Street that for the occasion had been lit up both outside and in. Above the front door which was swung open for guests, was a title of the Maya Angelou poem, 'Still I Rise'. Lena's fingers were laced through Quentin's as they entered, and she looked up at him, smiling.

The entryway was lined with narrow bookcases, and to the left there was a parlor in which small clusters of people milled, conversing with drinks in hand. Where there were walls, they had been painted a rich mustard, but otherwise, the exposed brick was left bare and somewhat distressed. Wooden beams, crown molding and tin ceilings maintained the historical fidelity, and made it feel as though for a split second they had stepped into another era altogether. In the background, jazz played, the wail and whine of a saxophone providing a pleasant backdrop to the hum of human voices.

"This is nice," Quentin leaned over to murmur in Lena's ear. "Maybe we should look around for something like this."

"God, I would love it," Lena said back to him. "How much do you think a place like this goes for?"

"A lot," Quentin said.

Together they wandered over to the table that had been set up at one end of the parlor as a bar. Quentin got a Heineken while Lena chose red wine, then they turned to survey the room. Along the walls, framed inspirational posters hung with quotes from notable Black women. Words of wisdom from Harriett Tubman, Sojourner Truth, Angela Davis, Alice Walker and Toni Morrison were all represented, and each was about strength, pride or self-worth.

"Who's the woman who told you about this place?"

Lena looked around. "I don't see her yet. Her name's Trisha. She looks like a cross between a fashion model and a voodoo priestess."

Quentin laughed.

Moments later, Trisha entered the room. Without even asking, Quentin knew it was she. Wearing a long, colorful caftan and a head-wrap, she seemed to glide when she walked, and had an expression of otherworldly contentment. Her complexion was fair and clear, and she had deep, dark eyes.

Smiling, she looked around the room and nodded in Lena's direction before rapping a fork against the side of her wineglass to command everyone's attention.

"Greetings, family," she said when everyone had quieted down.

A chorus of voices returned the pleasantry.

"I am so pleased you all joined me tonight," she continued. "It's been a long journey to this place. And I want to tell you about it ..."

For the next several minutes, Trisha recounted a little of her family history, a little folklore and a little bit about her personal evolution from what she called "corporate drone to communitarian."

"For many years I've known—though I pretended not to know—that my personal success," she said, "was meaningless when juxtaposed against the continuing struggle of Black and brown girls all around me." There were murmurs of assent all around the room. "So with my grandmother's passing and the revelation of her wishes for this place, I was liberated. My lack of courage to make the change I knew needed to be made was no longer relevant. I had to do what my grand-momma said needed to be done."

Trisha opened her arms like a benign ruler welcoming her subjects.

"And so here we are. Manifesting her dream. Welcome."

Quentin forced himself not to roll his eyes. While he appreciated what Trisha said she was trying to accomplish, he found her tone sanctimonious and self-congratulatory, not to mention that pretentious get-up she was wearing. Trisha was one of what he liked to call The Enlightened Ones—Black folks who, having had a personal epiphany about the need to 'give back', spent fifty percent of their time giving back and the other fifty percent shaming others who had not yet "evolved" to that point themselves. He could only hope Lena had not been too taken in by Trisha's shtick.

After her speech, Trisha was approached by several well-wishers, while Quentin stood back and watched.

"She's cool, right?"

Q looked down at Lena and smiled. "Yeah. It's a cool project."

"She says she already has a couple city contracts lined up, so she should have her first class of girls in here by the end of the month."

Noticing the excitement in her voice, Quentin gave Lena his full focus.

"What's on your mind, baby?" he asked on a hunch.

"What d'you mean?"

He lifted one eyebrow and watched as Lena blushed, and scrunched her lips together the way she did when she was trying not to smile.

"You thinking of ... volunteering here or something?"

"*Well.*" Lena let the word drag out. "Something like that."

"Tell me."

"Trisha might have mentioned that they were looking for a Director of Operations ... someone to help negotiate contracts, work with the city, stuff like that."

"So, a job," Quentin said.

"Yeah." Lena narrowed her eyes and scrunched her lips tighter, but this time as though bracing herself for his objections.

"What could a place like this afford to pay you though, Lene?"

"I don't know. I'm guessing probably about half what I made in DC."

Quentin winced inwardly. That would mean just under a hundred grand a year. For the average person, that was a nice salary. For a corporate lawyer with five years' experience under her belt, that was a pittance. But he had known for some time now that corporate law was probably a thing of the past where Lena was concerned. He just hadn't considered what that would mean in dollars and cents.

Above all though, he wanted his girl happy. So, if this was what it took, then this was what it took.

"So, you planning to throw your hat in the ring or what?"

"I've been thinking about it. Wanted to talk to you first though. Because it means maybe a different kind of future than we ..."

Quentin smiled. "We're good," he assured her. "I can take care of us, even if you never worked again."

Lena's eyes softened at that and she took a step closer to him. Quentin put a hand at her waist and pulled her against him.

"Never worked again? Are you out of your mind?"

Quentin laughed. "I'm not recommending it or anything. Just sayin'."

"I'd never expect you to do that," Lena said. But if I took this kind of job, it'd be different. Money-wise, I mean. You sure you wouldn't be upset?" Lena asked. "You wouldn't see it as me not pulling my weight financially, or ..."

"No, baby."

"But who knows? She may have someone in mind already. And I don't have any experience in the non-profit sector, and ..."

"Don't talk yourself out of it," Quentin said, shaking his head. "If you want it, go after it."

"You think so?"

"I know so," he said. He inclined his head in Trisha's direction. "Go on over and talk to her. Feel her out. Let her know what you're thinking."

"If I do, there'd still be a lot of steps before anything definite," Lena said, looking at him with her large brown eyes. "I could still get another job if this doesn't work out. Like in a firm. Right?"

Quentin nodded. "Yeah," he said, smiling encouragingly.

"Okay." Lena took a deep breath, her shoulders heaving. "I'm going to talk to her."

Watching as she made her way over to Trisha and the small crowd surrounding her, Quentin couldn't shake the feeling that their lives had just changed.

15

———

"Is this for real?"

Emerging from beneath the car, the man stood and dusted off the back of his jeans and jacket, rubbed his hands together, then clapping to get his circulation going again.

"What do you mean is it for real?"

"You're not asking a lot for it, the mileage is low and everything looks pretty clean. There's got to be a catch. Something wrong with it that you're not telling me."

New York and Washington DC weren't that far apart geographically, but in some ways, they may as well have been on different planets. DC was the Land of Obfuscation. No one was ever completely direct about their thoughts and feelings. Maybe it had something to do with being so close to Congress, so littered with politicians. By contrast, New Yorkers were brutal truth-tellers. Even when that meant telling a stranger they thought you might be a liar.

"Nope. No catch and no hidden defect. I just want to unload it quickly that's all. And looks like you're the lucky guy."

"*Could be* the lucky guy," he said stroking his long goatee. "Or maybe not-so-lucky guy if there's something you're not telling me."

"Look," Lena said, shifting her weight. "If you can't make yourself do it, don't do it. I have a few other people interested and I'm sure one of them will take it off my hands."

He grinned as though amused by her attempt at playing hardball. "Lemme see the keys again?" He held out his hand.

Hesitating a moment, Lena dropped them into his palm and watched as he got in, once again starting the engine to her three-year-old Toyota 4Runner. Leaving the door open and one foot on the pavement as he did, he kept his eyes on Lena when the engine purred to life, as though checking her face for signs of concealment.

It was getting colder, and the sky had turned grey. There would probably be an early season snow.

Lena fished into her coat pocket and pulled out her phone, intending to check the weather app, but instead seeing that Quentin had texted her.

What you up to?

She smiled and typed back. *Selling my car! Yay!*

Moments later he responded. *To who?*

Some guy.

Seconds later, her phone rang. Lena answered, stepping a few feet away from her would-be buyer.

"You didn't invite him in, did you?" Quentin asked. "Or let him see where you live?"

"Stop being such a worry-wart," Lena said.

"I'm not. You need to be careful, Lene. You know the kind of shit that happens to women selling stuff on Craigslist? I told you don't make any appointments for times when I'm not around."

"I think I can handle selling my car without your help, Q. Honestly." She turned her back to her buyer and lowered her voice.

"Don't let him talk you down on the price," he said. "It's more than fair. It's a steal. And if he decides he wants it, tell him you'll meet him this evening to turn over the title and he needs to bring a cashier's check."

Lena rolled her eyes.

"Lene? You hear me?"

"Yes, Dad, I hear you. Cashier's check. Title transfer this evening when you're around."

"Exactly. Okay, call me back when you're done with him and back in the apartment."

"*Miss?*"

Lena turned to face her potential buyer again.

"Is that him?" Q said on the other end of the phone.

"Yeah. I'll call you back. Bye." She hung up and turned her full attention back to the guy sitting in her car.

"I'll take it," he said.

"Good."

Lena tried not to look as elated as she felt.

After three weeks of casting about in the apartment, jobless and without a mission, she was beginning to feel uncomfortable with not contributing much to her and Quentin's now-shared expenses. The eight thousand from her car would go into a joint account they had opened, and which, so far only Q had deposited anything into.

"I'ma stop through with my boy who works on cars and then we can sign the final paperwork. Five o'clock work for you?"

"Ahm. Could you make it seven-thirty?" Lena asked, thinking of Quentin's desire to be around for the final exchange.

The guy grimaced.

"Sorry," Lena shrugged. "My boyfriend wants to be there."

"You got a boyfriend?" the guy asked, stroking his goatee again, and tilting his head to one side. There was a hint of a smile on his face.

Was he *flirting* with her?

Lena shook the thought loose and nodded. "Yeah. He wants to be here when you bring the payment."

The guy nodded. He was tall. Taller than Quentin by about two inches, and looked solid beneath his army-green jacket. It was funny how she compared every man she met to *her* man now. Not as tall as Quentin, or taller. Lighter in complexion, or darker. Good-looking but never *as* good-looking. Lena almost smiled at the thought.

In another time and place, she wondered what effect flirtation from this tall, handsome man with Brooklyn swagger might have had on her.

"I'll make seven-thirty work," he said. "Wouldn't want your man to be mad at you. It means I won't be able to bring my boy, but I guess I'ma have to trust you."

Lena ignored that last bit of editorializing.

"Wonderful. Thanks."

She extended her hand for the keys and he shut off the engine again, stepping out of the car and placing, rather than dropping them in her open palm. His fingers lingered on hers as he withdrew, and he smiled again at some private amusement.

"I'm Mitch, by the way," he said.

"Mitch?" she asked with raised eyebrows.

He grinned openly this time. "Yeah. Want to make something of it?"

"Nope." Lena shook her head. "Just can't quite remember ever meeting a Black guy named ... Mitch before."

Was *she* flirting with him?

"I'm one-of-a-kind," he said, his eyes holding hers.

Lena looked away quickly, startled by the little frisson of pleasure the obvious appreciation in his gaze caused her.

"So, seven-thirty then," she said, turning, and beginning to walk away.

She was halfway down the block before she realized she'd forgotten to hit the fob to lock the 4Runner's doors.

"He's late." Lena glanced at her phone.

"By ten minutes. Relax. If he flakes, believe me, someone else will step up. With that crazy-ass price?"

Quentin was standing at the kitchen sink, shoveling the last of the food from his plate into his mouth before leaving the dirty dish and silverware behind.

"Quentin," Lena said.

He looked at her, his mouth still full. "What?"

"Could you at least unload, and then load the dishwasher?"

He turned back to the sink and looked at the pile of dishes as though he had no idea how they'd gotten there. Since she was the one who was home all the time, somehow chores like dish-washing had become hers alone.

"Oh. Yeah. Sorry," he said, beginning to take everything out.

Just then, Lena's phone buzzed. It was Mitch, telling her he was standing next to the car, but could she meet him at the Star-bucks on the corner since it was freezing out. Except the phrase he used was "colder than a witch's tit."

"That's him," she told Quentin. "He's at Starbucks."

"Then let's go get this money."

At the door, as they both got bundled up for the block-and-a-half walk to Starbucks, Lena looked up to see Quentin watching her with an unreadable expression on his face.

"What?" she asked, smiling.

"You just took my hat," he said, indicating the beanie she had pulled down over her hair.

"Can't find mine," Lena said, hunching her shoulders.

"That's cool." Quentin pulled her against him. "You look cute in it."

And when she let her head fall back so she could look up at him, he leaned in to kiss her. His lips barely brushed against hers and Lena heard a soft '*hmm*' escape her.

"Let's go, hat-thief," he said, zipping up the front of her coat. "Because when we get back, I got somethin' for you."

Lena didn't bother asking what that was.

Mitch was waiting at a table in the center of Starbucks, his large hands wrapped around a cup of coffee. Spotting Lena as she entered with Q, he stood, and Lena saw him look Quentin over, sizing him up in that way men did. And next to her, Q did the same once he realized that Mitch was probably the person they had come to meet.

Exchanging greetings, Lena quickly introduced the two men, and they all sat.

"So, here's the title," Lena produced the yellow manila envelope from her coat and slid it across the table toward Mitch.

He slid it out and gave it the once over. "So y'all moved up here from DC?" he asked, looking up again.

"Yup." Quentin said, his tone businesslike and discouraging of pleasantries. "You got a cashier's check, right?"

"Yeah." Mitch produced his own envelope and set it in the center of the table.

Opening it, Quentin looked it over, and then up at Mitch again. "You didn't sign this?"

"Nah. The truck is for my sister. She signed it. For a little project she's got going on."

Lena took the check from Quentin and glanced down at it, then back up at Mitch.

"Your sister?" she asked, studying him a little more closely. Now that she looked, there was a resemblance. Slight, but it was there. "*Trisha* is your sister?"

Mitch looked surprised. "You know her?"

"Yes! Small world!" She looked at Quentin. "You remember Trisha. From the girls' program we went to the opening of?"

Next to her, Quentin nodded slowly. "Oh yeah."

"I've been talking to her about maybe working with her!" Lena said leaning in. "Do you work there? At the program?"

Mitch laughed and shook his head. "Nah. Just helping her out a little bit while she gets things set up. If it was up to me, I'd make her sell the place instead of trying to be Mother Teresa."

"But from what I understand, she's just following her ... and your, I guess? Your grandmother's wishes."

Mitch shrugged. "It was a suggestion. Not a directive. But Trisha does her own thing, so yeah ... I guess she feels she has to save every little Black girl in New York now."

"Or help them save themselves," Lena said.

"So, are we doin' this or what?" Quentin interrupted.

"Yeah, let's get 'er done," Mitch said.

"So who're we signing the title over to?" Quentin asked. "Just for our records. Your sister, or ..." He looked down at the check again. "Ida's House?"

"Is Ida your grandmother's name?" Lena asked.

Mitch turned his attention to her again. "Yeah. Real old-fashioned name, right? Won't be too many more Idas out there for sure."

"Kind of like 'Mitch'," Lena said, smiling. "At least not Black ones anyway."

"It's actually Michel. French for Michael. My father's Haitian. But Mich is a girl's name, the way you shorten 'Michelle'. So my people call me Mitch."

"Your people as in ...?"

"Anyone I vibe with."

Quentin cleared his throat.

"Sorry," Lena said, reaching for the title. "Yeah. Lemme sign this and let you go."

"I FEEL LIKE THAT WAS PREORDAINED," LENA SAID, HER MOUTH full and frothy. "Don't you?"

They were brushing their teeth, getting ready for bed and Quentin listened to her without comment.

"I mean, what are the chances, right? After going to Trisha's mixer and then having the *first person* interested in my car be her brother? And in a place as big as Brooklyn? That had to be preordained."

Quentin grunted.

"And I feel better, y'know? Knowing that the truck is going to a worthwhile effort and everything? Don't you think it's a worthwhile effort?"

Quentin spat into the sink and turned the faucet on so he could rinse. "So, how's things coming along with you and her negotiating whether you'll work there?" he asked ignoring her question.

"She's not very responsive to email," Lena said. "But I hope she's interested. I don't know if my coming from the corporate world might be a turn-off to her."

"She came from the corporate world. So if she holds that against you, she's a hypocrite."

"Whoa. *That's* harsh. She has every right to want someone with non-profit experience, Quentin."

"I don't think you should take it," he said. "Something else will come along."

"But ..." Lena stopped brushing and looked at him, trying to meet his gaze in the mirror. "This is perfect. I'd be walking distance from home ... it gets my feet wet in the social justice world ..."

"And pays next to nothing," he added.

"You said you didn't care about that." A slight whine had entered Lena's tone.

"Yeah, but ..."

"But what, Q?"

But he didn't like the way that Mitch asshole had looked at her. He didn't like the way *she* looked at him. Quentin knew how a man and woman acted when they were feeling each other. Even though Lena might not even know it, she was putting out those signals—the ones women exuded when there was something about a man they found intriguing.

Right now, Q would call her reaction to Asshole Mitch curiosity, but on his end, it was more than that—it was 'interest'. The idea that Lena might be working with his sister could also mean she would run into the Asshole on a regular basis. And why borrow trouble? It was best to short-circuit all that right now.

"But I think you're acting real thirsty when there's no need to be."

"*Excuse* me?" Lena pulled back and nudged his shoulder so he would turn to look at her.

"I'm just sayin'. Don't chase after that fake-ass prophetess like you wouldn't be doing *her* a favor by working at her little makeshift girls' home."

Lena stared at him. A tiny dribble of toothpaste was making its way down her chin, but she still looked cute. He almost smiled, except that he was pretty sure they were about to have a fight.

"You're being an ass right now," Lena said matter-of-factly.

"Why? Because I don't want you to sell your expensive law degree for next to nothing."

"This is what I want to do. With my life, I mean. I want work that's meaningful. Not just something to pay off my student loans. Something that ..."

"But the loans do have to get paid, Lene. That's the thing."

She stared at him. "Of course I'll do the math. Make sure it makes sense. Give me *some* credit. It's not like I'm planning to live off you."

He rolled his eyes.

"Don't act like that wasn't what you were thinking! You said you were cool with this, but suddenly, now that it looks like it might happen, you're backtracking?"

"I'm not backtracking and that's not what I was thinking. I think you just need to ..."

"I don't want to hear anymore from you about what I '*need to*'," Lena said. She turned to the sink and leaned forward to rinse and spit. "Turns out I'm a grown-ass woman. And perfectly capable of figuring out on my own what I 'need to' do."

"Except you're *not* on your own," he said before he could stop himself. "This is a joint decision, Lena."

"Was it a joint decision when you decided to move to New York in the first place?" she demanded, yanking a towel from the nearby rack and wiping her mouth and chin.

Quentin opened his mouth, but couldn't think of an adequate retort.

"*Exactly*. So don't tell me you get to decide where I work. Because you don't. The fact that I even asked you was nothing more than a courtesy."

It was his turn to be taken aback. "Oh so it's like that?"

"Yeah. It's like that." Lena tossed the towel across the bathroom where it missed the hamper by mere inches and fell to the floor. Grunting in frustration, she went over to deposit it into her target and then shoved past Quentin and into the bedroom.

When he went in, she was already under the covers and had

pulled them all the way up to her chin and turned her back to his side of the bed. Undressing and tossing his clothes aside, Quentin walked back out into the living room to make sure they were all locked up tight then returned, and turning off all the lights climbed in behind her.

Ignoring the rigidity of her posture, he moved in closer and wrapped his arms around her waist and pulled her closer.

"Are you serious right now?" Lena's voice broke the silence.

"What?" he asked, trying to sound innocent.

"I'm mad at you!" Lena hissed.

"Yeah," Quentin said against her neck, reaching down and sliding his hand between her thighs. "But *she's* not."

"Well, she belongs to me. So she'll do what I tell her to do," Lena returned.

She was trying to hold on to her anger, but he could hear the hint of a smile in her voice.

"Will she?" Quentin maneuvered so that Lena was on her back and he was on top of her, weight resting on his forearms. "How about we test that theory?"

Lifting the sheet over his head, he slid down until he was between her legs, making short work of removing her underwear.

"*Quentin ...*" She stopped short with whatever she intended to say when his tongue touched her and instead issued a low moan.

"Yeah?" he lifted his head long enough to ask.

But Lena said nothing, Instead, he felt her hand atop his head, gently pressing downward just as she arched her hips up. Smiling, Quentin went to work.

As she squirmed and moaned, he forced out of his mind the image of the way she leaned toward Asshole Mitch when they were sitting in Starbucks. *She was his*. And it didn't matter where she worked, or who she worked with, he wasn't letting anyone or anything mess that up.

When he made her come, good and hard, he would apologize. He would tell her she should take whatever job she wanted, wherever she wanted. He would tell her that she didn't need his approval, but that no matter what, she would have his support.

"Baby …" Lena was groaning now, her voice hoarse as she spoke. "Get up here."

Quentin obeyed, sliding back up the length of her body until they were face to face again. Lena's eyelids were heavy, her expression one of dazed pleasure. When she reached up to wipe the perspiration from his brow with a forefinger, he smiled.

"You're right," she said.

"I knew it," he said. "She doesn't belong to you." He glanced downward and licked the residual taste of her from his lower lip. "She belongs to *me*."

Lena smiled and shook her head. "Yes, she does. But I wasn't talking about that …"

"So what *were* you talking about?" Q lifted his pelvis and lowered it again, surging forward and feeling himself slide deep into his woman's warmth.

Lena gave a soft gasp, reaching down and clutching his ass, pulled him closer. "The job," she breathed. "It is a joint decision. If you don't want me to …"

"Nah," Quentin said. Right now, she could tell him she was about to take a job as a street-sweeper and he would be cool with it. "Do whatever works for you, baby. You know I got you."

Feeling his own eyes drift shut, Q buried his face into the coarse softness of Lena's hair.

Yeah, he had her. But damned if she didn't have him too.

16

———

Lena woke with a smile on her face. Quentin was pressing his hard chest against her back, and something even harder between her thighs. Instinctively, she arched toward him, further opened her legs and let her head loll to one side as he kissed her neck.

"You leaving me today?" Quentin said into her ear.

She was flying to Miami later that morning to spend Thanksgiving with her parents and Marlon, and wouldn't be back in New York for a week. Quentin was heading to DC and staying until Saturday when he and Darius would drive back up, just in time for Darius to fly out of JFK on his way to Thailand the following morning.

"Uh huh," she said, her eyes still shut.

His fingers slightly callused, brushed against her already hard nipples. Sighing, she turned to face him.

"Don't go," he said.

Lena opened her eyes. "I have to go," she said, draping a leg over his thigh. "Everyone's expecting me. My parents, my cousins, my grandparents ..."

"I know," he said after a moment.

Lena kissed the corner of his mouth. "Q. Did you mean that?"

He shrugged. At least as much as one could shrug lying on their side.

The last two weeks had been a whirlwind. Lena had begun her new job with Trisha's transitional girls' program, and it had turned out to be far more challenging than she could have ever expected. And more rewarding as well.

From the very first day, when she turned up at the Remsen Street brownstone, she realized she had her work cut out for her. Trisha was an Idea Person. Her execution of those ideas often left much to be desired. Through the force of her charm and personality alone, she had managed to land city contracts to have young women referred to her for diversion, or as they reentered the community from juvenile detention.

With her brother's help, she renovated the townhouse so that it had residences on the upper floors suitable to house ten girls, common rooms on the second floor and offices on the ground floor and in the basement. But that was about all. Trisha was a terrible project manager.

In her first week alone, Lena had to arrange for the transportation of three young women from juvenile detention to the home, file their paperwork with the court, take all three girls to get copies of their birth certificates and new social security cards since none of them had such in their possession; arrange doctors' appointments, and request records from their last school. And every step of the way, she had to wing it. None of that was within the ballpark of her prior professional experience.

And Trisha? Trisha seemed content to wander around in gauzy clothing issuing sage advice. *Her* role, she had informed

Lena, was to be the program director. She would arrange for classes and therapy for the girls, make sure they got the schooling and counseling they needed.

All the paperwork, all of the formalities of dealing with the various systems—that was what she expected Lena to take care of. Along with the more mundane matters like telephones, electricity, cable and internet service; and the hiring of any other staff that might be needed for the smooth operation of the Center.

And so, for almost fourteen days straight, Quentin and Lena had precious little time together. He worked late, and now often so did she. Most nights, they collapsed next to each other in bed and barely exchanged a dozen words before falling asleep. Lena, who most often got home before he did, left him a plate with his dinner, warming on the stovetop, covered with aluminum foil.

"Do I mean what?"

"That you don't want me to go. Because if you mean it ..."

"Of course I mean it. But I also don't want your father to hate me any more than he already does, so you should go."

"He doesn't hate you."

"Okay, dislike. Abhor. *Revile.*"

Lena laughed. "He doesn't feel any of those things about you either. He just needs time to get used to the idea, that's all."

"The idea that his daughter is living in sin ..." Q rolled over atop her, bracing himself on his elbows on either side of her head. "Having unspeakable things done to her ..."

He kissed her neck and Lena hunched her shoulders at the sensation.

"Speaking of the unspeakable, I think our next-door neighbor is a hooker," she said, closing her eyes at the sensation of his lips on her neck.

Quentin froze, his mouth still pressed into her skin. "*What?*" he laughed. "Talk about a non sequitur."

"Only a lawyer could use a phrase like 'non sequitur' while in the process of having sex."

"We're not in the process yet," he returned, reaching down with one hand to slide her underwear off her hip on one side. Lena arched off the bed to help "I was *trying* to get there but then you mentioned the prostitute next door and that kinda put the brakes on all the action."

"I would've thought it would speed up the action," Lena said winking.

"No, for real. What makes you say she's a prostie?"

"A 'prostie'?" Lena said. "That's such a white boy word. You're all just all over the map with the weird vocabulary this morning."

"Okay, how's this?" Quentin cleared his throat and when he spoke again, there was considerably more bass to his voice. "What make you think the trick over there ho'ing?"

Smacking him against his chest, Lena spluttered into uncontrollable laughter. "What the hell was *that*?"

Quentin lowered his head again, kissing along the length of her neck. "That was me trying to ... blacken it up a little."

"You're a goofball."

"You're worried about my vocabulary? Don't use words like 'goofball' when we're about to ... you know. It'll make my dick soft."

Lena was about to laugh again, until she felt him between her thighs and gasped. "I don't think it had any effect on your dick."

"Don't say nothin' right now," Quentin said, amping up the bass again. "'Cause we about to do the nasty."

"Oh God, it's getting worse. No, Q. Just ... *no*. No one says that anymore."

"They don't? I was just getting into character again. Being that dude. That Blacker-than-Black dude ..."

"Shut up," Lena said. "I don't need you to be anyone other than who you are."

She lifted her ass off the bed and opened her legs a little wider. Quentin slid into her effortlessly, and she emitted a soft sigh. He bowed his pelvis toward her, so not an inch of room remained between them.

***

"So you never told me. What makes you think our neighbor's a hooker?"

Lena looked at him, her expression blank for a moment. They were sitting in the American Airlines drop-off zone at LaGuardia, and she was just about to get out to make her flight to Miami. After their morning quickie, which turned out not to be too quick, they'd shared a hasty shower and then sprinted the six blocks over to where the SUV was parked, Quentin carrying Lena's suitcase in his arms like a small child.

They made it with just ten minutes to spare before the one hour cut-off for check-in, so the blank look was probably called-for.

"Just curious." Quentin shrugged.

Lena narrowed her eyes. "Should I be worried about leaving you here alone with a hooker as a next-door neighbor?"

"Maybe." He grinned "But first tell me why you think she's a hooker."

"Well, when I wasn't working, she was always home. Like always. And since our walls are paper-thin, when she got a phone call, I could hear the ringing through the walls. And after these calls, she would run off, and be gone for maybe an hour or so. And then she would come back, and there might be another call and she would run out again, and ..."

This time it was Quentin's turn to look at her blankly. "That's it? That's all you got?"

"And her shoes!" Lena added, her eyes open wide as though that was self-explanatory.

"O*kay*, baby. Have a safe trip, a great Thanksgiving and tell your father we only did it twice this week, so you're practically still a virgin."

Shaking her head in exasperation, Lena leaned over and planted a long, wet kiss on his lips. "Be good. And don't try to like, hire our neighbor or anything while I'm gone."

Quentin watched as Lena disappeared into the terminal, assessing the sway of her hips under her lightweight winter coat and smiling because he was sure she'd added that extra little twitch just for him.

When he opened the door to the apartment, it seemed smaller, and lifeless. He wasn't due to leave for DC until the morning, but now, waiting until then seemed pointless. He cleared the half-empty coffee cups from the table, emptied and then loaded the dishwasher, leaning against it when the cycle started. Lena's flight would just be taking off right about now, and he had the expanse of a Wednesday and no plans for what to do with it.

He and Lena had been living together for what? *Fifteen minutes?* And he already had no idea what to do with his time when she wasn't around. That was his life: work, Lena, and then more work, and more Lena. Pathetic. He needed a hobby or something. And because he knew exactly whose voice he was hearing in his head telling him so, Quentin reached for his phone and called him.

"Yo, D. What you up to, man?"

"The hell you mean what am I *up* to? It's nine-fifteen on a Wednesday morning. I'm not up at all."

"Oh. Shit. Sorry. I was ..."

"What you want?" Darius asked gruffly.

"Nothin'. Lena just left so ..."

"And so ... what? You need a binky or somethin'? Call me later. "

Quentin found himself listening to the echoing silence. He'd forgotten what an asshole his brother was if you woke him up before noon. In his line of work, it wasn't as though he had too many demands before the middle of the day.

Grabbing his coat, Quentin shrugged it on and left the apartment again. Just as he turned from having locked the door, he collided with someone who smelled like fall—burnt leaves and something spicy, he couldn't quite identify. She must have read his expression, seen his flared nostrils because she nodded as though he'd asked the question.

"Frankincense," she said.

Not knowing what to make of her mind-reading, Q said nothing in response.

"So, you're my new neighbor, huh?"

Quentin's curious hazel eyes met a pair of lively brown ones. And then, because of Lena's comment, his gaze fell. To the shoes. They were high heeled boots, shin-high and laced up the front. Like witch boots, but much sexier.

"Hey," he said, extending a hand. "Yeah. One of them. I'm Quentin."

"Asha," she returned. "Good to finally meet you. I've run into your ..." She raised her eyebrows questioningly.

"Girlfriend," Quentin said. "Fiancée. I guess. Lena."

I guess?

And he wasn't the only one who thought that sounded lukewarm, because Asha pursed her full lips and nodded. "Hmm. Yeah." And then, as if trying to save him from himself, she pressed on. "Could I just say? I *love* her hair. I literally want to scalp her and steal it for myself every time I see her."

Quentin laughed. Asha was cute but he couldn't say he was buying her claim of hair envy, considering she'd shaved her entire head except for a curly dark brown tuft at the crown, streaked with bronze highlights. And Lena was way off. This chick—bad-ass body though she had—was definitely not a working girl.

"In fact ..." Asha looked over his shoulder as though Quentin might be hiding Lena behind his back. "Is she around? Today might be the day I have the guts to tell her that to her face."

"Tell her what to her face?"

"That I love her hair."

"Oh. She's not here. Just dropped her off at the airport. She's going to Florida for the holiday."

Asha looked perplexed.

"Thanksgiving?" Quentin prompted.

"Oh! Yes. I always forget."

"You always forget Thanksgiving?" Quentin asked. "How is that possible?"

Asha shrugged. "I know, right? With all the cartoon pumpkins and turkeys everywhere you look. But I don't do Thanksgiving. Or family, for that matter." She gave a short laugh.

"Hmm." It was his turn to sound bemused.

He and Asha stared at each other for a while, both at a loss for what to say. She had a narrow, almost angular face, a straight aquiline nose and lips that were identical top and bottom. With each feature isolated, she didn't look like she should be pretty, but for some reason, she was.

"So, if your girlfriend-fiancée is out of town for the holidays, what're you up to?" she asked, apparently finally thinking of something that would move the conversation along.

Quentin weighed the chances that her question was suggestive and decided that if anything, she was trying to change the subject, and shift the attention away from her and back to him.

"Driving down to DC to celebrate with my family, eat too much and then drive back up."

Asha smiled a polite smile. "Sounds like fun. Especially the part where you're stuck in traffic on I-95 for hours."

Quentin laughed. "Yeah, that's a definite drawback, but on the upside, there'll be lots of food that I don't have to cook, nor clean up afterwards."

Asha's smile grew even thinner, and Quentin wondered whether he sounded like a jerk.

"Yeah. That must be nice. So ... you ... enjoy that, and be sure to tell Lena, your girlfriend-fiancée that I covet her hair."

"Yeah. I will. It was nice meeting you, Asha."

"Same here. See you around."

Quentin watched she let herself into her apartment—the only other unit on the floor—and noticed for the first time that she was lugging a huge, curiously-shaped bag over one shoulder. It hung low on her back, and bumped heavily against her as she walked. But before Quentin could examine it further, or ask what it was, Asha slipped behind her apartment door with a brief wave and was gone.

LENA SAT ON HER SUITCASE AT THE AMERICAN AIRLINES PICK-UP zone and scanned the line of vehicles cruising by, looking for her father's Ford truck. Miami International was a zoo, just as she'd expected it to be, teeming with families either arriving, or departing for the holiday. But Lena found her eyes drawn to the couples, some of them walking hand in hand as they went to claim their luggage, or headed toward their departure gate.

She felt a surprising surge of something like sadness when

she saw those couples. They looked so assured of their couple-dom, it was difficult not to envy them even though she, too, was part of a couple. The only explanation she could come up with for her envy was that Quentin hadn't put up much of a fight when she told him her father was insisting that she come home for Thanksgiving.

And he hadn't so much as suggested that he come along, although it was probably up to her to issue the invitation in the first place. She didn't want there to be invitations, and acceptances of invitations. She wanted them to have the same assurance that those couples walking through the terminal had—that they were together, and came as a unit. Always as a unit.

"Hurry up, lazy! This zone is for loading and unloading only!"

Lena grinned and lifted her head at the sound of her brother's voice.

Marlon looked incongruous behind the wheel of her father's truck. It was surprising enough that their Dad had permitted Marlon to drive it at all, but to drive it alone? That was unheard of. Perhaps the thaw that had begun—the melting of the frosty relationship her father and brother had ever since Marlon came out to everyone five years ago. Not that Lena hadn't known practically her entire life that her brother was gay, but sometimes, a thing had to be declared to become real.

"Took you long enough!" Lena hauled her luggage toward the truck and with a grunt hoisted it up and over into the truck-bed.

"Careful!" Marlon warned as she climbed into the cab. "I'm not taking the heat because you messed around and scratched his baby. No ma'am."

Lena looked at her brother, already darker after only one day in Florida. Knowing Marlon, immediately upon arrival, he had probably headed for South Beach to look for what he called "his tribe" of The Beautiful and Idle.

"How's he been?" Lena said as they pulled away.

She wasn't asking after their father's health so much as his mood. He and Marlon had a complicated relationship, which sometimes made it unbearable for other people to be around them both at the same time.

"The same, I guess," Marlon said, shrugging. "I try to stay out of his way as much as possible so I don't have to find out."

"You guys seemed fine when you came to help me move."

"That's because he was preoccupied with you, and how you're 'giving up your life for some man'." Marlon took his hands off the steering wheel briefly to make air quotes.

"Q isn't just 'some man'," Lena said reflexively.

"I know, I know. He's the love of your life," Marlon sang.

"He *is*."

"Okay," Marlon said. "Touchy."

Lena glanced at her brother and saw that he had put a finger briefly to his lips. He only ever did that when he was literally trying to silence himself.

"What?"

"Nothing," Marlon said unconvincingly.

"You agree with Daddy? Is that it?"

"No, but ..."

"Spit it out, Marlon. *What*?"

"It's just that y'all went from zero to one hundred in lightning speed. And now you're talking about marriage, and the future and ... It just seems a little ... quick to me."

"Because we both know what we want. If I thought you'd be such a hater ..."

"Oh please, girl. Ain't nobody hatin' on your little relationship. I'm jus' sayin'. First good man in years so your ass packs up and moves to another state? I just think you should've given it a moment to ... breathe or something."

"We tried that. And we didn't like it."

"It's co-dependent."

"Maybe you should finish you Master's degree before you start throwing around words like 'co-dependent', Marlon."

"You know I'm right. That's why you're being such a bitch right now," Marlon said, unfazed by her tone.

"And you decided to bring this up now, why?"

"Because I was thinking about what you told me. About how he called himself proposing that time. At the kitchen table." Marlon made a scoffing noise.

"*Called himself* proposing?"

"You don't feel like it was kind of casual? Kind of like an afterthought? *'Oh, of course, we're getting married'*? I mean, it was the same thing when he asked you to move. Like ..."

"Just shut up, Marlon. It's not like I needed him to rent a plane to sky-write a proposal or something. We understand each other. And understand exactly where we want our relationship to go, that's all."

"People make a big deal out of marriage proposals for a reason, Lena. It shouldn't be an administrative detail, like getting your mail forwarded. That was a lame-ass way to ask someone to commit their life to you."

Lena felt her eyes fill. She blinked rapidly, and stared straight ahead. Moments later, she felt Marlon's hand cover hers.

"I'm sorry," he said, his voice softer. "I didn't mean to ..."

"Let's just drop it, okay? I'm here to rest and enjoy some family time. I don't need someone interrogating me about my relationship all weekend. I can already expect it from Daddy. I didn't think I'd be getting it from you, too."

"You won't," Marlon said, sounding chastened. "Sorry." He squeezed her hand. "You know I love him. Because I know he loves you. And anyway, how *is* big-head Quentin anyway?"

Lena tried to smile. "He's good. And more than that, *we're* good. So ..."

"You don't have to explain or convince me, Lena. I said I was sorry. Let's just try to have a good time while you're here. In fact, I got a club I want to take you to."

"Always party time with you," she mumbled.

"You know it, bitch. Tonight we get turnt *up*."

17

———

"You're a punk, man. Why didn't you just say no?"

"Shut up." Quentin walked ahead of this brother and toward the old Saab that looked like it had been in a fire, Darius' poor excuse for transportation.

Darius unlocked the doors and waited until they were inside and pulling away before resuming his taunt.

"Punked out. The one time you get tested, you just ..."

"What was I supposed to say?"

"No! You were supposed to say, 'no'. Plain and simple, end of story."

They had been standing in line in HoneyBaked Ham, waiting for the two hams their mother had ordered for tomorrow's dinner when Quentin's phone chimed. Thinking it was Lena, he reached for it. But it wasn't Lena.

Are you in Maryland for Thxgiving?

He waited a moment until the second chime before answering. *Yes.*

If it's not too much trouble, I'd love to see you. To clear up some things.

It was then that Darius grabbed the phone and looked at it, shaking his head in disgust.

Quentin took it back, and after playing with it for a few minutes, finally responded.

Sure. Call me in about an hour.

"What could Mara possibly have to say that you should give a shit about?" Darius asked as he pulled out onto International Drive.

"I was married to her, D. She at least deserves a conversation."

"She doesn't deserve jack. I mean, have you forgotten all the bullshit motions she had her lawyer file to delay your divorce?"

"Divorce is hard."

"It shouldn't have to be."

"But it is!" Quentin snapped.

Darius held up a hand in surrender and fell silent.

He didn't mean to take his brother's head off, especially since Darius was only looking out for his best interests. But thinking about his ex-wife and the nasty way their marriage ultimately ended still put him on edge. There was just something fundamentally wrong with having a relationship that was supposed to carry you through to the end of your days become contentious and fraught. It was one thing to decide that they weren't meant to be man-and-wife, but it was another thing altogether to decide that it meant they were supposed to be enemies.

He didn't admit it to anyone, and sometimes not even to himself, but he thought of Mara still. Not with love, or even affection. But with regret. If they could get to a place of at least wishing each other well, he would sleep much better at night.

Sometimes he looked over at Lena—getting out of the shower, messing around with that crazy hair of hers, or just sitting on their sofa watching the news—and he wondered whether they would make it work, or whether somehow, someway, they might one day find themselves where he and Mara now were.

Nah, he would think. *Never. Not me and Lena.*

But hadn't there been a time, not that long ago when he had believed the same about him and his ex-wife? That thought scared him. Whatever happened with Mara was something Quentin still felt like he needed to decode. If he didn't, maybe he would never be able to properly move on. On good days, he was sure he already had. But because of Mara's out-of-the-blue text message, today wasn't a good day.

"We need to go get the wine, too," Darius said. "You remember what kind she said?"

"You told her *you'd* remember," Quentin said.

"I only said that so she'd let us out of the house and not add more errands to the list,"

Quentin laughed. "Yeah, well you're on your own because I wasn't even listening."

Darius uttered a curse and then reached for his phone to call their mother.

"This is hardly what I would call neutral territory," Mara said.

The sun had set, though it was only five-thirty, and they were sitting in her car in his parents' driveway, the engine running, and the heat turned up full-blast. Mara's hair was longer, still natural, but back to a shade of dark brown.

And as usual, she was made up impeccably, projecting an image that to Quentin now felt untrue. She looked well put-together, but their divorce had shown that Mara could, when she wanted to, come complete unhinged.

"The war's over. All territory is neutral."

Mara gave him a skeptical look. "If that's the case, why aren't we in your parents' living room, sitting down and having a cordial conversation like normal people?"

"Because no one but Darius knows you're even out here. Ma's in the kitchen cooking her heart out, and my father's watching some movie with D in the den. I don't want to disrupt their evening."

Mara sighed. "I wouldn't want to do that either. I guess they all pretty much hate me now, huh? Since I'm considered a ... disruption?"

"No one hates you, Mara."

"Not even you?" she asked quietly.

"Not even me."

"I was surprised when I heard about your move," she said. "You managed to keep that pretty well-concealed until the final papers were signed. Was that because of me?"

"Was what because of you?"

"The move."

"There you go again," he said. He felt unsettled sitting this close to her. The closeness was intimate and uncomfortable at the same time. Maybe he should have given in to her wish to meet for a drink at a restaurant nearby.

"There I go again, what?"

"Thinking that everything is about you."

Mara gave a brief laugh, absorbing the insult. "We could do this all night, I guess. Trade the same snide remarks we tossed at each other at the end of ... everything. But I didn't call you for that. And I'm guessing that's not why you answered my call."

Quentin said nothing.

"Believe it or not," Mara continued, "I'm not proud of how I acted. And now I still have days where I'm downright ashamed of how bad things got."

"Really?" Quentin asked, trying not to sound sardonic. "Because at the time, you seemed pretty invested in making it every bit as terrible an experience as you could possibly make it."

"I was hurt, Quentin," Mara said unexpectedly. "I was hurt by Richard. And I was hurt by you. It felt like both of you were going to make out just fine; and I was the dumb bitch on the sidelines who had messed up her life chasing after a mirage."

"Well, you said it, not me."

Mara pursed her lips and looked away.

Sighing, Quentin reached out and put a hand on her thigh. "Sorry," he said. "That wasn't called-for. I didn't mean to ..."

"Can we just ..."

Holding his breath, Quentin hoped she wasn't about to say what he thought she might.

"At least be friends?"

He exhaled silently with relief.

"I don't know about that, Mara. But we can *not* be enemies. How about we start with that?"

She gave a wry smile and then nodded. "I can live with that for now, I guess."

As the silence between them lengthened, Quentin glanced in the direction of the house. It was past time for him to call Lena, and any minute now his mother would go in search of her men and find him gone.

"I'll let you go then," Mara said.

"Yeah." Q reached for the door handle.

"How long are you here for?" she asked, just as he shoved the door open.

Cold air rushed into the car and Quentin hunched his shoulders and lowered one foot out onto the pavement.

"Till the weekend."

"You want to give this not-enemies thing a shot and go have a drink somewhere on Friday?" Mara asked. "Maybe even a meal that doesn't involve turkey?"

Remembering that she wasn't close to her own family, Quentin wondered what she was doing for the holiday. But he didn't ask. It would be too depressing to hear that she was spending it alone.

Quentin offered her a smile. "Give me a shout Friday morning," he said.

"Okay, good." Mara nodded and leaned in.

Not wanting to embarrass her, Quentin gave her cheek a quick peck and beat a hasty retreat back into the house.

When he entered the den, only Darius looked up. His father's eyes were glued to the television where football was on.

"What's playing?" Quentin asked.

"Some third-rate bowl game," his father responded.

"Oh."

Darius was still looking at him and Quentin shrugged, telling him without words that the encounter with Mara had been a non-event.

"I never did ask you how Lena's doin' up there," their father said. "She getting settled in that new job of hers? Settled in New York?"

"Yeah, pretty much. Since it's cold out, we don't do a hell of a lot other than work and come home."

At that, Darrell Thomas looked up, giving Quentin his full attention. "Well son," he said, "you can't do that."

Quentin stared at his father for a few beats, confused. "Do ... what?"

"Have her move all the way up there, on a slender promise of an engagement, and then turn her into your roommate."

Snorting Quentin shook his head. "Believe me, we're not ... roommates."

"What I mean is, don't start taking her for granted right off the bat. You all just got together. Treat her like it. Take her out, romance her a little."

"Thanks, Pops, but I think I got this."

"That's the problem. You think you 'got this' so you ain't doin' nothin' to keep it."

Darius cleared his throat. "He has a point, Q."

"Tell me the point. Especially coming from you, this ought to be good."

"Jus' sayin'. Lena's one of the good ones, and she practically fell into your lap. I mean in spite of you and your dumb ass, you have her. And since you do ..."

"For your information, I already proposed to her."

"You did?"

Quentin was gratified to see the surprise on both their faces.

"You never told me you were ring-shopping or anything. When was this?" Darius asked.

"I ... we haven't gotten to the ring part yet, but ..."

"Aww ... see?" Darius looked at his father for confirmation. "Then that's just some bullshit. Sorry Pops."

"No, you're right. That *is* some bullshit," their father confirmed. "When I proposed to your mother ... don't roll your eyes at me, boy. When I proposed to your mother I was makin' twelve thousand five hundred dollars a year. And I *still* went out and got her a ring that was worth three months' salary. Didn't eat but twice a week for more than a month, but I got her the ring she deserved."

"That was back in the day. Nowadays, as long as you and your woman have an understanding ..."

"That's what the ring is, boy! The understanding that you intend to make her your wife. Now I'm not sayin' you should rush down the altar if you're not feelin' it. But if you are, like you claim you are, then you need to make your intentions clear. All this shackin' up nonsense ..." Darrell Thomas made a sound of disgust.

"How much time you think he got, Pops? Before she starts actin' up."

Their father pretended to be doing calculations in his head. "She's been there a couple months now, is it? I'd say he's got another five weeks. Six at the outside."

Darius laughed. But Quentin did not.

"I CAN'T BELIEVE YOU WERE CO-SIGNING THAT MESS," QUENTIN said when their father left the room to go check on the progress of the cooking.

"Because it's true. You know how I feel about marriage in general. And in your case, just coming off that nightmare situation with Mara, part of me feels like telling you to let her go."

Quentin sat up in alarm. "Let who go?"

"Lena. I mean, are you being fair to her, man?"

"In what way, D?"

"I know you want her. But is it the right time? It's like you're halfway in and I can tell you, man, she is *all the way* in."

"So am I!"

"I know you want to be. Because you're that dude. They ought to call you The Closer or some shit, because you commit. I'll give you that. From the time you were like fifteen, you were the one in your crew who *always* had a girlfriend. And I'm not talkin' 'bout some honey from 'round the way that you kept around because she let you hit it whenever you wanted to. I mean you were committed when most of us knuckleheads didn't even know the word."

"So what's wrong with that?"

"Nothing. But it's just that it's your ... orientation or something. You choose someone and you try to stick. But sometimes the person ain't right—like Mara. And maybe with Lena, it's not the person, but just the time that ain't right."

"That don't make no damn sense. A minute ago, you were telling me I needed to marry her."

"Nah. I was telling you that you need to decide *whether* you're going to marry her. Not just keep her around until you make up your mind."

"I don't see the difference."

"Yes you do. You're just pretending not to."

As their father returned, Quentin stood.

"Where you goin'?" Darius called after him. "What? I hurt your little feelin's or somethin'?"

Darius' voice followed him out of the room.

"C'mon man. I promise—from now on we only talkin' football!"

Upstairs in his childhood room, Quentin sat on the bed, disconnected his cell phone from the charger and saw that he'd missed two calls from Lena. Hitting the 'call back' button he waited, but after a few rings, it went to voicemail.

"Hey," he said. "Sorry I missed you. But I decided to take the drive up today after all and then when I got here, Ma sent me and D on a run for her. And ahm ..." The fact that he'd met up with Mara wasn't something that would be wise to share in voicemail, so he stopped and changed gears. "I miss you. Call me back."

Breaking the connection, Quentin lay back on his bed and looked at the ceiling. When the lights were out, it turned into a constellation. There were dozens of little glow-in-the dark stickers affixed up there, his teenage approximation of the Milky Way when for a hot minute he had been interested in astronomy.

This was also the room he lived in when he first met Mara as a law student. He had been saving money while attending

Georgetown, and liked the stability of coming home to a hot meal and an already-made bed while he tried to find his legs in his chosen course of study. He didn't mind that he could be sitting at his desk reading a Con Law text and his mother might shove open the door without knocking, just to bring him a grilled cheese sandwich and a glass of juice for a snack.

And then he met Mara Stillwell.

She was the first girl who tested his resolve to put women on the backburner until he graduated—hopefully with honors and an offer from a prestigious firm—from law school. After their first few dates, and then for certain after they'd first slept together, Quentin remembered thinking, *'You can't put this one on the backburner, Q. If you do, you'll lose her.'*

And that feeling was only strengthened when he watched the way Mara handled herself with her career. She was already a meeting planner then, and when he was slaving away in the stacks with Torts and Commercial Transactions, she had no end of social engagements. True, they were her work, but Quentin imagined her meeting guys in suits, working the kinds of jobs he was still just aspiring to. So, he'd bitten the bullet and rented his own place.

Mara was the reason he had done that. The sole reason. He wanted a spot of his own where she could come to after her fancy parties; so he could keep tabs on her, to tell the truth. So he would know that if she was sleeping at any man's house, it would be his.

By his third year of law school, they were practically living together. And by the month before graduation—yes, with honors—Quentin knew he was going to ask her to marry him.

When he did ask, Mara was surprised. *Married though, Quentin?*

Yeah, he said. *I know what I want.*

He remembered sounding so sure. He remembered *being* so sure.

They had a small, chic wedding, organized by Mara herself. She and her best friend had a ball planning it, getting wine and even the location comped by vendors Mara did business with. Quentin remembered asking her why her mother didn't help more, and Mara saying in an offhand manner that not all families were as close as his. He didn't think much of it, because he was going to be her family now. His family was going to be her family. And then, when the time was right, they would have kids.

He was excited to say his vows and hadn't had a moment's doubt when he spoke each word. And when they took off for their Kenyan honeymoon, Quentin felt a sense of completion—like he was finally an adult. He was a newly-minted lawyer with a beautiful, ambitious, and driven wife and together they were going places.

Was Mara as bewildered as he by how things turned out between them?

She had to be. Otherwise, why now, all these months after the final papers had been signed, did she feel a need to suddenly 'be friends'? But maybe he owed it to her to try. Maybe he owed it to himself as well. Because after all his anger at her receded, he had to admit—the peace he thought he made with the end of their marriage still eluded him.

Reaching for his phone again, Quentin turned it back and forth between his fingers for a few moments. Then he took a breath, and called his ex-wife.

18

"Lena? Do you have a moment?"

Looking up from her computer monitor, Lena saw that Trisha was leaning into her office. The older woman's expression was grim.

"Sure. What's up?"

Trisha rarely looked worried about anything. She was one of those people who maintained a placid Buddha-esque façade at all times. The kind of person who made you feel petty if you dared complain about the weather, or traffic, or the fact that your trash hadn't been picked up. Trisha lived on the Planet of Zen, and never seemed touched by the concerns that occupied the minds of mere mortals. For that, she paid people like Lena.

But today, she looked unmistakably nonplussed.

"It's Nakiya. She didn't make it back from her supervised visit."

"How could that happen? If it was ..."

"*Supervised.* Yes. I know," Trisha said. "Apparently the social worker who brought her back must not have watched her come in. The security cameras show Nakiya walking up the path, someone letting her in, and then minutes later, her leaving again."

"But the protocol ..."

"I know," Trisha said, a sliver of impatience entering her voice. "So obviously, that wasn't followed either. And I don't need to tell you what will happen if word gets back to Social Services that we had a girl abscond in the first six months of our contract."

Lena sighed and leaned back in her chair. "How can I help?"

"We think we know where she is," Trisha said. "One of the other girls told us Nakiya has a twenty-three year old boyfriend in the Bronx."

Nakiya, Lena recalled, was only fifteen or sixteen.

"He's got his own place," Trisha continued, "and anyway, we have the address from her mother, so I want you to go up there and ..."

Lena opened her eyes wide, already shaking her head. "Trisha, I don't think ... First of all, I'm new to the city so I have no idea how to even *get* to the Bronx, and second, how am I going to wrestle Nakiya away from her boyfriend if she refuses to come? And if he's belligerent ..."

"Calm down, Lena." Trisha was using her imperious voice now. "I wouldn't send you alone. And I would go myself if I could. But someone from the state is coming for a home-visit for Shaundra."

Shaundra was one of their wards, a seventeen-year old who was six months pregnant. Lena had counseled Trisha against accepting her into the program, reminding her of all the liability issues, the medical risks and their vast knowledge gap about how to appropriately care for a pregnant teen who was prone to running away. But they all were prone to running away, Lena had come to learn. I

n the borough, there were few placements for girls of the

type they cared for at Ida's House. Girls, Lena had been told by a DSS worker, were a pain-in-the-ass. They didn't respond to the same interventions that boys did, and their problems were often multi-layered and complex. Some of them—like Nakiya—gravitated to the very dangers that the system sought to protect them from.

"Then, what's your plan?"

"My brother will take you. And he'll exert whatever pressure necessary to get Nakiya to come back."

"Whatever pressure?" Lena repeated. She shook her head again. "Trisha, I really don't think ..."

"Nakiya will be sent back to juvenile detention if this placement doesn't work out. Is that what you want? Do you see how small she is? She gets targeted in there. She could get seriously hurt, or worse."

Part of Lena wanted to say that those were consequences Nakiya should have contemplated before she ran off. But she knew as well as anyone that teenagers were impulsive, and often downright stupid. They didn't make decisions based on long-term outcomes, they made them based on whatever foolishness flitted into their underdeveloped brains.

"Oh my god." Lena exhaled, wiping a hand across her forehead.

"Thank you," Trisha said, interpreting the gesture, accurately, as one of capitulation. "Make no mistake, Lena. You may be saving this child's life. I'll tell Mitch you'll be right out."

Trisha disappeared from the doorway and Lena let her shoulders slump.

And that was another thing. Mitch.

Since she started the job at Ida's House, she had avoided running into Trisha's cheeky and flirtatious brother. Once in a while, from her office in the basement, she heard his voice upstairs and a few times, she'd spotted him through the window leaving the brownstone and getting into what looked like a work van. Those times, all Lena saw of him were the back of his head in a knit cap and his strong butt and thighs in dark-wash jeans.

Mitch did maintenance and repairs for Trisha, and odd jobs like mounting the flat-screen to the wall in the rec room for the girls. Lena had overheard a few of them making comments about how "fine" he was, and how they thought they would have had a shot if they weren't confined the way they were.

Out there in those streets, I woulda been *got that nigga,* Lena heard Sade, one of the older girls say.

Sade was at the home because she was a trafficking victim, but talked so tough it was hard to imagine her being anyone's victim. But that was how the ones who had been victimized most sounded.

There was a lot Lena still didn't know about this world, and a lot she was beginning to despair of ever learning. Trisha kept her so busy with paperwork, she rarely interacted with the girls at all. And when she did, Lena got the sense they thought she was naïve, or trivial, noticing how they looked her up and down, taking in her UGG boots, her cut-above-average parka, and well-coiffed natural curls.

She hadn't yet figured out how to talk to them without feeling self-conscious, or slipping into slang in a way that they probably justifiably, thought was condescending.

Grabbing her bag, Lena paused then thought better of it, instead fishing out her driver's license and a twenty and locking everything else in the bottom drawer of her desk. Everything at Ida's House had a lock on it. Even the refrigerator.

Upstairs on the main level, where what seemed like ages ago, Lena and Quentin had come to the open house, Mitch was waiting. Sitting on the arm of the sofa, he was chewing on a plastic stir-stick. His eyes registered her arrival but his expression stayed the same.

"So," Lena said. "Are we ready?"

He shrugged. "Let's roll."

Looking toward the stairs to the upper level where she presumed Trisha must be, Lena hesitated. "Should we tell her we're leaving?"

"I don't see why. I have the address. So unless she has some words of advice on how to reason with a dumb-ass nigga and his underage girlfriend, I'd say we're free to go."

The drive was a slow one. Mitch fidgeted with the radio in his van quite a bit, trying to get clear reception on a radio station with a radio that wasn't cooperating.

"You warm enough?" he asked about ten minutes in. "I keep telling myself to get rid of this piece of shit. But it doesn't give me nearly as many problems in the summertime."

"I'm fine," Lena said. She was a little cold, but by keeping on her hat—Quentin's hat—and keeping her hands shoved deep in her pockets, she would be able to handle it okay.

"What's your story?" Mitch said unexpectedly a few minutes later, having given up on the radio. "How'd you get roped into my sister's deal?"

"I wouldn't say I got 'roped in.' I believe in what she's doing."

"Do you?" he asked. "So maybe you can explain it to me. What is she doing?"

Looking at him, Lena tried to decide whether he was being facetious. He turned to look back at her and seemed perfectly serious.

"She's trying to interrupt the cycle of destruction and self-destruction that ..."

"Nah. That's a line straight out of her shiny brochures. What I want to know is whether you think she can do any of that. Isn't all this ... me and you drivin' up to the Bronx to save a girl who don't even want to be saved ... isn't all that just a ripple in the ocean?"

"I like to think we can make a difference."

"Like to think. But what I know? What I know is that half these girls will be dead before they're fifty."

"And the other half?" Lena prompted.

Mitch smiled. "Okay. You got me. The other half." He shrugged. "Will not."

They arrived at the building in the Bronx almost an hour later. The weather hadn't cooperated for the last stretch, so they had seldom went faster than forty-miles-an-hour. And by the time they got there, it was almost as dark as dusk even though not yet noon.

"We might have missed them," Lena said when Mitch found a parking space and shut off the engine.

"It's before twelve o'clock. In winter. And they're shacked up in an apartment free to do whatever for however long they want. You really think those two are up and at 'em already?"

Lena smiled. "Probably not."

Mitch took a breath and shook his head, preparing for the unpleasant task ahead. "So, let's go do this."

The lobby of the building looked like the interior of every slummy apartment that showed up in the old Blaxploitation films like Shaft and Cleopatra Jones. Lena could scarcely believe her eyes. And as if to round out the image, the elevator was broken.

"It's the third floor," Mitch said. "Might as well start hoofin' it up there."

Lena wrung her hands together, looking at the dim stairwell.

"Don't worry, I got your back. But if I tell you to run, don't pause, just book it the hell downstairs."

Lena's mouth must have actually fallen open a little because then Mitch was laughing at her.

"I'm messin' with you. C'mon. Ain't nothing goin' on around here except some multigenerational urban poverty."

She followed him up the stairs, which he took two at a time until they were at the third floor. He nodded in the direction of the door directly in front of them.

"You knock," he said, his voice lowered. "I'll stand off here to the side so they won't see me if they look in the peephole. Say you're Miss Lena from Ida's House and you wanted to drop off some things for Nakiya, including the money she had on her book."

"What?"

"Don't worry about it. He ain't that smart. Believe me."

"I wouldn't count on it. Why would you assume he's ..."

"And why would you want to argue with me right now?" Mitch hissed back.

Taking a deep breath, Lena gave a tentative knock.

Leaning over, an exasperated look on his face, Mitch knocked louder. Loud enough, Lena thought, to have everyone on the entire floor opening their door.

It took almost a minute, but finally someone inside answered, a gruff male voice.

"Who is it?" he sounded resentful, accusatory.

"It's Miss Lena, from Ida's House?"

"From where?"

"Ida's House. Where Nakiya ... where she used to live."

"There ain't no Nakiya here. Wait ... you said where she *used to* live?"

"Yes. I'm afraid she's been kicked out," Lena said, trying to sound regretful. "I have her things if she wants them." She purposely ignored his claim that there was 'no Nakiya' there.

"Kinda things you talkin' 'bout?"

From behind the door, Lena thought she could hear some whispering, one of the voices urgent.

"Hello?" she said, not wanting to give them sufficient time to get their act together. "If you want to open the door, I could give you what I have."

A few moments passed. "You don' have no bags or nothin' so what things you talkin' 'bout?"

"Your elevator's broken. I had to leave them on the landing. And there's …"

She heard a click then the sound of a chain being removed, and then the door opened a crack.

That was all Mitch needed. The next thing Lena knew, he had given the door a hard shove, sending whomever was behind it flying back into the apartment, and then rushing in himself.

"Yo, yo, *yo!*" she heard someone shout. "What the fuck …?"

"Shut up!" Mitch said, his voice just as loud. "You don' wan' none a this, pimpin'. Where Nakiya at?"

"Man, you can't just come up in here …"

"I can do whatever the hell I want. Because you don't want to go down on a kiddie rape charge. So get her out here before I get your dumb ass picked up."

After that, Lena heard scuffling, a few more curses and then Mitch emerged, holding Nakiya by the back of her neck like a puppy, firmly guiding her toward the door. Wearing a tank top and jeans, she also had a coat slung over her shoulders, slipping on one side and in danger of falling to the floor.

"Sherrod!" she screamed over her shoulder. "I won't say nothin'!"

Lena watched the scene unfold, mouth agape. When Mitch moved out of the way, she was able, finally, to see inside the apartment where a young man, shirtless and in sweatpants was still sitting on his rump in the living room, an overturned coffee table nearby. He looked shell-shocked and for one ridiculous moment, Lena felt awful about deceiving him.

Pulling his door shut, she turned and followed Mitch and Nakiya down the stairs.

During the entire ride back, the girl never stopped crying. Sitting in the center, wedged between Mitch and Lena, she still shivered a little until Mitch turned up the heat. But otherwise, he ignored her sobs until she started moaning about how he better not get Sherrod in trouble.

"Shut up. He got his own ass in trouble," Mitch said roughly. "And as for you ... the hell you think would happen? I should drop you off on the side of the damn road."

"Miss Trisha would ..."

"She ain't here," Mitch said. "I'd just tell her I never found you."

Though she *kind of* objected to the way Mitch was talking to the girl—because after all, she really was just a girl—there was part of her that was glad he had come, and was taking things firmly in hand. If in a moment's insanity Trisha had insisted Lena go alone, she probably would have gone, but things wouldn't have turned out like this. And ultimately Nakiya would have been found, and Sherrod would have been in a world of trouble.

When they pulled up at the brownstone, Nakiya waited until they came to a complete stop and shoved her way past Lena (she didn't dare try it with Mitch) and ran up the steps and to the front door where she banged on it until someone opened up.

From her vantage point in the van, Lena thought she saw Trisha pull Nakiya into a hug. Taking a deep breath—she had done a lot of that since this morning—she looked at Mitch, who was shaking his head in disbelief.

"Thank you," Lena said. "If you weren't there ..."

"You want to go to lunch?" he asked, cutting her off. "It's almost one-thirty and I'm hungry as hell."

"So Ida was more than a grandmother," Lena said, chewing her slice of pizza. "Sounds like a real force to be reckoned with."

"A 'force to be reckoned with'? She was mean as a snake," Mitch said laughing.

"But Trisha ..."

"Doesn't always live in the real world," Mitch said. He took a bite of his third slice and chewed energetically.

"Do you have other siblings?"

"Nope. Just us two. How 'bout you?"

"I have a twin," Lena said. "Marlon. He lives back in DC."

"You moved how long ago?"

"Just a couple months now."

"With that cat you came to Starbucks with? What's his name again? Quinton?"

"Quentin."

Mitch studied her for a few long moments. Long enough that Lena had to look down and away. She reached for the shaker with the garlic powder.

"What'd you do before you came to New York?"

"I was ... I am a lawyer. I was with a law firm."

Mitch's eyebrows lifted. "And you left that to work in my sister's basement? Dude must be a real persuasive brother. He a lawyer too?"

Lena nodded "Uh huh."

"Huh. What's he think about you out here scouring the streets of New York with my sister, scooping up the kids no one wants?"

"He thinks I should do what makes me happy."

Mitch smiled and leaned back, putting down his pizza to regard her properly. This time, Lena tried to meet his gaze, and for about three seconds, she succeeded.

"Sounds like you're one lucky chick," he said. And then he blinked, slowly. "But y'know what I think?"

She was afraid to ask, but did anyway. "What do you think?"

"I have a feeling he's an even luckier dude."

After they ate, Lena had Mitch take her home. She didn't even bother asking Trisha's permission first, just called and told her she was taking the rest of the afternoon off. She figured she had earned it, and Trisha didn't argue otherwise.

It was only once he had watched her let herself inside the building that Lena realized she had now divulged where she lived, something Quentin expressly told her not to do. But, she thought as she headed up the stairs to their apartment, it wasn't as though Mitch was a stranger any longer.

After the morning they had shared, she would even go so far as to call him a friend. You didn't have an adventure like that with someone and then consider them just an "acquaintance."

"Hey!"

Just as Lena was unlocking the apartment door, that of their neighbor swung open. Her hair was standing on end, spiked with what had to be some very significant doses of hair gel. Lena stared, almost forgetting to return the greeting.

"I'm Asha," she said. "And I have a package for you. Came this morning and they left it on the stoop outside. Like it's not about to snow or rain any minute. Like this isn't New York. Hold on. Let me get it."

When Asha returned, she was holding a flat cardboard box about eleven-by-thirteen in size. She handed it to Lena and smiled, arms akimbo.

"*Damn*, you've got fabulous hair. Did Quentin tell you I've been wanting to say that?"

Looking at her now, Lena decided she probably wasn't a hooker. And if she was, she would have to have clientele with very specific tastes. Because she was almost like a punk rocker, complete with a septum ring. She couldn't believe she hadn't noticed that before. But then again she had only ever glimpsed her before. And maybe the ring wasn't …

Asha reached up and touched it. "It comes off. See?" She yanked at it and it popped free. She held it up to Lena's inspection. "It's pressure, not a piercing."

"How did you know I was …?"

"I'm good at reading faces," Asha said, completely without sarcasm. "And you were staring at it, your mouth a little bit open like this." Let her bottom lip fall away from the top one.

Lena laughed. "Sorry. Before this I was in Washington DC. There isn't as much diversity there. Not like there is here."

"People are pretty buttoned-up, huh?"

"Kind of."

"Well, I think that's sad," Asha said, nodding contemplatively. "But the other day when your fiancée came back, he had a guy with him. He didn't look like *he* was too buttoned-up. And I remember Quentin told me he was doing a trip to DC for the holiday, so …"

Lena narrowed her eyes, realizing that this was the second time she had mentioned Quentin by name, and alluded to having spoken to him.

"You met Q?"

"Yup. On his way out the day before Thanksgiving. He said he'd just dropped you off at the airport and was looking kind of lost and forlorn."

Lena smiled. "He looks like that all the time."

"He does have a moody face," Asha agreed. "Not like that guy who …"

And it was the second time she'd mentioned Darius as well. *Ohhhh* …

"That was Quentin's brother. He was just passing through on his way to Thailand. He'll be back in a few weeks. I think he may stop through then as well."

"Hmm. Cool," Asha said.

And it was the first time something she'd said sounded false. Lena got the distinct impression that their neighbor was deliberately holding back her enthusiasm.

"I can introduce you if you're around," Lena offered.

"Yeah, if I'm around. See you, Lena."

"See you." Lena entered the apartment and was about to chuck her purse onto the sofa and begin to think about what to do for dinner when she realized she was carrying the package under her arm.

Shutting the door behind her she looked at it, then turned it over to see where it came from. Who it came from. *Where* it came from was Washington DC. And who it came from? Well, that was none other than Mara.

Mara Thomas.

19

———

THE APARTMENT WAS DARK WHEN HE OPENED THE DOOR, AND JUST as Quentin reached for the light switch he noticed the figure sitting on the couch and jumped. He might even have yelped like a girl a little bit.

"Damn, Lene! What you doin' sitting in the dark like a serial killer?"

She stood, and it was a second before Quentin realized she had something in her hand, and it was a few seconds more before he realized when she raised her hand that she intended to throw that something at him. He ducked just in time before it sailed toward his head and hit the front door with a thud.

"What the ...?"

"You must have read my mind!" Lena shrieked. "Because I was just about to start my sentence in almost *exactly* the same way. Like, '*what the hell is she doing sending you shit?*'"

"What the hell is *who* doing sending me shit?"

"Mara!"

Quentin froze, then turned to look at the package on the floor. Bending to retrieve it, he glanced over his shoulder lest Lena come charging at him with something else. But now she was just standing there, seething, arms crossed, and staring daggers at him. The package had clearly been opened, but remained intact now only because it had self-adhesive holding it together.

Pulling it apart again, Quentin slid the contents out. It wasn't even completely out of the box before he knew what it was.

Internally, he groaned, and let his chin fall to his chest. *Why the hell would Mara think ...?*

"Why the hell would she think you wanted that, Quentin? And how does she even know where we live? Did Darius ..."

"He wouldn't give Mara my address. *Our* address. And besides he's in Thailand. Maybe she looked it up?" He shrugged. "You can find anything on Google these days."

Lena was still wearing the clothes she had put on that morning for work. And there wasn't the aroma of anything cooking so he could only assume she had gotten the package directly after work and was sitting there, in the dark for two hours, marinating in her anger and waiting to confront him.

"Did you see her?" Lena asked, her voice deathly calm.

Lie, Quentin's gut counseled him. *Just lie. This is one of those times when nothing good can come of the truth, man. Just lie!*

"Yes. I did. But ..." He stopped, because just like that, the anger on Lena's face was replaced with hurt. And with a little bit of something else. Something that looked an awful lot like fear.

Then she was very still. Still as a statue. Quentin had the distinct feeling she was holding her breath. Like she was waiting for the inevitable bad news.

"How many times?" Lena's voice had fallen to a whisper.

"How many times what?" he asked.

"Did you see her, Quentin? How many ..."

"I just want to make sure we're talking about the same thing here," he said shedding his suit jacket and maintaining eye contact. "Because that's all it was. I *saw* her. We talked. Nothing more than that."

"Why?"

"*Why?*"

"Will you stop repeating everything I say! It makes me think you're figuring out ways to lie to me. Is that what you're doing? Thinking of how to *lie*, Quentin?"

"*No.* Baby ..."

"Don't you fucking call me that. Your ex-wife, whom you claim to hate sent you your wedding album! And now you tell me you saw her? So don't you call me baby."

"I never claimed to hate her, Lena."

"Okay. So ..." She shifted her weight, and seemed to not know whether to sit or stand. "Do you ... love her then? Is that why ..."

Quentin sighed. "Fuck, no. Of course I don't love her. I love *you.* I didn't even think that was in question."

"You didn't think that was in question? Are you kidding me? Did you see the note? Maybe you should read the note, Quentin. Because if you read it, you'd understand why it's very much in question."

"What note?" He picked up the package again and upended the entire thing onto the floor. A note card came fluttering out. It was cream, quality card stock with a tasteful satin-finish border. And in Mara's elegant, flowing cursive were the words: *Looking forward to building something new, but here's a reminder of the old. Love, M.*

"This says a lot about what she's thinking, Lene. But it doesn't say shit about what I'm thinking." Quentin took a few tentative steps in her direction and when she didn't step back, he took a few more, so that soon they were less than a foot apart.

"But you went to see her, and didn't tell me. That does say something about what you're thinking."

"I didn't 'go to see her'. She texted me out of nowhere when I was there for the holiday. Asked me whether I had a little time to talk. I said okay, and she drove over to my parents'. She didn't even come in."

Lena waited for him to go on.

"She said she was sorry things got so ugly. I said I was sorry too. She asked if we could try to be friends and I said 'fine'. That was the extent of it."

Except that it wasn't. He had called her that same night, asked her whether she was still up for meeting for drinks, and suggested they do it that evening. And they had. And then on Friday, they'd met up yet again, that time for dinner.

"How many times," Lena asked, "are you going to go looking for closure with her before you accept that maybe it just isn't ... closed?"

"Lena, she was my wife," Quentin said, repeating the words he'd used to Darius. "I can't just ..."

"Just what? Divorce her and move on? Yeah, maybe you can't," Lena said, her voice breaking. "Maybe you just can't."

Then she turned and left him standing there. Moments later, Quentin heard the shower. Bending down he picked up the wedding album and carried it to the kitchen, pressing down on the lever that lifted the lid of the trash can. He held the album, poised above it. But at the last second, he couldn't let it fall.

When Quentin lifted his head, April was standing at his office door holding a red seasonal Starbucks cup.

"Thought you'd like to refuel," she said coming in and setting it on his desk. "A grande dark roast. Just like you like it."

As the 'thank you' was about to pass his lips, Quentin got a fleeting rush of déjà vu and his smile disintegrated.

"April," he said. "You getting me coffee, that's not necessary. Thank you, but it's not something you need to do."

"Oh, I know that," she laughed, exposing that cute little gap-toothed grin. "But I don't mind. I want to. I ..."

"Don't," Quentin said.

Her face fell, and he knew he must have sounded too harsh, but he couldn't leave any room for misunderstanding.

"Don't bring me coffee anymore," he said. "Or snacks, or left-over birthday cake when one of the other associates has a party. Just don't."

April now looked mortified, and stood holding her own cup of coffee, looking at a loss for words.

"You're a good lawyer," Quentin said. "And someday you'll be more than that. You'll be a *damned* good lawyer. I have a feeling there'll be plenty of senior associates, partners even, who'll want to mentor you."

April nodded. "But it won't be you."

"It won't be me," Quentin confirmed. "But thank you for this." He raised the coffee cup. The last one he was ever going accept from her. And once she was gone, he took a long, deep sip.

On his desk, next to his keyboard, his cell phone sat silent.

Since their conversation a few days ago, Lena hadn't called him at work like she usually did. She hadn't even texted him. And when he got home, she had usually already eaten, and was preparing for bed, so that by the time he ate the food she left for him, she would be under the covers with her eyes closed even though it was barely even eight-thirty and Quentin suspected she wasn't asleep.

He was in the wrong. There was no question about that. Even more in the wrong than Lena knew.

Not only because had he seen Mara in DC a few times more than he had let on, but because he had a chance—if he wanted

—to see her again. The day after tomorrow she was going to be in the city overnight for a professional conference, and had only just texted to let him know, minutes before April arrived with the coffee.

Since they were only a week and a half away from Christmas, Mara said, her work schedule had slowed. This was the time of year she had her own industry gatherings. As Quentin remembered them, they were more social than anything else. Vendors and hotel chain reps gave out swag bags, and comped the meeting planners dinners and drinks in the best restaurants, or gifted resort vacations and free nights at their flagship hotels.

In the early days of their marriage, he had gone with Mara on a few of those junkets, and they made love on enormous beds, ordered room service and didn't leave their room for days on end. He tried to remember now what they had talked about, what they had in common, what made him so sure he would love her till the day he died, and he couldn't.

When in DC and they'd had drinks, it had just been more of the same conversation they had sitting in her car in his parents' driveway—Mara apologizing and him telling her he had made mistakes as well. And during their dinner, the day after Thanksgiving, more of the same. Quentin actually felt himself getting a little bored with the entire routine of them both revisiting their regret.

So the irony of her sending the wedding album, and of Lena finding it when she did, was that it happened just as he was finally getting the message: there was no point going to see Mara when she came to town. No point seeing Mara ever.

And no point responding to her messages either. Because he *didn't* remember what made him think he would love her forever, and even if he did recall, no number of reunions over drinks would resurrect that feeling. He had probably always known that, but knew it for sure the minute Lena looked at him the way she had—with hurt and fear. Her fear triggered his own.

Three nights of silence between them had been more than enough.

Quentin almost never made it home early. In law firm culture, it just wasn't done. Not in DC and definitely not in New York. Not unless there was an emergency at home at the level of a death or dismemberment.

But today, he was leaving at three. He wanted to be there when Lena got home. It would be too early for her to avoid him. Maybe they could go out for dinner at that Indian restaurant in the neighborhood that she said she was curious about.

Riding home on the train, he looked around at his fellow strap-hangers and realized that since he'd moved to New York, his subway time had been limited to two very rigid schedules. He rode to work between seven-thirty and eight a.m. and then again between six forty-five and seven-thirty p.m. And on weekends, he and Lena largely confined themselves to Brooklyn. He had never taken her anywhere more than ten blocks away from their home.

They went to an indoor farmers' market a few times, and grocery shopping. Twice Lena had suggested the movies and both times Quentin had talked her out of it, pointing out how cold it was, and how much more fun it would be to explore their new neighborhood in the spring.

Leaning forward, his elbows on his knees, Quentin exhaled a long, deep breath.

It was true. Everything his father said when he was home was true. He'd been selfish and had taken Lena for granted. Without even thinking about it, he had invited her into a life that as it shaped up, was beginning to look very much like the life he and Mara had just before they split—both of them throwing themselves into work, but otherwise going their separate ways.

Quentin never asked Lena about Ida's House. He didn't think he knew the names of any of the people she worked with, except for the eccentric Trisha. And if someone had bribed him to describe the flow of Lena's days, he would have had no clue.

By the time he arrived at his subway stop, he was eager to get home and jogged the entire way. He was breathless and fumbling at his door with the key when it swung open.

And ... Darius was standing there.

It took several moments for Quentin's brain to process it, and then he took his brother in from head to toe. He was unshaven and looked slightly unkempt. But that wasn't unusual after one of his trips. The things that were unusual, were the hard cast that encased his brother's left leg, and the crutches.

"Hey! D. What ..." He indicated his brother's leg.

Darius accepted his embrace and moved to one side so Quentin could enter.

"Good to see you too, man. Did she call you?"

"Did who call me? Lena?"

"Yeah." The look on Darius' face was strange, cautious.

"Nah, she didn't call me. How'd you get in?"

"I called her. From the airport. Thought I might surprise you and I remembered you said she works close to the apartment, so I asked her to meet me here to let me in."

"Cool." Quentin peeled off his coat and suit jacket. "What happened to your leg? How the hell did you ..."

Darius shook his head. "We got plenty of time for that later. Right now, you have much bigger fish to fry."

"What bigger fish? What's goin' on?

Darius grimaced. "I think Lena left you."

"*What?*" Quentin looked around wildly, as though he was being punked and Lena might come springing out from behind a piece of furniture. "What do you ...? Why do ...?"

"You have an iPad, right?"

Quentin's brow furrowed. "Yeah. But what does ...?"

"You left it at home today. On the dining table."

"Okay, *so what*? And what does that have to do with Lena ... leaving me?" He could barely get out the last two words.

Pushing past Darius, he went to their bedroom. Everything looked in order until he checked the closet and the dresser drawers. She hadn't taken everything but maybe a third of her things were missing, gaping holes in their shared space, where signs of Lena used to be.

Back in the living room, Darius was waiting, still balancing on one leg.

"What the hell happened? Tell me *everything* from the beginning," Quentin demanded.

Darius shrugged. "It ain't complicated, man. You left your iPad. She came home, let me in, was getting me set up and comfortable. Explained that if I wanted to get online, I'd have to wait because she took her laptop to work and y'all don't have a desktop. Then she spotted your iPad and picked it up to hand it to me, said she didn't think you had a passcode. And then she saw it."

"Saw *what*, D?"

"A message from Mara about being in town. Your iPad and iPhone use the same account, right? So when you get messages on your phone they sync to your iPad as well?"

"Fuck!" Quentin ran his hand over his face. "*Fuck!*"

"Exactly," Darius said. "She looked at the iPad and I swear to God, her face turned grey. Then she hands it to me, and without a word goes back to the bedroom. Now I read the damn message and I'm like ... *shit*. So I hear all the activity back there and figure she's taking some scissors to your clothes or somethin' but nope, fifteen minutes, calm as can be, she comes out with a bag, tells me there's food in the fridge and that you generally get home by seven-forty. And then she left."

"Then why didn't you fuckin' call me, D?"

"What the hell were you gon' do? I have no idea where she went. Do you?"

Quentin thought for a moment. "Not really. But maybe …"

"Q, what the hell were you thinkin'? Are you and Mara …?"

"There is no me and Mara."

"But you went out with her a couple of times when you were home."

"And now it's done."

"At least one of you doesn't know that." Darius said. He indicated the iPad lying on the sofa.

"I can't think about Mara right now. I need to find Lena. How did she …" Quentin thought about her face the night the wedding album arrived. "How did she look when she left?"

"That's the killin' part," Darius said, collapsing into the sofa and extending his injured leg. "By the time she had her shit packed, she was completely calm. That's when you *know* they're done; when they don't even cry no more."

"That's real helpful, D. Thanks."

"What do you want me to say? That '*it's not that bad, Quentin*'? I can't play you like that, man. It's *that bad*. Your woman just left you. For real."

20

CHRISTMAS CAME. AND THEN IT WENT.

In the last week leading up to the holiday, Lena felt like a fugitive, spending all her emotional currency on avoiding the one person she most wanted to see. By the time she left to spend the holiday with her family, she was exhausted and relieved; and disappointed and heartbroken that she had succeeded in not seeing him. For obvious reasons, she didn't exactly advertise what was going on in her personal life, though Marlon managed to pry it out of her the day before she flew back, and made her promise to take the train to stay with him.

They rang in the new year together in DC and Marlon to his credit, didn't say *I told you so* once, or even give Lena a hard time about wanting to spend New Year's Eve on the couch in flannel pajamas, with a glass of wine and a pint of ice cream as her only company. She probably looked too pitiful to pick on.

Predictably, she spent most of the night wondering what Quentin was doing. She could have asked, she supposed, since he had been calling her at least three times a day. She took a strange comfort just in seeing all the missed calls from him, the number in parentheses increasing each time she glanced at her phone, which she had set aside with the ringer off.

When she returned to New York there was a brief lull, a period when he didn't call at all, and Lena both hoped and feared that the calls had stopped entirely. She hadn't been back to the apartment since that day she discovered Mara's message, and had convinced Trisha to let her stay at Ida's House, living in the small, Spartan bedroom on the basement level. It was meant as a very temporary, emergency sleeping space for staff. On her first night back, trudging up the icy steps into brownstone, and then down the stairs into the basement, she cried hot, bitter tears and fell asleep fully-clothed on the small, uncomfortable bed.

The next morning, she heard from one of the girls that Quentin had come by a few times over the holiday, and only went away again when Trisha persuaded him that Lena wasn't there. The worst part was feeling pain for his pain. Because she knew in her heart of hearts that this couldn't have been easy for him either; and that no matter what happened with Mara, it had never been his intention to hurt her.

But even knowing that didn't relieve the ache, deep in her chest, like a wound that would not heal. The ache was her constant companion now. She didn't even have the energy any longer to wish it away.

ON HER FIRST DAY BACK AT WORK, AS LUCK WOULD HAVE IT, THERE was plenty to do, a backlog of paperwork a foot high from everything having been closed for the holidays. There was no time for moping. Lena almost worked through lunch until just after one when a rapping on the doorframe to her small office caused her to look up.

It was Mitch. He was wearing a plaid work-shirt and faded jeans with scuffed Timberlands and was grinning at her like he had told a joke she didn't understand, and had no intention of letting her in on the punchline. Lena smiled back at him.

"How was your holiday?" she asked.

"Same ol', same ol'."

Lena sat up straighter as something occurred to her. "Do you realize I don't know anything about you? Like whether you're married ..."

"Nope."

"... or have kids."

"Yup. One. A boy. Fifteen."

"*Fifteen*?" Lena repeated, leaning forward. "But then you must've been ..."

"Nothing but a baby myself. Sixteen when he was born."

"Wow. Now there's a story for you to tell me one day."

"How about *this* day?" Mitch suggested. "Trisha said you've been down here like a hermit all day so I thought I might as well come persuade you to join the land of the living and drive over to get some gyros or something."

Lena grimaced. "I don't like gyros."

"That's because you've never had them in New York. C'mon. Grab your coat and meet me upstairs."

He didn't wait for her answer, just ducked back out, and moments later Lena heard the clomping of his heavy boots as he made his way back to the main level.

Sitting in her chair for a few moments more, she considered. She had to eat. And working in a basement in winter—the same basement she now lived in—was a recipe for Seasonal Affective Disorder if there ever was one. May as well go out and try to squeeze whatever Vitamin D there was to be had from the pale winter sun.

Mitch was waiting for her in the living area upstairs, sitting on the arm of the sofa the way he had that day they went on their grab-and-run mission to bring Nakiya back to the House. When Lena came into view, he stood without comment and opened the front door, letting her pass ahead of him.

It was bright out; one of those winter afternoons that were so vivid one could almost be fooled into thinking it was warm until a chill arctic breeze slapped them in the face. Still, Lena lifted her face up toward the sun willed herself to absorb its rays.

When she opened her eyes, Mitch was looking up at her and smiling. While she had been standing there giving herself solar therapy, he had descended the steps and opened the door to his work vehicle and was holding it for her.

Trotting down to meet him, Lena climbed in, noting that it was balmy inside. He must have just arrived when he came down to the basement to get her. She wondered whether she was the only business he had at Ida's House today.

"So you're going to school me about the New York gyro?" she said when he climbed in on the other side.

"Yup. It's gonna change your life."

Lena laughed. "It better. Because it's so damn cold out here, only a gastronomic miracle justifies leaving the building for lunch."

"I'ma try to deliver on that," Mitch said.

They drove in silence for a few minutes, and then Mitch was pulling over, eyeing a parking space that a woman in an old Toyota was torturously trying to get out of. She turned her wheel this way and that, maneuvering one slow inch at a time even though there was a foot of room on either side of her vehicle.

"C'mon!" Mitch finally yelled, banging on his steering wheel.

"Impatient much? Maybe you should go offer to pull out for her," Lena teased. "And what was it anyway? Ten blocks? We could've walked."

He looked at her. "I didn't want you to freeze your skinny little tail off."

"Skinny little tail?" Lena said. "That's the nicest compliment I've had since ... last year."

Mitch grinned. "Now why would you want to be skinny? You women kill me with that."

"I don't really want to be skinny," Lena admitted. "I guess it's just cultural indoctrination that makes us think we want to be."

"Yeah, but whose culture though?"

This time Lena looked at him, her eyes lingering longer than she had ever allowed them to linger before. Mitch came across as alternately glib and gruff, so it was difficult to get past that to whatever might lie beneath. It was funny that with one offhand comment like that, she was suddenly curious about him again.

Finally, Toyota Lady managed to get going, and with three turns, Mitch parked in the space she had vacated.

"Show-off," Lena said, when he killed the engine.

The restaurant was a decidedly no-frills joint, with old Formica countertops and stools that had been bolted to the floor. The grill was in view, as was a large slab of meat on a spit, standing vertically. Two men in soiled aprons prepared fries and gyros at lightning speed while a plump dark-haired woman—who might actually have been Greek—stood behind the cash register and took orders.

Lena let Mitch order for her, and took a seat at the counter, waiting while he paid for them both. She wasn't kidding when she said she didn't much like gyros, but that didn't matter. She hadn't been eating that much lately. Everything tasted basically the same to her—like cardboard. So sure, she would try a New York gyro, because chances were, her taste buds would respond to it in exactly the same way they had to the bagel she had for breakfast, which is to say, not at all.

"Sprite?" Mitch asked.

"Sure." Lena shrugged.

Looking around, she saw that the walls were decorated with old, faded pictures that she could only guess were of places in Greece; and interspersed with those were portraits of grim-faced peasants. One of the things she had always liked about New York was that it was a city of contrasts—the very rich living practically alongside the very poor; the modern juxtaposed against Mom-and-Pop places like this.

When she and Quentin agreed that she would move up here, that was one of the things she had looked forward to, exploring these contradictions. Going to the Met, and then to galleries in the outer-boroughs that featured outsider art; buying knock-off designer purses in her neighborhood, and then splurging on a ridiculously expensive pair of shoes from a boutique on Fifth Avenue.

And in all the pictures she had in her mind, Quentin was right there with her; because living here was new to him as well. It was to be their grand adventure as a couple, while they built something new together and left the old behind in Washington DC.

Except Quentin hadn't left the old behind. He had brought it, brought *her* right along with him.

Feeling her nose clog with threatening tears Lena sniffed and reached for a napkin from the nearby dispenser.

"You good?" Mitch fell onto the stool next to her.

"Yeah," Lena said. "It's so cold out, you can't even tell when your nose is dripping."

He nodded but said nothing. It was only moments later that their number was called and two red rubber baskets, lined with checkered red-and-white wax paper were set in front of them. The other of the cooks unceremoniously slid a squirt bottle of tzatziki sauce and another of ketchup in their direction as well.

"You have to love the white-glove service around here," Lena said under her breath.

"Hey. You want good food, or you want all the frou-frou stuff?"

"I hear there are places where you can get both for one low price," Lena said.

"One price, but it might not be so low. Don't knock it. This whole lunch cost me under fifteen bucks."

Not wanting to disappoint him, Lena reached for a french fry and tried it. It was good. Crisp and not too greasy, but nothing to write home about.

"You have to go for the main event right away," Mitch recommended. He had already bitten into his gyro and was talking with his mouth full.

Sighing, Lena picked up her gyro and first nipped the edge of the pita, which she knew she would be able to tolerate. Then finally, she braved a full bite. Immediately her mouth was flooded with flavor and bold spices—raw white onion, the creamy, cool sauce she had squirted on, and the star of the meal, the tender, juicy lamb.

"So ..." Mitch prompted.

"It's good," she admitted. "I like it. A little short of the miracle I was hoping for, but I don't hate it, which ..." she shrugged, "is probably a miracle in and of itself since I generally don't like ..."

"Yeah, yeah. Don't try to talk around it. I saw you. You closed your eyes when you took your first full bite. That's a dead give-away that you had a food-gasm."

Lena spluttered. "I did not have a food-gasm. At best, it was pretty good foreplay."

"Well, that's probably about right. Wouldn't want you to nut on a first date. Because that would make you a food 'ho."

Lena reached for her cup and took a sip. "Is that what you think this is?" she asked. "A first date?"

"Depends," Mitch said, taking another bite of his gyro.

"On what?"

"On why you're living in my sister's basement. Are you and ol' boy on a break? Or breaking up?"

Lena blinked quickly and cleared the clog in her throat. "I don't know," she admitted. "I guess that's what I'm living in the basement trying to figure out."

"Let me know when you do," he said.

"Mitch, I don't know. I'm not in a position to ..."

"To what? Occasionally go grub with a brotha?"

"When you put it that way ..." Lena let her voice trail off.

"That's all I'm asking. Let's just get to know each other. And if somewhere along the line you figure out that he's gone for good, maybe we take it to the next level. And if you're letting the sorry-ass nigga stick around, then I guess I'll just be that dude you once went to the Bronx with to snatch up a little hot tail from her boyfriend's apartment."

Lena smiled. "He's not a sorry-ass nigga."

"I beg to differ. Because if I was him, ain't no way in three hells I would have some dude like me giving you food-gasms on a Monday afternoon all out in public and shit."

Lena rolled her eyes. "Let's just finish up this food and get back to the office, Sweet Talker."

They had a lot more to say to each other on the short ride back. Funnily enough, Mitch confessing his interest in her had made her more comfortable with him instead of less so. There was no more subtext. He had deftly eliminated all the awkward guesswork, so now they were just free to hang out and enjoy each other's company if that's what they wanted to do.

When he pulled up in front of the brownstone, there was a

car in the space he had vacated about an hour earlier. Mitch let the truck idle and Lena glanced over at him.

"You not coming back in?"

"Nah. I better get back to work. And besides ..." He inclined his head in the direction of the building. Lena turned to look and her heart leapt.

Standing outside, at the foot of the steps that led to the entrance of Ida's House, was Quentin. He was shifting from one foot to the other, his shoulders hunched, rubbing his gloved hands against each other. He wasn't wearing a hat. That was the first thing that stuck her—how cold he must be. She had taken his hat with her when she left, and he obviously hadn't replaced it.

Turning once again to Mitch, Lena thanked him for lunch and he nodded, giving her a wink as she opened the door and exited the van.

"Hey."

Lena spoke before he saw her, and when Quentin spun to face her, it was impossible not to smile just at the sight of him. He smiled too, at first with pure, unvarnished joy, and then with a little more caution.

"Hey," he said back, his voice hoarse.

"You want to come inside?" she asked. "You must be freezing. Why didn't you wait in the living room?"

"Trisha said she wasn't sure I was a welcome guest, so she was loath to let me wait inside. She actually used that word —*loath.*"

Lena giggled despite herself. "Trisha takes herself a little too seriously sometimes."

"You think?"

"Well, c'mon. I can even make you some coffee, or tea."

"That'd be great. So I can get some feeling back in my face."

Lena walked slowly as she led Quentin back up the steps and into the brownstone, taking the time to try to slow her heartbeat, compose something to say; and to fortify her willpower so she didn't throw herself into his arms and beg him to take her back home.

Inside, when he removed his coat, she shook her head.

"No. Bring it with you," she said. "Downstairs to my office. We don't let visitors leave their stuff lying around. For obvious reasons. And also, contraband, you know ..."

He nodded but he didn't seem to know what she was talking about. Quentin didn't speak as he followed her downstairs, and when they were in her office, he draped his coat across her spare chair and looked around.

Lena took in her space as he did—the overcrowded book-shelves, the messy desk, small window that was level with the front path and the shabby secondhand furniture that had been crammed into the room.

"This is where you work all day?" Quentin asked, his voice quiet.

Lena nodded, resisting the urge to apologize for her humble workspace.

"D'you like it?" This time, he was even quieter.

"I didn't expect to move into a place that's like Fox Cheatham." She shrugged. "They don't call this work non-profit for nothin'."

"Is there any reason you need to be here, though?" he asked. "I mean, you could have worked from home, or ..." Quentin stopped and shook his head as though realizing he was getting off-topic. "Anyway, I ..." He stopped again and ran a hand across his forehead, shoving aside his coat and collapsing into her spare seat.

"It's not that bad, Quentin. It's ... winter. So it makes it look and feel dank down here."

"You've only been here in the winter," he said, sounding impatient. "So this is how it's been ever since you got here. And where are you staying?"

"You don't get to come here and start tossing out judgments about where I work, or asking where I live, Quentin."

"I'm not *judging*, Lene. I'm worried. Can I be *worried*? You run out on me, you don't answer my calls and I come here to find out you're working in this ... in these conditions? And where the hell are you living? Please don't tell me you live here too."

"Maybe you should go," Lena said, folding her arms, and looking down at the floor.

The truth was, she was desperate to get out of this stupid basement. It was fine working here, but she didn't want to admit that living here was just about driving her insane. And if Quentin kept heaping it on like this, she just might give in and go home for the sake of a warm comfortable bed, when she knew good and well that would be a huge mistake.

"No. Look. I'm sorry. It's just that it took me so long to catch up with you, and ..." Quentin ran a hand across his face again and Lena saw for the first time just how tired he looked. There were dark circles under his eyes. And he had a three-day shadow.

"Have you been going to work?" she asked.

"I have a couple more days off. I go back day after tomorrow."

"Oh."

"Why? Do I look like shit?"

Lena gave a small smile and nodded.

Quentin laughed that laugh of his. The one that warmed her from the inside out, and made him look like the handsomest man on earth. Lena looked away, fighting what felt natural—just going over and falling into his arms. He always felt so solid against her, and made her feel so safe. Or he had, before.

"I look like shit because I miss you," he said. "And because my life isn't even *my* life without you in ..."

"Don't do that," Lena said, cutting him off. "Don't try to placate me with pretty words."

"They're not just words."

"Well I'm not ready to hear them."

Quentin looked down. "Fine. That's ... I get it. You probably have a lot of questions. And you deserve to have every one of them answered. So ... let's have at it."

Lena sighed. "Did you sleep with Mara?"

"No."

"Are you ... do you love her?"

Quentin exhaled. "No, baby. *No.*"

"Did you tell me the truth about when you saw her?"

With this one, Quentin took a moment. And then he looked up at her, meeting her gaze with a steady one of his own. "No," he said finally. "Not completely."

Lena made a sound of disgust. "Not *completely*? See, that's what I can't ..."

"Can we just agree to one thing?" he cut her off.

"*What*, Quentin?"

"That when I call you'll answer. When I come by, you'll see me. That you won't disappear on me again."

"That's three things."

"Lena."

"Okay. Fine." That had been excruciating for her as well, so the promise was an easy one to make, though she was pretending otherwise.

"Do you have anything else you want to ask me?" Quentin's voice was smooth, almost coaxing.

Sometimes he made her just want to ... scream. *Why couldn't he even fight right?* They were supposed to be having a knock-down, drag-out right now. Things were supposed to get broken, and messy, snotty tears shed. Preferably his, because she had shed plenty as it was.

Looking away from him, she shook her head. "That's all I have right now."

He stood. "Then I'd better go. You're working, and ... I'm losing my shit being underground for this long."

Lena rolled her eyes.

Quentin shrugged on his coat and before Lena could react, had closed the distance between them, kissed her quickly on the lips, and was gone.

21

———————

"I'M SORRY, I DON'T THINK I CAN."

Quentin looked at phone and tried to contain his frustration. This was the third time he'd called to ask Lena to meet him—for coffee, drinks, *anything*—and the third time she'd told him she had to do something with "the girls" at Ida's House.

This time, it was for MLK Day. He had a rare day off on Monday, which meant a long weekend, so he'd been hoping that ... Hell, he'd been doing a lot of hoping lately where Lena was concerned and very little of it had borne fruit.

"So how about Friday?"

"That's tomorrow."

Quentin looked at the ceiling. "You need more notice than that?"

At the other end of the line, Lena fell silent.

"Sorry. That sounded ..."

"Sarcastic?" she supplied.

"Yeah. Sorry. Look, I just want to see you, Lene. I know you're still pissed, and that maybe we won't ..." *Stay positive, man. Keep it positive.* "I know there's a lot to talk about. But for now, if we could just table all that and spend some time together."

"Table it?" Lena echoed.

"Yeah. Put it on a later agenda."

"I know what the phrase means, Quentin. I just don't get how we 'table' something like you lying to me!"

"Well I'm asking you to," he said, going out on a limb. "Because you know me, Lena. You *know* me. I would never do anything to hurt you."

"But you did!"

The unexpected sharpness of her tone rendered him silent for a moment.

"And I'm ..."

"Look, I have to go," Lena said abruptly. "I have a meeting upstairs."

And then she hung up.

Quentin dropped his phone on the dining table and leaned back, exhaling a hard puff of breath.

"So, that went well I take it?"

"Shut up, Darius."

"Okay. But first, can I make an observation?"

"No."

Darius was in full mountain man mode lately. Having not shaved for weeks, he was sporting an almost full beard now. After arriving back in the States with a leg broken in two places, he had somehow just stayed on at Quentin's. They drove home for Christmas but returned two days later and Darius had been there ever since. He said it was because with a bum leg, he needed Quentin to 'look out for' him, but they both knew it was probably the other way around.

The day she left, Quentin had gone directly over to Lena's workplace and was told that she wasn't there and had taken the rest of the day off. And in the week following, she ignored all his calls. He alternated between thinking that she was overreacting and would probably have a better sense of perspective if he allowed her to cool off, and panicking because he had no other way, besides her job, of reaching her.

That last one had been a humbling realization—he didn't have her father's number, nor her brother's. He didn't know a single friend of hers back in DC who could give him some insight into where Lena might have gone. It was like she was a ghost, who had easily slipped into his life and could just as easily slip away.

Only then had Quentin started to accept just how much she had given up for him. She was living this life because it was *his* life. Because it was the one he chose for them.

"I'ma make it anyway," Darius said.

"Go ahead. Make your observation," he said wearily.

"You're still talking to her like she's your woman, bruh."

"Because she is!" Quentin spat.

"Okay, fine. Calm your ass down. But right now, in her mind at least, maybe you're not her man."

"So what're you sayin'?"

"Stop talking to her with that ... that freakin' ... *tone* in your voice, man. Like you're entitled to have her. Like it's a foregone conclusion that she's coming home, and it's only a matter of time. At least act like you lost her for good and you're trying to win her back. Because if you don't, Q? You *will* lose her for good."

He hated to admit it, but that made a certain kind of sense.

Quentin staggered toward the kitchen, eyes still clouded with sleep, and almost right into an unfamiliar contraption sitting in the middle of his living room. Standing upright, he focused on his surroundings, disoriented for a moment.

"Good morning!"

His next-door neighbor, Asha was standing at the doorway to his kitchen wearing only a tank top and leggings, and fluffy socks. Her spiky hair pointed due north, and she was holding what looked like a crock pot. But as far as he knew, Quentin didn't even own one of those.

"Want to get in on the action, Q?" Darius' head stuck out into the doorway just above Asha's.

"What kinda ... action are we talking about?"

"Asha," Darius said pointing at the top of her head. "Is a massage therapist. She's about to give me a hot stone treatment."

"A massage therapist?" Quentin grinned, thinking about Lena and her imaginative interpretation of Asha's comings and goings. And then just as quickly, his chest tightened, because she wasn't there to laugh about it with him.

"I'd be happy to hook you up when I'm done with Darius," Asha confirmed. "Hot stones can do wonders for tight muscles. And in the wintertime we have a tendency to get a lot of stiffness here, and here." She indicated her shoulders and lower back. "All that hunching over to protect us against the cold."

"Thanks, but I think I'll just leave you guys to it. All I need right now is coffee."

"Coffee is terrible for muscle tension," Asha said conversationally as he slipped by her and into the kitchen.

"I'll take that under advisement," Quentin said as he began setting up the Keurig.

While waiting for the coffee to brew, he listened to Darius and Asha in the next room, laughing, and then heard Darius yelp as the first stone made contact with his back.

"Don't be a baby about it," Asha said. "It's going to be hot, otherwise it doesn't work. And I strictly control the temperature, so it's not like you'll get burned or anything."

"Alright, well keep those stones moving, and quit flapping your gums," Darius returned.

Quentin knew his brother. That was the way he spoke to women he either *had* bedded, or planned to. Teasing, with just a little edge to it, keeping them off-balance and unsure of his interest. The Bro Code dictated that he should shower and find something to do outside of the apartment today; something that kept him gone for a few hours at least.

He could go to the office, and win a few brownie points for coming in on a Saturday. But he didn't feel like it. Or he could find a matinee and check out a movie. But it didn't matter where he went; it was obvious he had to go somewhere. Not just to give his brother some much-needed room, but because if he stayed home, he would only sit around thinking pointless thoughts, like about all the free time he suddenly had on his hands.

After drinking only half his mug of coffee, he showered and got dressed. When he re-entered the living room, Darius was still facedown on the massage table, but Asha had abandoned her hot stones and mounted the table, straddled Darius at the hips and had her elbow pressed into his back. Sensing that the situation was about fifteen minutes away from getting out of hand, Quentin grabbed his coat, and after a mumbled '*see you later*' got the hell out of there.

Outside, it was the kind of cold that would normally have had him hightailing it back inside and reconsidering whether anything was important enough to justify freezing his butt off. But for all he knew, Darius was a faster worker than he was giving him credit for, and the situation upstairs had already taken a turn. So he pulled up his hood and headed for the Starbucks three blocks over.

When he got there, the line inside was ridiculous. It snaked past the pastry case and around to the rear where the restrooms were. Then Quentin remembered a place Lena had told him about, just one street over from Ida's House.

It's so freakin' cute, baby, she'd said. *A real, authentically inde-*

pendent operation. The kind of place we ought to be supporting instead of that behemoth Starbucks.

He remembered, too, that he had stifled a smile and thought how freakin' cute she was, his little baby-revolutionary. But that was what their neighborhood was like—chock full of privileged do-gooders. He didn't knock it though. At least they were looking to do some good.

As Lena described the spot, it was a brownstone that, like Ida's House, had been converted to another purpose. Except the owners had done minimal remodeling so the interior still resembled a home, with comfortable overstuffed couches, and a smattering of tables and chairs; and each room had its own unique menu dedicated to coffee, tea and desserts from different parts of the globe. There was a Colombia Room, a Jamaica Room and so forth.

Armed with only that memory, he went in search of the place, and after only a few wrong turns, finally located it. It was unimaginatively named World Java and inside, was just as crowded as Starbucks had been. There was a difference in the nature of the crowd though. There were couples in World Java, leaning against each other, cuddled on the couches and drinking from soup-bowl-sized mugs; and families with small children bouncing babies on their laps, or trying to coax toddlers into trying a bite of crepe.

Wandering from one level to the next, Quentin finally chose France as his final destination and ordered a strong dark roast and a chocolate croissant. The room was both quaint and kitschy, with inexpensive Eiffel Tower statuettes in the center of each table, and a sloppily hung French flag just above the fireplace. Lena was right, the place was cute. And if he had his guess, he would say its owners were two starry-eyed recent college grads armed with trust funds and a lot of ideals about fair trade coffee from the developing world. Or maybe a middle-aged widow whose kids had finished college and started their own lives out on the West Coast, leaving her unmoored and lonely.

Quentin took a seat near the window and looked out and down onto the street below, wondering whether this was where Lena stopped in to get her morning coffee. And if it was, did she do so alone. And if so, was she lonely? She had left everything behind in DC for him—her brother, her friends, her job, her apartment ... And he had taken that, and her, for granted.

At the table next to him, a couple was having an argument, exchanging sharp and angry whispers. Finally, the woman leaned back and folded her arms, her eyes brimming with tears which she tried to hide from the man by turning away from him. Her lower lip trembled, and Quentin felt a surge of sympathy for her, even though he didn't even know who had been in the wrong.

Pushing aside the uneaten croissant, he gulped down the remainder of his coffee as quickly as its temperature would allow, and shoved back from the table.

***

"You here for the discussion group?"

"The discussion group?"

"Yeah." The young woman at the desk looked bored when he first entered, but now her expression was bordering on aggravated.

"No, actually I was hoping you could tell me if Len ... Miss Chambers is here today," Quentin said.

"I think she in the group," the young woman said. And when Quentin didn't move, she sighed. "You want me to go get her?"

"Thank you."

Sliding out of her seat at the makeshift reception desk, she cast Quentin a suspicious look over her shoulder intended to warn him not to be up to anything funny while she was gone. She took her time climbing the steps to the second level, her hand dragging along the banister as she did.

While he waited, Quentin looked around, noticing the signs of life that hadn't been there when he and Lena first visited for the open house not even three months earlier. Now, there were umbrellas by the front door, and the coat closet appeared so stuffed, the door didn't completely shut. Little nicks and scratches marked the floor of the foyer and the wall leading into the living area looked a little smudged, where many hands had leaned against it.

"Quentin."

He looked up and watched Lena descending the stairs with the young receptionist. She was wearing close-fitting jeans and calf-high brown boots with an oversized peach sweater. Her hair was pulled back into a high curly, messy puff and she wore lipstick and dark eyeliner, as though she had made a special effort to look nice for an event.

"What're you doing here?" she asked when she got to the foot of the stairs. Then, seeing that they had an audience, she pulled him into the living room.

"I told you I couldn't this weekend, because ..."

"No, I know," he said. "I was just in the neighborhood, so ..." He laughed at the skeptical look on her face. "No, I was! At that coffee shop you told me about."

"You were at World Java?" Lena asked. She stared at him for a moment and a smile tugged the corner of her lips. "You said it sounded pretentious when I told you about it."

"Did I say that?"

She nodded.

"Okay, so it was a little pretentious. But it was nice too. I liked it. Is that where you go?"

"It's too cold to go much of anywhere, but yeah, sometimes."

They stared at each other for a long time and Quentin felt his hand at his side, the fingers twitching as he yearned to reach up and touch her face, trace her lips the way he always did just before he kissed her.

"You ..." She began, stopped to take a breath and then began again. "You want to come upstairs and join the group?"

"The discussion group your receptionist was talking about?"

"Yeah. I'm having like a little conversation with the girls. We do themed discussions every Saturday."

"Really? I didn't know you were involved in any of that," Quentin said, surprised. "I thought you just did the paperwork and stuff."

"Mostly, yes. But since I ... lately I've gotten a chance to participate in a few of these."

"I don't want to intrude. Especially if it's a bunch of girls."

"Scared of a handful of teenagers?" Lena teased.

"Nah. But ..."

"Then c'mon." Lena inclined her head in the direction of the stairs. "I have a feeling the girls would love a male perspective on this particular topic."

The topic was Black Sexuality.

And since Quentin was the only dude, when Lena led him into the room—where about nine girls were arranged in a rough circle, sitting on a couch, and cushions laid out on the floor— they all whooped and squealed as he entered.

"Miss Lena!" one of the girls called out immediately. "Is this your man?"

"This is Mr. Quentin," Lena said, sidestepping the question before Quentin had a chance to answer 'yes' on her behalf. "And he's here to join the conversation if you all don't mind having him."

"Hell *nah* we don't mind," a very pregnant girl sitting on the floor with legs outstretched said. "He fine as shit!"

The other girls laughed raucously and Quentin tried not to be intimidated by so much scrutiny directed his way by a bunch of brash teenagers.

"*Ooh*, she cussed, Miss Lena," another girl said when the laughter subsided. "You s'posed to dock her ten points for that."

"I'll give her a one-time pass," Lena said. Then she looked at Quentin. "Because she's right, he *is* fine."

The girls all collapsed into new peals of laughter. And this time, Quentin blushed.

"Sit anywhere you want, Mr. Quentin," Lena said with a hint of teasing in her voice. "When I stepped out, we were just talking about images of Black women in popular culture, and the girls were doing pop-ups."

"What're pop-ups?" Quentin found a place on the floor, leaning back against his arms extended behind him.

"That's when you think of something and you just holler it out," one of the younger-looking girls explained.

She couldn't have been more than fourteen but had the kind of mature beauty that would keep a father up at night, with thick dark hair, full pink lips and a wide, amber-eyed stare. And if her being in Ida's House was any indication, perhaps the worst had already happened to this particular girl.

"Exactly," Lena confirmed. "So who's next? Let's just go around the circle so we can keep the rhythm going. What are some images we see of Black and brown women in our culture."

"*Hoochie!*

"*Video 'ho!*"

"*Remy Ma!*"

More howls.

"*Ignorant!*"

"*Always fightin' somebody!*"

"Uneducated!"

"Okay, so let's talk about whether those images are true," Lena prompted.

"Yes," one girl said. "They true. But at the same time they not."

"That's interesting," Lena said nodding. "Explain that a little more for us, Daisy, or anyone. How can something be both true, and not true?"

"Well, it's like when you see a picture of somebody screamin', right?" A lanky, light-skinned girl with waist-long braids spoke up haltingly. "And if she Black you might, you know, jump to conclusions and think she screamin' at her man, or jus' actin' a fool or whatever. But if they show the whole picture, you know, you might see she screamin' 'cause it's a fire or ..."

"Kenitra, you ain't makin' *no* kinda sense," another girl said shaking her head.

"I don't know. Let's work with Kenitra's example a little bit," Lena said. "If I understand her correctly, she's saying that the image isn't altogether untrue, it's just ... incomplete."

Kenitra looked pleased and nodded at Lena, her eyes grateful.

The room fell silent for a few moments while the girls all contemplated this perspective.

"Wait." The pregnant girl spoke up. "So you sayin' we *are* hoochies and ign'ant and ..."

"No," Lena said. "I'm saying that those labels are interpretations of Black and brown women that some people make. Without having the full picture."

Quentin watched as the girls all nodded, some of their eyes lighting up in new understanding.

"So Mr. Quentin," Kenitra said shyly. "What you think? Do Black women have a bad image with Black men? 'Cause all I ever hear is Black men callin' us out our name and sh ... and stuff. So if we got a bad image, it's not just White folks that be feedin' into it, it's Black folks too. 'Specially you men."

Quentin cleared his throat. "I think that's true. I mean, I know it is. But there are other Black men too. Who only love and value our women. And who would never ..."

"Aw, he jus' sayin' that because he into Miss Lena!" the pregnant girl cackled, and the others followed suit.

"Wait, but hold up," Quentin said, putting up a hand to quiet them down. "I won't front. I *am* into Miss Lena." More laughs and a smattering of *oohs*. "But I guess what I'm tryin' to say is that the beauty I see in her? You all deserve to have someone, someday see in you. Because as beautiful as she is, not one of you is any less beautiful. And that's the truth."

And when he looked up and met Lena's gaze, he saw that this time, he was the one who had succeeded in producing a blush.

22

"You want to walk me home?" Lena asked, once the girls had filed out of the room, leaving her and Quentin alone.

But when she saw the look in his eyes, a mix or frustration and something akin to desperation, she knew she should have chosen her words more carefully. He didn't want this to be her home. It wasn't her home. But she was being cute when she shouldn't have been.

"Sure," he said, recovering quickly. "You can show me your digs."

"Don't expect much," she warned.

Her glib tone was fake, her casual demeanor ... fake. He couldn't know it, but her heart was beating painfully in her chest, and she couldn't seem to stop swallowing. And each time she did, her mouth filled again with a bitter taste that usually meant she was about to throw up.

Lena felt his eyes on the back of her neck as she led him downstairs to the main level. She felt the heat of his presence, a mere foot behind her. He hadn't touched her in so long, her body hummed with need for him.

It was only once she left that Lena realized how quickly she had become reliant on having him close. The first few nights away had been brutal, and cold. Not only because of the chilliness of the basement, but because she had grown used to Quentin's constant reaching out, touching and holding her. The way, in the middle of the night when asleep, he tugged her closer until she was practically on top of him; and how, when awake, he never let the chance for even the smallest contact pass him by. He touched her hair, her face, her ass; he pulled her legs onto his lap when they were watching the evening news, or briefly massaged the back of her neck when he walked by her washing up at the sink.

God, she missed that.

"So you *do* live here," Quentin said, as she led him to the back of the house, and down the basement stairs. There was tension in his voice, controlled ... something. Not anger, but something just short of it.

"It's not so bad," she said, trying to sound lighthearted.

But as they made their way past her office to the rear, the bareness of their surroundings made a liar out of her. The walls were institutional grey and the light in the hallway an anemic yellowish glow. Though he said nothing, Lena felt Quentin's concern, even when she opened the door to her marginally brighter sleeping quarters. She had a bed and dresser, a small television and an en suite bathroom, but there wasn't much else there. When she moved her things in, it had struck her how much a person could do without, if they had to.

Mitch offered to paint the walls something other than ecru but she refused, reminding him that her situation was temporary, and didn't merit him going out of his way. She didn't know for sure what might happen with Quentin, but she certainly wasn't going to live in this tiny room for much longer.

"There's a zero-tolerance policy against boys in the rooms,"

Lena said, in a last-ditch attempt at changing the dour mood. "So we probably shouldn't stay here for long."

Quentin said nothing, but he sat on her bed and looked right and left, taking in the lack of space, her toiletries arranged in a sad little island in the center of the dresser, and in front of a small foggy mirror.

He swallowed, and Lena saw his throat bob once, twice, three times.

"You can't ... you can't stay here, Lene," he said, his voice sounding choked. "*I'll* move out. If that's what you want. You just ... you can't stay here."

Lena blinked back the tears before they started.

"You're not the one who should be uncomfortable," he continued. "You're not the one who ..."

"Quentin." She sat next to him. "Stop acting like I'm in prison or something. Or like I'm punishing myself. I hardly spend any time in here anyway. It's just a place to sleep until ..."

"Until what?" he asked, his voice cracking. "Tell me what you want me to do. I'll do it. Just *tell* me."

"I don't kn ... I don't need you to do anything. This is like a ..."

She was about to say something about it all being a new experience, or an immersion course in the new world she was working in now. She was about to say that she liked having meals with the girls, getting to know them better, and learning about their lives. But Quentin wouldn't have been listening and she wasn't convinced of the words, even if she had said them.

"I fucked up," he said, almost to himself. "I *know* I fucked up. But you shouldn't be living like this. Come *home*. Please."

Not knowing what to say, she put her hand on his thigh and immediately his hand covered hers, like he had been starving for some contact, just as she had. Touching him right then had been a moment of weakness, but when she looked at him, the hunger in his eyes was unmistakable.

Lena moistened her lips and before she could blink, Quentin was kissing her, pushing her back onto the rigid and uncomfortable bed. She exhaled, soft bursts of air, gulping and fighting to regain a steady rhythm to her breathing. But she couldn't because he was everywhere: his mouth on her neck, his hands under her sweater, and then tugging at the waist of her jeans.

Without stopping to think of time, place or consequences, Lena lifted her hips to aid him, and while he worked on her jeans, removed her boots, and shrugged the sweater over her head. Only when she was naked did Quentin slow, and then pause altogether. He looked at her. For almost a minute he just looked and did not touch. But just having his eyes on her was arousing, so Lena was the one to reach out.

She lifted his shirt from the hem, slowly peeling it upward, and with it the extra layer he had underneath. With the tips of her fingers, she traced the muscles of his chest, the ripples and ridges on his abdomen. When goosebumps rose on his arms she smiled, and then met his gaze again.

"I miss you," he said, as though in explanation of his body's reaction to her touch.

She could have said she missed him too, but there was still a small part of her that wanted to withhold something. Because she was too weak to do otherwise, she was about to give him her body. So, she had to reserve *something*.

When she reached for the button of his jeans, Quentin captured her wrist and shook his head, shoving her back once again so she was looking up at him, and he down at her. Taking an ankle in each hand, he spread her legs and pulling back until he was kneeling on the floor at the edge of the bed, he bowed his head between her thighs.

Lena tensed in anticipation of the feeling she had missed.

And when he touched her, it was better than anything her memory could have conjured. His tongue was hot and hungry, moving not in small tentative strokes, but in a broad, sweeping and deep exploration. Opening her eyes long enough to glance down, Lena saw the determined bob of his head, moving in time to each shock of pleasure.

Still, she withheld something.

Where she might normally have gripped his head, encouraging him, unable to prevent herself from arching toward his face, Lena instead pressed her tailbone down into the covers. Rather than touch him at all, she grabbed ahold of the sheets on either side of her, digging her nails in, and forcing herself not to moan out loud.

"Baby," Quentin paused long enough to gasp. "I need to hear you ... let me hear you ..."

She wouldn't give him that. So Lena bit down on her lip, bearing the pleasure as though it was pain, and feeling small, angry tears squeezing from the corners of her eyes.

He owned her. He didn't know it, but he owned her.

He could have her when he wanted her, and for however long he wanted her. She didn't leave him because she was angry, she left him because she was scared.

She left because if she confronted him once again about Mara, maybe this time, he would have said the things she was most frightened of hearing—that he made a mistake, and that maybe there *was* some unfinished business with his ex-wife; and that he was sorry, but he had to find out what that was.

"Baby," Quentin was saying, his warm breath on her inner thigh. "*Please ...*"

It was the '*please*' that did it. The raw need in his voice cracked something open inside her and she was crying, and crying, and crying. Tears of a different kind, that she had held back not just from him but from herself. She didn't know where they came from, but thought they would never stop; and while she was letting them carry her away, Quentin was removing the rest of his clothes and moving atop her, kissing her face, and saying words she couldn't hear.

He entered her, and her body welcomed him like he had never been gone.

Lena pulsed around him and Quentin jerked a little. But he was more focused on her face, staring into her eyes, trying to read her. Lena turned her head to one side, but he reached up and with his thumb and forefinger held her chin.

"Look at me," he said as he bowed and flexed, stroking her slowly and in the way he knew full well drove her insane.

Lena looked, intentionally blurring her focus by allowing the tears to pool in her eyes so that all she could see of him was a vague haze with the shape, colors and contours of a man.

"Lene," Quentin breathed, sounding almost desperate now. "*Look* at me. I didn't mean to hurt you. I love you ... I love you."

She loved him, too. But that, too, she would withhold—or at least the words. Because what other power did she have right now, besides the sounds she didn't make, the words she didn't say?

Quentin moved with more purpose now, intent on making her body respond, even if her mind resisted. And soon they were both perspiring, the bed beneath them groaning, and the sound of their connecting flesh filling the small room. Lena's pants and Quentin's groans joined the symphony. For a while they only sounded angry, and then they really were angry and their sex became hard, and fast, and frantic.

With her head tossed back, Lena tried to disappear, but Quentin would not relent.

"Look at me," he said over and over. "Look at me."

But she didn't. When he grasped her chin, this time cupping it with his palm, Lena squeezed her eyes shut, forcing herself to take pleasure from him without giving anything more than that in return.

Finally, with a long, almost tormented sound, she came and Quentin's mouth covered hers, his tongue insistent, taking that scream from her because she had given him nothing else. Moments later, he pulled back from the bruisingly hard kiss, but only long enough to issue an anguished cry of his own.

For a long time, they lay there in silence, Quentin next to her, both of them staring up at the ceiling.

There were water stains up there, one of which looked remarkably like the State of Florida. Lena was well-acquainted with that shape because whenever she traveled there, it was emblazoned all over the chintzy items in the airport gift shops. Last time she was there, she had to remind herself that it wasn't necessary to bring something back for Quentin. It annoyed her now to remember it, how she had almost broken down right there in the store.

The entire holiday had been a marathon of near-sleepless nights with her mind playing its own little horror reel of Quentin in the arms of some other woman, faceless and yet achingly beautiful. She had never seen Mara, but somehow that made it infinitely worse, and gave Lena's imagination just enough fodder to envision the other woman as everything that she was not.

"You made me feel stupid, Quentin," she said into the silence. "You made me feel so fucking stupid."

"I know. I ..."

"Just shut up," she said, not unkindly. "I don't want you to apologize. I just want you to understand how ... dumb you made me feel. She sent you your wedding album with that sweet little note about starting over and I was standing there and realizing that I had nothing in this city, and almost nowhere to go because I *trusted* you."

Quentin said nothing.

"I'm not coming back to the apartment," Lena said quietly. "And I think ... I just ... you should just go."

SHE COULD STILL FEEL QUENTIN INSIDE HER.

Sitting there at the table with the girls, all of them buzzing around with excitement because Trisha had ordered pizza and allowed them to pick the toppings, Lena was having a difficult time concentrating.

Because she could still feel him. Not just where he had been inside her, but the roughness of his face against hers, the hardness of his chest, the weight of him.

From moment to moment, her feelings changed—from anger to sadness, from longing to resignation. But the emotions themselves weren't that important. What was important, what she realized since he left, was that Quentin still had power over them. He could shift her mood as easily as the moon shifted the tide. All she was doing here, was hiding out.

Taking two slices of pizza, Lena slipped out of the room while the girls were being particularly raucous and didn't notice her departure, seeking out the quiet of the front room. They weren't allowed to eat there, so she knew she would be alone.

Or so she had hoped. But Trisha was there, sitting in the window seat, wearing one of her flowy skirts, and a long-sleeved white blouse, her neck festooned with beads. She turned and smiled at Lena, for a second looking remarkably girlish.

"Come," she said, noting Lena's hesitation because of the plate of food in her hand. "Sit. I know, they can be a little taxing on the nerves, can't they?" She nodded her head in the direction of the kitchen where the girls were eating. "Nobody ever said this work was easy."

"It's rewarding work, though," Lena said, taking one of the armchairs and balancing the plate on her lap.

"It is, it is." Trisha nodded. "And I heard you did well with the group this morning. Several of the girls were talking about it. And you had your young man join, I heard?"

"That was impromptu," Lena said apologetically. "He stopped by, so I ..."

Trisha waved away her explanation. "Every encounter they can have with a man who's about something is good." Then Trisha seemed to think of something. "*Is* he about something? Or, is he the young man that's responsible for you living in our little basement?"

Lena said nothing and instead took a bite of her pepperoni slice. She hardly tasted it. Between her legs, there was a dull, almost pleasant throb. All she could think about was Quentin. She wasn't sure she was up to talking about him too.

"You know what I've found? *Falling* in love is the easy part," Trisha said, in that tone she took before she made one of her pronouncements. "*Loving* is hard."

Making a noncommittal sound Lena wondered whether she could simply wish the conversation away, to make Trisha stop talking. Her boss seemed to read her mind and laughed, turning to look out the window again.

"I'm sorry," she said. "I know what you must be thinking: what the hell does *this* ol' broad know about falling in love and loving?"

"I wasn't thinking anything of the sort." Lena swallowed a hard lump of pepperoni a little too fast so she could speak. "First of all, you're hardly old."

"I've got a few years on you," Trisha said, nodding. "But, having been married three times, I know a little about falling in love. Lawd yes."

"Three times?" Lena said, leaning forward.

She hadn't exactly bonded with Trisha. The woman wasn't exactly the kind of person it was easy to get to know, walking around as she did, with her head in the clouds, her mind reserved for some other, loftier plane. And if pressed, Lena might even say she didn't like her that much. She respected her, but Trisha had yet to arouse anything akin to affection just yet.

She couldn't imagine Trisha "falling" for anything, let alone "in love."

"I know. Three times. It speaks to my optimism." Trisha laughed. "At least that's what I like to tell people."

"Well, what happened? If you don't mind my asking."

"Mind? Girl, I love talking about my romantic history. As you get older you'll find the same thing. When you pick up a few years in age, society neuters you. So, you use any little opportunity you get to remind them that you are still a woman."

Lena smiled. Actually, sometimes Trisha said things that were pretty cool.

"My first husband I married too young and loved too hard; the second I married because he loved me much harder than I loved him; and the third I married because he was a good friend, and I didn't want to die alone."

There was something about that brief synopsis of her love-life that made it all sound so sad, but Lena knew there were probably rich and layered stories associated with each of those men, and with those times in Trisha's life.

"Only my first husband was my husband in the way God intended. I loved him hard. But we were young and wild and foolish. And so *uncompromising*."

"Some compromises aren't worth making though," Lena said. She had completely set her meal aside now, and was giving Trisha her full attention. "Some compromises you make, you'll lose your self-respect."

Trisha smiled. "Why don't you just tell me what compromises you're talking about?" she suggested. "It's not like I'm about to go spread your business in the street. And once romance is dead in your own life, all you have to look forward to is living vicariously through others."

"Now why does romance have to be dead in your life?" Lena asked, half-teasing, and half as a delay tactic while she decided whether it was wise to share details of her personal life with her employer.

"Girl, I don't need the rollercoaster anymore. And I've gotten comfortable with my own company. Not afraid of dying alone anymore. And of course, there's them ... in there. Those girls."

Trisha was looking at her expectantly and Lena took a breath and decided to take the plunge. She had no girlfriends in New York yet. And the ones in Washington she would rather die than confess she had left the city for a man then found herself in her current predicament. So, she let it all come pouring out— the friendship, the romance, the move, and the heartbreak.

While she spoke, Trisha listened, occasionally nodding or making sounds of understanding, but never interrupting. When Lena was done speaking, she smiled that maddening, knowing smile of hers.

"You young girls," she said, shaking her head. "Sounds like you left him for just being the man you fell in love with."

Lena bristled. "What does that mean?"

"You left him for being a man who likes to honor his commitments, and doesn't walk away from them easily. Who is consumed with the need to make sure he does right by the person he said he would love forever, even though she did him wrong."

"But what about the commitment he made to *me*?" Lena demanded. "When I came here ..."

"Baby, I don't hear anything in what you said that tells me he's broken that commitment."

"Not yet."

"So you left him for something he may do."

"And for the lie! He saw her, he met with her and he didn't tell me. And then she sent the ..."

Trisha shrugged. "That was wrong."

"That was *wrong*?" Lena echoed, almost shouting now. "That's all you ..."

Trisha held up a hand. "You should do what your head and heart tell you, Lena. But in *my* experience, the things we love about a person are almost always the same things that we try to change—a man who's strong we start to accuse of being overbearing, the ones who are tender, we accuse of being too weak. And so it goes.

"But if I were you? I'd think long and hard about walking away from a man whose only sin—so far as I can see—is that he regrets that he and his wife were unable to keep the vows they made in front of God and family."

"At some point, though, he has to decide to move on. Or not."

"Yes. At some point. But you can't dictate what that point is. And his mourning his marriage doesn't preclude him from loving you. Does it?"

Lena said nothing.

She did believe Quentin loved her. She had seen it in his eyes, that very morning. That was why looking at him had been so difficult, because when she did, she couldn't deny the love was there. And seeing it, made her weak, and she thought, foolish.

But now she wondered. Maybe what had been foolish was afterward, when she let Quentin walk away.

23

———

"I have two words for you, Q. Bi-sexual."

"That's actually one word," Quentin said shutting the apartment door behind him. He pushed past Darius and dropped the paper sacks containing their Thai takeout dinner on the dining room table. "And what the hell are you talkin' 'bout anyway?"

"Asha," Darius said with satisfaction.

Quentin shook his head. "So?"

"You don't see the potential?"

"For what?"

Darius frowned as though disappointed his brother could be so obtuse.

"*Threesomes?*" Quentin laughed. "Just because she has girl-friends as well as boyfriends doesn't mean she would be looking to share the girlfriends with you. You do see that, right?"

"Maybe so. You have to admit, it increases the odds."

"D, I love you, man." Quentin pulled out the styrofoam plates and opened up the carton containing the pad thai. "But it's time for you to take your ass home."

"Why? What'd *I* do?"

"Don't you have a business to run? Women in DC to coerce into deviant sex?"

"There's nothing deviant about a threesome. As long as all parties are consenting adults not unduly under the influence of any substances, legal or illegal."

Quentin sighed and gave him a blank stare. "Go home, Darius."

"I have another week. Remember I was planning to be in Thailand anyway. So the business is all taken care of. And I need you to ..."

"You don't need me to look out for you," Quentin said. "Hobblin' around here trying to screw all the neighbors. And I appreciate it, but I don't need you to take care of me either. Not anymore."

Darius said nothing.

"I know that's what you were doing. And I'm good. I've *been* good."

Still, his brother said nothing.

"I know it looked really bad those first two weeks, but I'm straight man. For real."

"But ..." Darius inclined his head in the direction of the west side of the apartment. "*Asha* though."

"Come visit," Quentin said firmly. "Or better yet, have her visit you. I need my space back."

"Damn. A'ight. I'll look at the train schedule for tomorrow."

"No, I'll drive you. It's not like I have plans for the rest of the weekend or anything."

"Cool," Darius reached for one of the takeout cartons. "Maybe we can make it for Ma's Sunday dinner." Then, peeking in the carton he grimaced. "Pad thai *again*?"

ONSCREEN, THANDIE NEWTON WAS BEING FELT UP BY MATT Dillon while Terrence Howard silently seethed. Quentin barely registered the emotion in the scene, until next to him on the couch, Darius muttered a curse.

"Every time I see this …" he said. "Messes up me, every damn time. If that was me, I know I'd have to take a bullet that night."

"Uh huh." Quentin didn't have to work too hard to figure out what he would do. Even thinking of Lena being touched by someone she *wanted* to touch her made his entire body grow hot with unexpended rage.

Shifting in his seat, he considered whether a night at the office might be a good idea after all. At least when he was working, he wasn't thinking about anything but the job. This morning, he had been given a brief respite when he was with her in the discussion group. She smiled at him, she teased him and he thought he saw a break in the clouds.

And then he went downstairs to that shitty little room she was staying in and couldn't hold back any longer. But it backfired. His begging her to come home only reminded her of why she didn't want to be there in the first place. Even the sex had been an expression of the distance between them, rather than the closeness.

The knock on the apartment door caused him to sit up expectantly. He looked at Darius who shrugged.

"Don't look at me. I'm the one with the broke leg."

Shoving himself up, Quentin went to answer it. When the door swung open, Asha was standing there.

"Well damn," she said laughing. "Has anyone ever told you your face gives away like, *all* your emotions?"

"No, never," his said, his voice flat. "C'mon in."

His neighbor laughed again, then stepped aside. "Ta- *daaa!* Look who I found!"

Standing behind Asha, a bag on each shoulder, bundled in her heavy puffy parka, a scarf wrapped high on her chin, and wearing his hat, was Lena.

"Hi," she said.

"Hi," Quentin said back, staring at her, not sure what he should do next.

She hoisted the bags off her shoulders and handed them to him.

Behind them, the apartment was silent except for the sounds of Terrence Howard and Thandie Newton having a screaming argument in surround sound.

"You want to ...?" Sensing they had an audience in Darius and Asha, Quentin indicated the direction of the bedroom.

Lena gave him a wan smile. "Sure. But could we ... could we not ...talk? At least not now. I think I just want to take a long, hot shower and go to bed, if that's okay."

"Yeah. Cool. Of course."

Lena walked around him and lifted a hand in Darius' direction, waving as she passed on her way to the bedroom.

Following a few moments behind her, Quentin found that she had already shed her coat, boots and scarf on the floor and shut herself in the bathroom for that "long, hot shower." So he picked them up, taking them out to the living room and tossing them over the back of a chair, ignoring Darius' and Asha's inquisitive stares.

When he returned to the bedroom, he had to wait, sitting on the edge of the bed for almost twenty minutes more before she finally emerged. He stood.

Lena had a towel wrapped around her, another in her hair, and a flush of pink beneath her medium brown complexion. But best of all was the smile on her face.

"You don't know how I missed that shower," she said. "The

water pressure at Ida's House was terrible. And it never seemed to get even one degree above lukewarm. I feel like a new woman now."

Quentin attempted a smile back, and said nothing of what he was thinking, which was that she had never had reason to suffer through those lukewarm showers in the first place.

Removing the towel from her hair, in front of the dresser mirror, Lena raked her long fingers through the coarse, unkempt curls, or at least tried to. Groaning, she let her shoulders sag.

"What's the matter?" Quentin asked.

"I never should've washed it. Now I have to spend the next hour combing it out and twisting it. And all I want right now is to just go to sleep."

"I'll do it for you," he said.

Lena's eyes met his through the mirror, and she smiled again. But this smile was different, and reminiscent of the smiles he used to be able to take for granted from her—soft, and laden with feeling.

"You don't know how to twist hair," she said. And then, "*do you?*"

"You could show me."

She thought about it for a few seconds then shrugged. "Worth a try. Because otherwise, I'm waking up with locs."

Quentin watched as Lena opened the top drawer on her side of their enormous dresser, and pulled out fresh underwear, pulling it on underneath her towel. Then she let the towel drop and from another drawer pulled out a tank top which she lifted her arms to pull over her head. The unselfconsciousness with which she performed this familiar ritual, made Quentin, for the very first time since she walked in that evening, feel like it wasn't a trick. And that she might actually, really be back and to stay.

He watched Lena noticing his eyes fall to the dark rounds of her nipples and like she always did, she blushed a little at the desire he knew must be plain in his eyes.

"C'mon," she said. "Let's do it on the bed."

Q grinned and she shook her head.

"You know what I mean." She blushed again.

She was a little shy around him, and he could only assume that it was because she had shown up unexpectedly, after decidedly showing him the door only hours earlier. But she said she didn't want to talk, so he would honor that.

Taking with her a large pick, a tub of oil and some other creamy liquid in a bottle, Lena sat cross-legged on the bed and then pointed at the towel on the floor.

"Bring that," she ordered. "You're going to need it. Your hands are going to get pretty greasy.'"

Quentin followed her instructions and returned to the edge of the bed. "Okay, so where do you want me?" he asked.

"First I'm going to need to comb it out, all the tangles and everything. And then I'll show you how to twist with two strands, okay?"

Nodding, Q watched as Lena went to work on her stubborn mass of hair with the pick, after first slathering it with the creamy stuff. He grimaced each time she encountered a knot, and yanked at it almost viciously until the comb came free.

Pausing, Lena laughed at him. "It's fine. It doesn't hurt or anything. I'm not tender-headed like some women. God, if I was, could you imagine?"

"Tender-headed?" Quentin said, sitting at the edge of the bed.

"Yeah, I guess having only a brother, this is all new to you," she said, looking amused.

"I have two female cousins though. On my mom's side. Sometimes they'd come visit for a couple weeks in the summer.

And I remember how Ma always liked combing their hair. They never seemed to enjoy it too much though."

Lena nodded. "Tender-headed. I never was. Marlon used to comb my hair when we were thirteen, because he was so much better at it than I was. And one time my father walked in in the middle of him giving me this intricate, really beautiful cornrow style and flipped his lid. And then I was left with half a head done, because he wouldn't even let Marlon finish what he'd started." She seemed to disappear in the memory for a moment then looked at him again. "Did your mom want to have a girl, you think?"

Quentin shrugged. "I don't know. Maybe sometimes. But she's never said anything, never done anything to make me or Darius think we weren't enough, y'know? Or that we weren't exactly what she wanted."

Lena smiled. "That's nice. I wish Marlon could have had that kind of experience with our parents."

It was the first time that Quentin could remember them talking about their families in quite this way. He wondered why they hadn't. Life, probably. Just the busy-ness of life. Him moving, the aborted attempt at a long-distance relationship, then her moving ...

"Were they hard on him?"

Lena was still combing, and now her hair was standing on end in a massive afro. Quentin reached out and touched it. She smiled.

"They were always just a little harder on Marlon. In every-thing. I think they always knew he was different. They just didn't want to come to terms with *how* he was different. My mom got over it pretty quickly, but Daddy? I guess you could say that's still a work-in-progress."

"When did Marlon tell you?"

Lena paused, letting the hand with the comb drop again. "I

don't think he ever did tell me. It was always just … understood or something. I mean, I just always knew." She shrugged, and when she lifted her hand to begin combing the last untamed section of hair, Quentin took it from her.

"So how do I do this?" he asked. "I mean, I know how to comb hair, but how do I do it so it doesn't hurt you?"

"It isn't going to hurt me." She said it reassuringly, that soft smile crossing her lips once again.

Resting a hand gently on her forehead, Quentin combed her hair from roots to ends, feeling the crackling resistance at first, and then the smoothness and release. After a few strokes, he found a rhythm and soon Lena's eyes became heavy-lidded. He moved to the back of her head, sitting on the bed behind her, working on the hair at her nape. He didn't even know how long he had been going at it, because the repetitive motion, the feeling of her hair in his hands, and having her that close were almost hypnotic. Then Lena's head bobbed forward, then up again.

"Hey," he said quietly. "Don't fall asleep. We have to twist it all, remember?"

"Uh uh," she said, shaking her head. "I don't think I can. I'll put a scarf on it and go to sleep. Tomorrow. I'll twist it tomorrow."

"Okay, where's your scarf?"

She pointed vaguely in the direction of the bags she'd brought with her and Quentin went in search of the scarf, finding it in the second one. He handed it to her and watched as she fashioned a quick head-wrap and then reached for the bedside lamp.

"G'night, Q," she said.

Then she curled onto her side, and without even pulling the covers up, rested her head on the pillow and closed her eyes.

HE AWOKE TO WEIGHT ON TOP OF HIM, AND A CLEAN, FRESH, vaguely fruity scent. The room was dark, and the apartment was quiet. It took Quentin a few hazy moments to recall the balance of the evening after Lena fell asleep with his hands in her hair. He'd spent it watching movies with Asha and Darius, then eating cold noodles in the kitchen just before retiring for the evening and leaving them in the living room to their own devices.

The scent he smelled now was hair lotion, and the weight was Lena. He opened sleepy eyes just in time to see her sit up, straddling his hips as she removed her tank top. She was already naked otherwise, and Quentin could just make out the small, light patch of hair at the juncture of her thighs. Lifting her weight a little, she reached down and tugged at his boxer briefs, and Q responded immediately, more on instinct than out of intention, lifting a little so she could pull them down.

When she had, Lena returned to him, lying atop his chest so the softness of her breasts were pressed into the hardness of his chest.

"Lene ..."

He tried to speak, but she kissed him, her tongue insistently pushing past his unresisting lips. She tasted like toothpaste. Between them, Quentin felt his body jerk in response.

Feeling that as well, Lena opened her legs wider and her hips began a slow, wave-like motion, as she stroked him, and herself without breaking the kiss. When Quentin tried to grasp her hips, she gently shoved his hands away, instead gripping them, and interlacing her fingers with his. Using that as leverage, she moved more insistently, becoming warm and liquid as she did.

Tearing his lips from hers, Quentin lifted his torso from the bed and captured a nipple in his mouth, licking, sucking and nipping at it until Lena was making a low-throated groaning noise and increasing the pressure if not the pace of her hips. Releasing his hands, she reached up and cupped his face, her lips descending on his again. This was more assertive than Lena had ever been in bed and the shift was overwhelming, disorienting and so damn good. Quentin wasn't sure how much longer he was going to be able to hold out with this bump-and-grind thing she was working with. But he sensed that he needed to let it play out the way Lena wanted, with her in control.

Whatever he wanted to think about what happened with them earlier in the day, *this* was how it was supposed to be. Lena was with him now, fully, unreservedly and with all the love he had never doubted she felt for him.

Moving her mouth from his, Lena kissed along his jaw, tongued his neck and bit his shoulder. Unable to keep his hands out of the action, he reached between them, wanting to touch and taste her. But again, Lena resisted, and redirected his hand to her breast. He squeezed her nipple, and she arched against him in response, grabbing his other hand, putting it on the other breast.

"Lene," he breathed. "You're killin' me, baby ... let me ..."

She kissed him again, probably to shut him up, but Quentin didn't mind. She wanted control? She had it.

He let himself give in, and even closed his eyes. And just when he thought he knew what might come next, she wrenched her lips from his and slid down the length of his body and took him in her mouth.

He had to have been awash in her essence, but Lena didn't hesitate. For this, Quentin had to look. He lifted his head up just enough to watch Lena's head bob as she worked him over, lips sucking, tongue licking, teeth grazing, just short of dangerously hard in the places where he was most sensitive.

Gritting his teeth, Quentin hissed, feeling the tightening at the base of his stomach. Fighting the urge to pull back, he resigned himself to letting go when Lena lifted her head. In the dim light, he made out the expression of her face: wild, possessive, her eyes on fire.

And that was what did it. He erupted, semen iridescent in the almost dark room, hitting her chest and neck.

"*Fuck!*" he grunted.

But Lena, unperturbed, bowed her head again and in an act of sensual benediction, covered him once again with her mouth. This time though, she was slow and gentle, for several seconds just holding him on the flat of her tongue until implausibly, he was almost completely hard again.

Sitting up, her chest heaving, Lena locked eyes with him—hers intent and determined, his torpid and almost completely shut. While Quentin watched, almost unable to move, she lifted and then lowered herself atop him. It was only then that her eyes softened, and he lay there helpless and near-spent as she began to move.

His inactivity didn't last long, because she felt too good for him not to participate in the experience. And this time, when he reached up to grip her by the waist, Lena let him. She moved slowly, her back bowing and arching, her head falling backward with each forward motion of her hips.

Her head scarf had long come loose so how, what Quentin saw when he looked up was a halo of hair surrounding her head. When he sensed her growing weary, he held her tighter and flipped them both so she was on her back and he was above her. This time, he was the one taking and claiming, sucking her lower lip and her tongue, and nipping on her earlobe as he moved in and out of her.

"Don't ever leave me again," he said. "Don't leave me ..."

"No," she said. He was almost startled to hear her voice. It was the first word she had spoken. "I won't." Her breaths, feathering against his neck caused him to shudder in pleasure. "I'm not going anywhere. Because you're mine now."

The way she said that ... it moved him.

"She messed up, and now you're mine ... *You're mine.*"

Goddammit, he thought before it happened. *Not again.*

THE NEXT TIME HE OPENED HIS EYES, IT WAS TO A SERIOUSLY messed-up bed, the bright light of morning and a vague sense of something close to humiliation at the memory of how Lena had pretty much made him her bitch last night. Rolling over, he collided with a leg, and looked up. Lena was sitting there, legs outstretched in front of her. She had been watching him sleep.

"Hey," he said, his voice hoarse.

"Hey," she returned.

Quentin noted that she was wearing leggings now, and an oversized sweatshirt with socks. Her hair had been twisted and was pulled up and back into a sloppy bun. He had to have been pretty wiped-out for her to have managed to accomplish all that without him hearing or feeling a thing.

"There's coffee," she said. "And eggs and toast. And after that you'll probably want to get showered and dressed. Apparently we're driving Darius to DC?"

"Nah, I don't hav ... *we?*"

She shrugged. "Why not? I can see Marlon and you guys can make it to Sunday dinner."

Quentin shook his head. "We'll all go to Sunday dinner."

"It's okay. I really should go see ..."

"No," Quentin said. "I mean Marlon too. We'll all go."

Lena looked like she wanted to smile but was afraid to. Like he might retract the offer.

It made his heart quake to think that she had that kind of doubt. Part of him wanted to tell her that he didn't deserve that —he made a mistake, but it shouldn't have thrown everything they had into the tailspin it had.

"Okay," she said. And then she opened her mouth to say something else and seemed to change her mind, instead just once again saying, "okay."

"No. What is it?" Quentin asked.

"Last night," she said. Then she started again. "I know it wasn't just what you did. Everything with Mara ... that wasn't the only reason I reacted the way I did. I think ..."

He waited, and she took two deep breaths.

"I meant what I said. I'm not going anywhere. But I think we just didn't have that much of a foundation, Q. That's part of why I reacted the way I did. Not that what you did wasn't wrong, but it wasn't wrong enough for me to move into Trisha's basement. That's all I'm saying."

Thank you! He wanted to scream.

But he didn't, because the rest of what she said was right as well. They had moved really fast, and in the middle of their moving fast, there were all these enormous life changes—he lost a mentor and a job. He got a divorce. She decided to change her career; and move to another city, and live with him, for a time without working. It was a lot for any couple, let alone a brand new one.

"I want to be here," Lena said. "And I want to be with you. But I want us to be on the same page. About being ready to build something."

"Lena, I've been *wanting* to build something with you. That's always been true since we got together, and it's never changed. I'm ready to marry you tomorrow, if ..." He sat up.

"Don't say that." She closed her eyes.

"*Why?*"

"Because it's not true. You're not ready, Q."

"I am."

"Okay, then let's just say *I'm* not ready."

"Well then I guess I'll just have to work on *making* you ready."

Lena gave him a wan smile. "For now, let's just work on getting you ready for the drive to DC. Darius and I'll be waiting for you in the living room."

Quentin showered and threw on his jeans and a couple layers of shirts, then pulled on his boots. By the time he made it out to the living room, Lena and Darius were sitting there, apparently waiting for him. Darius' bags were packed and at the front door, and Lena too had a duffel sitting at her feet.

"What's that?" Quentin asked, indicating her bag.

"I thought we might make a night of it. Stay in DC," she said. "It'll be a long day if we drive back right after dinner at your parents'."

Quentin scratched the back of his neck and tried to act like he hadn't just experienced a moment of panic that she might be planning another 'break'.

"Oh. Yeah. Cool. So maybe I should pack something too."

"No. You grab something to eat real quick. I'll throw a couple things into a bag for you while you do that, and then we can leave."

When she'd left the room, Quentin exhaled and was about to head for the kitchen when he noticed Darius giving him an amused look.

"What?" he asked, trying not to sound too defensive.

"She really straightened your ass out last night, huh?"

"Shut up."

"I thought I heard some high-pitched squealing coming from y'all's room and I'm pretty damn sure that wasn't Lena."

Quentin shook his head. "I can't wait to get your ass out of my crib, man."

"Yeah," Darius laughed as Quentin walked past him and into the kitchen. "I bet you can't."

24

———

Lena looked around the room that had been Quentin's childhood bedroom, taking in all the law enforcement paraphernalia—the pictures from the Police Athletic League, the Explorers Program completion certificate, and the tin badges scattered across the desk. While she looked, Quentin tossed their overnight bags in the corner.

"Your parents are being so cool about us sleeping in the same room," she said, running her hand across the headboard before sitting on the edge of the bed.

"What would the point be in separating us? We live together."

"I know. But my father wouldn't be as cool, I can tell you that. Regardless of the whole living together thing."

"Yeah. I figured. Maybe we should take a trip sometime soon. Go visit. So I can suck up to him for a couple days and maybe earn my way into the same bedroom as you."

Lena gave a brief laugh. "No, thank you. I was there twice recently. For Thanksgiving and then again for Christmas. So it'll be a while."

"How was that?" Quentin asked her, sitting at the other end of the bed and beginning to remove his boots.

"How was what?"

"Christmas."

"I don't know." She stood again and feigned interest in the books on the bookshelf. The last thing she wanted to do was get into the details of her depressing, weepy Christmas without him. "The same as Christmas always is, I guess."

"I came here," he said. "It was kind of shitty."

Lena turned and looked at him, studying his face.

"It was," he said with emphasis.

"Marlon had a great time tonight," Lena said in a pointed change of subject. "And I think your mother got a real kick out him."

"I think the minute he called her a 'silver fox' he had her eating out of his hand," Quentin agreed.

Lena laughed. "I don't think your Dad was diggin' that too much though."

"Darrell Thomas isn't too crazy about anyone looking at his woman," Quentin said. "And for that matter, neither am I."

Lena laughed. "*What* are you talking about?"

"Dude at Ida's House. What's up with him?"

Lena froze, wondering for a moment when it could have been that Quentin ...

"Yeah, I saw you. That day when I stopped by. Just after the holidays," he supplied. "I saw you get out of his van. I pretended I didn't, because at the time ..." He shrugged. "I didn't have a leg to stand on. But now ..."

Lena lifted her eyebrows. "But now?" she prompted.

"Now, I think we're in a different place. The kind of place where I wouldn't want you thinking it would be cool with me for you to be getting all chummy with some dude who's always going to be hanging around at your job."

Because their reconciliation was less than twenty-four hours old, Lena figured her sense of outrage was to be expected.

"I won't be getting chummy with him anymore," she said. Because it was the mature thing to say. And because if they were in a different place, or at least wanted to get there, she would have to start doing the mature thing. Like not running away whenever there was a conflict, or looking to hurt him back just because she had been hurt.

"Good," Quentin said. After getting both boots off, he sat with his legs apart and beckoned her over. Lena went to him, standing between his knees. "How chummy did you get exactly?"

His hands were on her hips as he asked the question and though she should have been focused on the matter at hand, Lena couldn't help it that her mind drifted away to the night before, and his hands on her hips then. She was probably bruised from how hard he had pressed his fingers into her sides. But oh God, the rest of it ... she felt a tiny pulse begin at her core.

"Lene? How chummy?"

She smiled. "It was a couple lunches. Nothing more."

Quentin nodded, his expression still solemn.

"I would never do that," she said. "Get even with you because of something you did."

"Something you thought I did," he corrected her.

"No. Something you did, Quentin. You *did* see Mara. You *did* conceal it. Those are not things I thought happened. Those are things that *did* happen."

"Okay, fair enough. But I didn't let it go beyond that. And for the record, it's not like I invited her to New York, or implied that I would see her if she came."

"But did you? See her?" He hesitated and Lena felt her skin grow cold. "Quentin?"

"Yes," he said.

Lena tried to pull back but he held her fast.

"No," he said firmly. "You didn't give me a chance to tell you before, but you're going to stay here and let me tell you now. We are *not* going through this dumb shit again."

Lena bit in her lower lip, all the better to prevent herself from screaming something at him. And to remind herself that just moments ago, she had promised herself she would be mature.

"I went to her hotel," Quentin said, keeping his eyes fixed on hers. "We sat in the lobby. I returned the wedding album, and told her that I didn't need it, I didn't want it, and that once and for all I was letting her go.

"I told her I was in love with someone else. And that I didn't think a friendship between us would be good for either of us. And then I walked out of there, never looked back and haven't spoken to her since."

Blinking twice, Lena let her shoulders finally drop. "And that was it?"

"Yes. That was it. Before that, I saw her at Thanksgiving. Three times. The first time when she came here after texting me. The second time was again that night for drinks and then a third time for dinner the Friday after Thanksgiving."

"*Why?* What were you looking for, Quentin?"

He shrugged. "Clarity. Understanding. Closure? I don't know, Lene. But once you left, I had all the fucking clarity I needed. Losing you was not something I could accept."

"You never lost me."

"Well it sure felt like it."

"I didn't even last a month away from you." Lena scoffed.

"Good."

She lightly slapped him across the top of his head. "Shut up."

"Are we done with this now? Can we lay it down for good?"

"Yes. We can lay it down for good."

THEY HAD BREAKFAST WITH QUENTIN'S PARENTS ON MONDAY morning, MLK Day. Afterward, there was a long afternoon of doing nothing at all but reading in bed and then gossiping with his mother. Later, while Quentin and his father retreated to the den, she helped his mother take down the family Christmas tree and painstakingly wrap the heirloom ornaments.

Each one had a story, which Mrs. Thomas told with smiling eyes. Lena didn't speak much, but just enjoyed the companionship and listening to funny stories about Quentin and Darius' childhood.

"Quentin has always been my serious one," Mrs. Thomas said. "Serious, purposeful and driven. And always way too hard on himself."

"I can see that," Lena said. "I remember that from when we worked together. But I always thought that's part of what made him so good at what he does—the fact that no matter how good, he's always trying to be better."

"He's like that in every way." Mrs. Thomas smiled. "I remember one time we thought we lost Darius."

Lena's eyes widened.

"I don't mean it like that. I mean *literally* lost him. Quentin was just seven at the time and I took him and Darius to the Mall. And I did that thing that mother's do: *'Hold your brother's hand, Quentin!'* And he did, at first. But I looked away for a few minutes and when I turned, Quentin was distracted by some toy or other, and Darius was nowhere to be found.

"Longest fifteen minutes of my life until we found him. And of course, I was just frantic. But when we found him—he had run off, I can't even remember where, but store security caught up with him—I just hustled them both out of there and went home. And that night after baths, I went in to tuck them in.

"Darius was fast asleep without a care in the world and Quentin was crying. So I ask him what's wrong and he says, *'it was my fault. I need to be a better big brother, Mama.'* Oh my goodness ..." Mrs. Thomas put a hand over her heart. "*Broke* my heart. It didn't matter that I explained that Darius was my responsibility, and it was *my* job as the mama to look after them both. He wasn't buying it. For months after that, he wouldn't let Darius ten feet out of his sight. And knowing Darius as you now do, you can only imagine how that went over. Even then he was a live wire."

Lena smiled, imagining a serious little seven-year old Quentin, looking after a rambunctious five-year old Darius. Some things never changed.

"He's like that," Mrs. Thomas said, closing the box with the last of the ornaments. "Still. He takes relationships seriously. And sometimes takes on the weight of burdens, and of blame that is not his to bear."

The older woman's eyes met hers in a way that made Lena think she knew more than she would ever let on directly.

"I know he's one of the good ones," Lena said nodding. "I feel very lucky to have him."

Mrs. Thomas laughed. "Yes, but don't feel too lucky, sweetheart. Remember he's lucky to have you, too."

Lena smiled. "Thank you."

"It's only the truth. But that's enough of that. How's that new job coming along?"

"It's coming," Lena said. "Although ..."

"Although?"

"I guess it's not what I thought it would be. What I do is mostly administrative. The pay is low, and the aggravations are high. Don't get me wrong. I don't regret the experience, but ..."

"You don't think you're going to stay."

Lena shook her head. "I don't think I'm going to stay," she confirmed.

Quentin's mother shrugged. "Trial and error. That's all life is. So what're you thinking? You'll return to practice?"

"No. I don't think so. I was mulling over working in policy, legislative affairs. Something like that. It's rewarding being with the girls and getting to know them and everything, but it's so incremental, the change we make, y'know what I mean? Just one girl at a time. And I'm not saying that isn't important work, but ..."

"But you're a big-picture person."

"Yes! Exactly. I want to help these girls, and work on the issues that will help them. I know that. But ..."

"Just in a different theater."

Lena nodded.

Once she'd started speaking she could hardly believe how much she said. She was spilling her guts about things she hadn't told Quentin, or Marlon, or even fully articulated to herself. Her time at Ida's House had helped her come into her own a little more, no matter how brief it had been. She wasn't going to leave them high and dry, but now she knew for sure she would leave them.

"That's exciting," Mrs. Thomas said, beginning to remove the garlands from the tree, and handing each strand to Lena as she did.

"You think so? It's scary though. It's starting my life over. *Again*-again."

The other woman laughed. "Well, in my experience, exciting things are often scary things as well."

"*What's exciting?*"

Quentin came striding into the room and winked at Lena when he saw the activity she was engaged in with his mother.

"I'm sure Lena will fill you in later," his mother said smoothly. "Quentin, hand Lena that bag over there, would you?"

"I'ma have to take your little helper from you, Ma. We need to hit the road if we want to make it back to New York before it gets too late. They're talking snow later further up our way."

"Oh. Well, I suppose you two do have work tomorrow." She took the garlands from Lena and the bag from Quentin. "You two should go ahead and load up the car. And take some of the food from yesterday with you. Especially that cake. Your father doesn't know when to say when with treats like that."

Once they were packed and ready to go, Quentin and Lena said their goodbyes to his parents at the front door, Lena accepting kisses from them both before getting in the car. In the rearview mirror she watched Quentin's last warm embrace with his father before he got in beside her, clapping his hands to generate warmth in them once more.

"Let's do this," he said.

"I can drive part of the way if you want," Lena offered.

Quentin looked offended. "No. I'm good. You take a nap or read or listen to music. I got this."

Remembering the story of the Serious Seven-Year Old Quentin, Lena smiled.

"Okay," she said. "You got this."

They drove in silence, and despite her resolve to keep Quentin company, Lena felt her eyes begin to grow heavy. The night before, they had kept each other up, trying to make quiet love and mostly succeeding. She fell asleep in his arms, just three hours before the sun came up, feeling more connected to him than she ever had.

But it wasn't just the lovemaking. It was the fact that she was with him in his parents' home, and that they had been so accepting and affectionate with her. Before she drifted off completely, Lena's last thought was that she finally, truly felt like part of a couple.

"Hey, Miss Lena."

Lena didn't bother looking up from her monitor. "You know I hate it when you call me that, right?"

"You know that's probably why I do it, right?"

It was almost one p.m. and Mitch was hovering in her doorway again, as she had known he would be when she heard his noisy van pull up forty-five minutes earlier. There had been something awry with one of the bathrooms upstairs, so Lena knew he would probably stop in to take care of it. With that many girls living together, clogged pipes seemed to be an almost weekly occurrence, as were Mitch's visits to take care of them.

"I was thinkin' we'd check out this Dominican joint over there on Flatbush today," he said. "You into it?"

Leaning forward, prepared to accept, Lena caught herself just in the nick of time.

"I probably shouldn't," she said, shaking her head.

Mitch nodded. "Yeah. Trisha told me you moved your stuff out of the basement this weekend. So the break turned out not to be a break*up* after all, huh?"

"It turned out not to be," she confirmed.

"Well, you sure look happy about it, so how can I be mad? I guess I'll just go back to being the dude you went to the Bronx with one time to snatch up a little hot-tail fifteen-year old."

Smiling, Lena shook her head. "You'll never be just that. We're friends. But I have to respect my relationship. And Quentin ... he wouldn't be comfortable with ..."

Mitch grinned and nodded. "Damn right he shouldn't be

comfortable letting you out with me," he said. "Turns out he may not be a sorry-ass after all."

Lena rolled her eyes. "What did I tell you about that?"

"Yeah, yeah. Well, see you 'round, *Miss* Lena." Mitch ducked out of her office and was gone.

Not too much longer afterward, she heard his heavy tread in the hallway above her office, the sound of the front door shutting, and then that of his noisy van pulling away.

***

"Did you want to be a cop when you were a kid?"

Lena and Quentin were lying in bed, in the dark, in those last few minutes before sleep grabbed ahold of them both, when she remembered the question. All of the police memorabilia in his room had been striking and she had tucked it away as something she would ask him about later. And as the tiniest, most seemingly trivial things had a tendency to do, it resurfaced just as her mind was clearing all the decks and preparing for rest.

"I wanted to be like my father more than I wanted to be a cop. It took me a while to recognize the difference," Quentin said, turning to face her. His fingers played lazily with one of the twists in her hair.

"What was it about him you wanted to be like?"

"Everything. He's just ... a solid, decent guy. Who sees things broken and wants to make them right. Always trying to make things right."

"You succeeded, Q. You are like your Dad," she said softly.

"Thank you, baby."

"I mean it. I've been thinking about what happened with Mara ..."

"Lene. *C'mon.* We said we were done with that."

"And we are. But I was thinking about it. And I understand

what you were trying to do. Your mother helped me understand. You were trying to make things right in any way you could. So I just wanted to say that I see that now."

"My mother? What did she ...?"

"Nothing. She didn't say anything about it. I just read between the lines I guess."

"Well let's be done with it now. For real this time. Okay? I'm sick of talking about Mara. I want to talk about you, and me. *Us.*"

"Hmm," Lena said, feeling sleepier now that she had gotten out what she wanted to say. "We can do that. But not tonight."

"Not tonight," Quentin said.

Then she felt his lips, soft against hers. And if he pulled away, Lena didn't feel it, because she was fast asleep.

EPILOGUE

SPRING

"Lena. For the millionth time, hurry *up*."

"I'm moving as fast as I can, Quentin. I told you a six-thirty flight was madness with rush hour and everything, but you wouldn't listen to me. I wanted to take the eight."

"The time you're taking right now? To flap your gums? We could be on the Belt Parkway headed to the airport."

"I just need to get my ..."

"Then stop talking about it, and *get* it. Whatever it is."

Flouncing past him in her maxi skirt and tank top, her halo of hair framing her face, Lena was clearly holding in one of her smart-ass retorts. But Quentin didn't care. All he cared about was that they got on that flight to Florida and made it to her parents' house before ten p.m.

When he spoke to her father, Winston Chambers had made much of the fact that they would be arriving at a time that was apparently his definition of late. And he had even implied that he just might not be at the airport to pick them up, because most "reasonable folks" were considering bed at that hour. By "that hour" he meant 9:18 p.m., Lena and Quentin's arrival time.

He's practically hazing you, and you're letting him do it, Lena said when Quentin reported the conversation back to her. *My father doesn't even* think *about sleep a minute before midnight.*

Okay, maybe all of that was true, but Quentin would not rest until he had Lena's father's approval. They didn't have to be golfing buddies or anything, but Lena was a Daddy's Girl, and for the sake of future good relations, he wanted the man to get to a place where he could at least look at him without creasing his brows into a frown.

It'll happen, Lena assured him just that past weekend when they were in Prospect Park. *Just be patient*, she said, her voice dreamy and unconcerned.

It was an unseasonably warm day and she was lying on her back, eyes shut, and arms bare, with a Mona Lisa smile on her lips.

But he couldn't be patient. He was officially out of time.

Because also that past weekend, they found out that Lena was pregnant.

Quentin was terrified and elated, and then terrified again. He was going to be a father. But it was all out of order. They hadn't planned for it to happen, and Lena had only two weeks ago given her notice at Ida's House. She didn't have another position yet, and now it was doubtful that she would look for one. Quentin hadn't broken that to her yet, but he wanted her to stay home—home for the duration of her pregnancy, and then for at least a while afterward.

But today, he just needed to get her butt on that plane on time.

"*Lena!*"

"Jesus. I'm right here! I'm ready, so let's go."

She tried to hoist her bag over her shoulder but he grabbed it before she could—which made Lena roll her eyes—and with his own in the other hand, shoved his way out of the apartment. Lena followed, and paused to lock up behind them, fidgeting with her keys in a way that made him want to bang his head into the wall.

"Okay." She finally turned to look at him. "Good to go."

At the airport, after a harrowing twenty minutes looking for parking, they were just in time to check in, but a little too late to check their bags, so Quentin wound up hustling both through the airport while Lena chattered away on the phone with Marlon. This was possibly the most stressful trip of his life, and she was yapping with her brother like she hadn't a care in the world.

Finally, at the gate, he collapsed into a seat and Lena next to him, now checking her email.

Actually, Quentin thought as he watched her out of the corner of his eyes, she *hadn't* a care in the world. Since peeing on that stick and seeing the plus sign, she had been almost serene. And once, when she was at the sink brushing her teeth, he'd seen her hand steal down to gently massage her abdomen.

Watching that, his heart sped up a little, with excitement and terror in equal measure. She was already eleven weeks along according to her doctor. And twelve was the magic number. *Twelve weeks made it real.* After twelve weeks, a majority of pregnancies went successfully to term. The force of how much he wanted that "successfully-to-term" to come to pass practically knocked him to his knees.

"You're looking at me funny," Lena said now without glancing up from her phone. "What's the matter?"

"Nothing."

"Are you still worried about Daddy? Q, he's going to be a jerk to you for at least a couple more years. So you may as well reconcile yourself to that. And not take it personally. He'll get tired of it and before you know it, find a new target."

"I wasn't thinking about your father."

Lena looked up, setting her phone aside. "What then?"

"I was thinking about you."

Lena smiled. "What about me?"

"I was wondering if ..."

Lena looked bemused. "Wondering if what?"

"If you'd marry me."

"*Quentin* ..." Lena's chin dipped and she looked left and right as though afraid someone might have overheard.

He had asked her before. Many times before.

He asked her once when they were in a grocery checkout line. He asked her before sex. After sex. And of course, several times *during* sex. He had even asked her once in the middle of a fight. And every single one of those times, he had meant it.

But now he meant it more. He wanted to give her his name, just as she was giving him this baby. He wanted to give her the right to hold up her left hand in front of her friends, her co-workers, and yes, her father. And he wanted that hand to have his rings on it when she did.

Reaching into his pocket he pulled out the box, thinking the entire time, *I'm not that guy. That flashy-proposal guy who rents a Jumbo Tron. I'm not that guy.*

But he needed to do something. Anything to get her attention. To get her to understand that this time was different from all those other times.

Upon seeing the box, and watching Quentin fall to one knee, right there in front of the gate, Lena looked momentarily confused before her eyes opened wide. And other passengers at the gate, seeing what she saw, started whooping and applauding.

It was embarrassing as hell, but Quentin made himself tune all of that out, and focus only on Lena. He hadn't planned to do it here and now. He had a vague idea he might do it in front of her family, or while they were in bed—hopefully the same bed —at her parents' house.

But right now felt right. Especially when he looked into

Lena's wet, happy, and very shocked eyes. She was laughing and crying at the same time, and had put a hand to her throat. Then she was sliding off her seat so that they were on the same level, and eye to eye.

"*Quentin*," she said again. Tears pooled in her eyes anew and she wiped them away.

"I mean it, Lena. I don't want to wait any longer. I need to know if you're in this."

Her eyes softened. "Baby," she said. "You're so ... of course. What do you think we've been ...?"

"No," he said firmly, pressing his forehead against hers. "Not what we've been doing. I want *more* than we've been doing. I want to be your husband. I want you to be my wife. *Are you ready for me?*"

Her nod was the smallest of nods. With his forehead against hers, he felt rather than saw it.

"Yes," she said, her voice strong. "I am. I'm ready."

ALSO BY NIA FORRESTER

The 'Commitment' Novels

Commitment (The 'Commitment' Series Book 1)

Unsuitable Men (The 'Commitment' Series Book 2)

Maybe Never (A 'Commitment' Novella)

The Fall (A 'Commitment' Novel)

Four: Stories of Marriage (The 'Commitment' Series Finale)

The 'Afterwards' Novels

Afterwards (The Afterwards Series Book 1)

Afterburn (The Afterwards Series Book 2)

The Come Up (An Afterwards Novel)

The Takedown (An Afterwards Novel)

Young, Rich & Black (An Afterwards Novel)

Snowflake (An Afterwards Novel)

Rhyme & Reason (An Afterwards Novel)

Courtship (A Snowflake Novel)

The 'Mistress' Novels

Mistress (The 'Mistress' Trilogy Book 1)

Wife (The 'Mistress' Trilogy Book 2)

Mother (The 'Mistress' Trilogy Book 3)

The 'Acostas' Novels

The Seduction of Dylan Acosta (The Acostas Book 1)

The Education of Miri Acosta (The Acostas Book 2)

The 'Secret' Series

Secret (The 'Secret' Series Book 1)

The Art of Endings (The 'Secret' Series Book 1)

Lifted (The 'Secret' Series Book 3)

The 'Shorts'

Still—The 'Shorts' Book 1

The Coffee Date—The 'Shorts' Book 2

Just Lunch—The 'Shorts' Book 3

Table for Two—The 'Shorts' Book 4

The Wanderer—The 'Shorts' Book 5

À la Carte: A 'Coffee Date' Novella—The 'Shorts' Book 6

Silent Nights—The 'Shorts' Book 7

Not That Kind of Girl—The 'Shorts' Book 8

À la Carte: The Complete 'Coffee Date' Novellas

Standalone Novels

Ivy's League

The Lover

Acceptable Losses

Paid Companion

The Makeover

ABOUT THE AUTHOR

Nia Forrester lives and writes in Philadelphia, Pennsylvania where, by day, she is an attorney working on public policy and by night, she crafts woman-centered fiction that examines the complexities of life, love and the human condition.

She welcomes feedback and email from her readers at authorniaforrester@gmail.com or tweets @NiaForrester. Or visit with her, at **NiaForrester.com**